The Passion of Broken Things

By

Susan Lamanna

For P

Purple Owl Publishing
Newton, MA 02461
Copyright 2021
www.purpleowlpublishing.com

Introduction

If I had known then what I know now, would I have done it? Would I have taken that first step? An unanswerable question. I did take it; it did happen. It can't be undone. But perhaps it was too late anyway. Perhaps it was too late the moment I met him.

I met him on a blind date.

Here is how it happened.

Chapter 1

Seeking Younger Man. That's what the title of my ad read. I liked younger men. I had always looked younger than I was, and I found men my own age somewhat sedate and boring. So, I was seeking someone younger. Someone hot. Because I had to have sparks. I had to have fire. I had to have a conflagration.

Maybe my need for unstable men was rooted in my childhood. My dad was alcoholic. My mom was distant and unavailable much of the time because she was so focused on him and his latest binge, his latest affair, his latest job loss due to his irresponsibility. So, what did I learn about men? That they were unstable, unfaithful, irresponsible. But oh, my dad could be fun. He was handsome and exciting. He would take my sister and me on adventures. The playground would become an alien planet, the swings would become a rocket ship, the slide a trip to the ocean's depths. He could be so much fun when he wasn't too drunk. We would laugh and play, and my mother would look on, worried and sad, because she knew the fun would not last. She knew that there was not enough money to pay the rent the next month or the electric bill. But my dad never worried about things like that. And then something had happened. He had…

But I did not want to think about that now. I wanted

to look toward the future. I wanted to meet someone new. Someone exciting, someone I could love, as well as lust after.

I had been intensely attracted to my last boyfriend, Miguel. We had met at a dance. I was wearing a short tight dress and high heels, my usual costume. I got a lot of attention that way. Miguel had walked in with his friend, tall and cool in a long overcoat, looking out of place in that rather ordinary crowd. Within minutes I was flirting madly with both, and within a few more minutes I knew I wanted Miguel. I made it clear I was interested. It didn't take long for him to ask me out.

We became inseparable immediately. The affair only lasted for six months, but it was hot. Flaming hot. But in the end, he was gone, and I was hurt. He cared for me but could not commit. In the end, he told me he wanted to see other women, not just one. Not just me. And he ran.

For this one, though, I was excited. We had spoken once on the phone. His voice was deep, a voice I called a chocolate voice, dark and deep. I love deep voices in men. I was 34. He told me he had just turned 28. I had asked him for a photo so I could recognize him when we met, but he had said he wanted the mystery of not sending a photo beforehand. He wanted the element of surprise.

The phone conversation had strengthened the pull. He seemed to want the same things as me. He told me he had been seeking a relationship for some time. He did not just want a quick affair, a fling. He had been hurt by his last girlfriend and wanted someone who could stick it out, who could talk things over, who would stay even through the rough times. It was exactly what I was seeking and what I wanted to hear. I couldn't wait to meet the man this voice was attached to.

I had flutters of excitement in my belly as I walked toward the restaurant where we were to meet. I had dressed carefully, but not ostentatiously. It was a chilly

November evening, and I had put on a long-fitted sweater and tight jeans, with low-heeled boots. My loose wavy hair came down to my shoulders. I had put silver hoops in my ears that glowed against my dark hair. I took a deep breath and opened the restaurant door.

He was sitting at the nearest table. He was the only lone man there. Seeing me, he stood.

"He's hot," was the first thought in my head. He was a smaller man than I had pictured but seemed tightly built, though his sweater was too loose for me to tell what his body looked like. His face was craggy, very masculine. His hair was reddish brown and wavy. The instantaneous attraction was like a wave that pulled me in, pulled me closer. I walked over and sat down. I barely remember what we said to each other. But when the dialogue came, it sparkled, it was like a river, flowing and undulating, strengthening the immediate connection between us.

We talked for two hours while we ate our dinner. I told him about my work with troubled teens, and he told me he did "this and that," usually working on construction sites. We spoke briefly of our last relationships. I mentioned Miguel, saying it had only lasted a short time without going into detail. He told me that his previous girlfriend had been a drug addict and he had finally left after a year when things got too crazy.

When it was time to leave the restaurant neither of us wanted the evening to end, so we went to a nearby bar, taking both cars. We sat, talking, and listening to the music. A man walked by, selling roses. He bought me one perfect rose. His name was Ian.

"I don't want to leave," he said when we finally walked to our cars. My heart thrilled to hear his words. I had known him but a few hours, yet I felt a tie between us, a connection, a bond that I feared to break by parting from him.

"Do you want to come over tomorrow?" The words

were out of my mouth before I was aware that I would say them.

"Do you want me to?" His blue eyes bore into mine. I knew I shouldn't be asking him to come to my place so soon. This was against the blind date rulebook. I didn't really know him. This was not the way a woman was supposed to play it. I should wait, go on more dates with him, get to know him, make sure he wasn't dangerous. But I wasn't listening to reason. My heart and body were demanding him already.

"Yes," I almost whispered. "I want you to come."

I gave him the details, we agreed on a time. Then he bent down and gave me a kiss on the lips.

It was a light kiss, a butterfly kiss, just a cool press of his lips against mine. But a sizzle went through my whole body, from my head to my toes and kept tingling as he moved away, as though I had gotten an electrical shock. I stood for a moment then slowly got into my car. I watched him drive away, then I drove home, almost in a dreamlike state. I was drunk on this man, high on him. He had somehow gotten to the core of me without seeming to try. I felt that I knew him. I was excited by him the way I had not been by the other men I had been meeting since the breakup with Miguel. I knew we would be lovers. Very soon.

I went to work the next day thinking of him, thinking of the night to come. I was a caseworker and activity coordinator for an agency that worked with disadvantaged teens. I loved the kids and loved the work, but my mind was preoccupied that day. "Ms. Taggert!" someone said, and I turned to see one of my favorites, Pedro, who was 16. He grinned. "I been calling you. You in dreamland or what?"

"Oh, sorry, I didn't hear you, Pedro. What is it?"

"I got a B on my math test."

"I'm so proud of you!" I truly was delighted for

him. He had really struggled in school and I had helped obtain an older honor student as a tutor for him. Until that he had been going down the wrong path, smoking weed, and hanging out. His single mother, who worked hard to feed her children, hadn't known what to do with him. But since he had been matched up with Barry, the older student, he had decided he wanted to turn things around and make something of his life.

He grinned again and went to join some of the other kids, who were playing basketball at the hoop outside. This was what was rewarding about my job. Sometimes you really did get to see progress in the kids, some of whom had been abused, who came from poor homes, or who just didn't fit into the traditional school program and had trouble learning.

I went about my day. At lunchtime I met my friend Ginny, who gave me a look as she got her sandwich out of the refrigerator.

"Ok, spill. How was it?"

"How was what?"

"Don't be obtuse, Dana. Your date?"

My cool broke. "Ginny, he was hot. So hot! We seemed to hit it off. We talked and talked and…"

"Did you do it?" She lowered her voice into a whisper as others came into the room.

"No! I just met him."

"Well, it wouldn't have been the first time."

"I didn't, ok? But I want to!" I added and sat down to eat. We didn't talk much more since others were with us. As we left, I said quietly to her, "I'm seeing him again tonight."

"Ok!" she said, giving me a little bump with her hip. "Let me know how things go."

I smiled, but part of me didn't want to report to her, as I usually did when I met someone. We had spent hours talking about this man and that, whether he was cute, how he was in bed. Ginny lived with her boyfriend of five years, so she had no more spicy stories to tell. Derek was attractive, steady, and had a good job. She loved him, but she liked to live vicariously through my rather wild and varied dating adventures. She was a good friend though. She had been a shoulder to cry on when Miguel had left me. She had made tea, had me stay at her apartment, and let me cry, calling him a bastard and not good enough for me to make me feel better.

But this felt different. There was something about Ian that was special. I didn't know if I wanted to report every detail to her. I felt that I wanted to keep him all to myself for now.

That evening I put on a soft sweater with tight jeans that outlined my slender body. I put on some music and lit a candle. I kept watching out the window for Ian's car. I was nervous, excited, alive as I had not felt since I had met Miguel the previous year. I had even purchased condoms for the occasion. Ian was supposed to be there at 7:00. When that time came and went, I began to feel scared flutters in my stomach. What if he wasn't coming? But at 7:10 I saw his car pull up.

He apologized when he came to the door. "Sorry, I was later getting home from work than I thought." His eyes looked me up and down and in a softer voice, he said, "You look beautiful."

He took off his coat. And I caught my breath. He had on a fitted t-shirt and jeans. His body was taut, his abs beneath the shirt were flat, his chest was broad. I could see the curls of chest hair in the V-neck of his shirt. Oh my God, I am in trouble, I thought.

"Would you like some wine?" I asked.
"Sure."

I poured some white wine and we sat at the table, sipping our drinks, and talking. I wanted to know all about him. "What is important to you?" I asked at one point.

"My own well-being," he said, after thinking for a moment. "I didn't really take care of myself in my last relationship. I was always trying to take care of Patty. She would snort coke and smoke weed and get into trouble and I would run in to rescue her. It got old."

He didn't reciprocate by asking me the same question, but I told him anyway. "I really want a relationship where we can talk, where my feelings matter. When I was with Miguel, well... he was great in some respects, but it was usually his way or nothing. And if I was upset, he would just blow me off. He didn't really want to hear it. He would just give me a hug and say that it wasn't worth worrying about or something like that. He just didn't want to bother. It was as though he didn't care enough."

Ian looked at me for a moment, then said, "I wouldn't be like that. I would care," in a quiet voice. I looked into his eyes. He repeated, "I would care."

We finished our wine and went to the living room, sitting side by side on the couch. I wanted him to touch me but was not sure how to begin. But I was also afraid to have him touch me. I was so attracted to him I felt I could hardly breathe, sitting so close to him. I wanted to just sit next to him for hours, but I also wanted to jump his bones. Who would make the first move?

I heard Ian say, "I want to touch you, Dana. I want too so much. But maybe it's too soon. Maybe we should go a bit slower."

I looked up into his eyes again. Every time I looked into his eyes, I felt that I was drowning in an ocean of blue. His eyes were large, heavy lidded, what they call "bedroom eyes." There were promises in them. I could hardly look away.

"Is that ok with you, Dana? I want to get to know you....in every way."

"Ok." My voice was barely a whisper. Then he

kissed me, softly, gently, and the electric shock went through me again.

"It will happen," he said.

"Ok," I said again.

We sat together and talked. We talked about our lives, what was going on in the world, our beliefs, everything under the sun. And finally, he got up to leave. "I want to see you again," he said. "Soon."

"Do you want to make plans now?" I asked.

"I have a busy work week. Can I call you?"

"Of course."

I could not help but feel a bit of a letdown as he drove away. While the night had been wonderful in many ways, and I had gotten to know Ian better, to see how he thought and what was important to him, I had been so sure that we would become lovers that night. I thought he had wanted me too. But he had held back. And he had not made definite plans with me. I would just have to wait for his call. It would come soon.

The rest of the weekend went by without a call. Monday came and I went to work. At lunchtime I fended off Ginny, who eagerly questioned me about what happened. "We just talked, I wanted to get to know him better," I told her.

She scoffed, saying, "Wow, that's not like you. It usually doesn't take you this long."

"Well, he's important. He matters. He isn't just fly-by-night, ok?" I felt a bit irritated.

"Ok, don't get bent out of shape. That's good. Don't give in so soon." I didn't tell her that he had been the one to put on the brakes.

I waited for his call. Monday, Tuesday, Wednesday, I waited. But it did not come. At first, I was a bit nervous, but kept telling myself he would call. But by Thursday I was jumpy and worried. I must have said something he didn't like. I must have done something wrong. It was too close to the weekend. He should have called by now. Should I call him? No, that's too forward. He must not want to see me. And on and on and on.

I obsessed, I even dreamed about Ian, dreamed I was kissing him on the couch, but then it became a boat on the sea, and Ian was gone, I was alone. I woke up with my heart pounding. Why did he have such a profound effect on me? I had just met him! I could live without him. I didn't need this crap. I would just keep going on dates with the other men who had answered my ad. I didn't need him.... why didn't he call???

Ian called on Friday, just as I was getting in from work. A bit breathless, I scrambled to grab my cell phone out of my purse.

"Hello?"

"Dana," said that deep voice. "It's Ian."

My heart started pounding hard. "Oh, hi."

"Sorry I didn't call all week. This job has me wiped out. Working long hours."

"That's ok," I heard myself say, though it really hadn't been.

"Can we get together tomorrow?" he said.

I should play hard to get. I should say no, I have plans. I should...

"Sure."

We made a date to meet and hung up. The next night I drove to meet him at the restaurant he had chosen. I had forgotten my nervousness over him not calling all week, choosing not to dwell on the fact that he could have picked up the phone for a quick call or even a text sooner than he had. I was just happy to be seeing him. And it was wonderful. We talked and laughed and bantered and flirted. And at the end of dinner, he asked if I wanted to follow him to his home. I didn't have to think about it. "Yes."

When we got there, he did not waste time. So much

for taking it slow. As soon as our coats were off, he turned to me, kissing me with open lips, with tongue, probing my mouth. He put his hands behind my back, pulling me to him. He pushed me slightly away then pulled me in again, closer, harder. He kissed me again. We started moving toward his bedroom, as he pulled his own shirt off and started slipping my dress down off my shoulders.

And we made love. It was ecstatic, it was amazing, it was…there are almost no words for what it was. I had never had sex like this. It was not just sex. It was a joining, it was mystical, it was magical. The word love floated through my mind like a cloud. I wanted this to never end.

When it was over, he held me, whispered in my ear, "You're amazing, you're beautiful." We dozed, then awoke and made love again.
I stayed the night.

And so, the relationship began.

From my journal:
December 11
It's hard not to not have a relationship and it's hard to be in one. I am in one at the moment; I don't know the definition of it, or the boundaries, but it exists, whatever it is. It's like a dance; sometimes it's almost like a battle. Only I don't always know the rules. It feels like I'm living on edge again. He keeps me quite off balance. Yet he pays attention- to what I say, to who I am. He is far from perfect, but he shows his flaws clearly. So far it seems to be reality based, there don't seem to be any illusions or fantasies. There have been no promises. No promises that could be broken, like in my last relationship. I've known him for a little over a month. I have feelings for him, but I'm not sure how to define those feelings. Sometimes it feels like deep tenderness, sometimes desire, sometimes burning anger and frustration. He's not easy with me; he pushes my limits. When we talk it's like verbal sparring. It can be exhausting. But he keeps my interest, like most men don't.

Chapter 2

Ian had done it again. Distanced himself.

We had been dating for over two months now. He was erratic, at times calling frequently, flirting, making plans to see me. When I saw him, it could be magical. The sex remained phenomenal. He made love like a young god. He paid such close attention to my needs, my desires. He focused wholly on me, as though there were only the two of us in the whole wide world. He kissed me with such passion, he undressed me with desire, he touched me with tenderness. He would move his kisses from my mouth down my body and back up, then kiss me with my own juices on his mouth. He told me I was beautiful, desirable. He never said that he loved me. But he would gaze at me with those deep blue eyes, gaze at me with passion so that I felt wanted, I felt loved.

A hobby of mine was writing poetry. I had even

been published a few times in poetry journals. I taught a class at work to my kids, teaching them to write poetry, to put their feelings, their frustrations, their loves and hates into words. Now Ian was my inspiration, my muse. I wrote poetry to him that I never shared.

Dragons

When we make love
The dragons come
White, yellow, red, purple
And the galaxies swirl
Their spiral arms
And I feel your spirit merge with mine
In brilliant colors
Our spirits make love
Like shadows above us
Mirroring our movements
And I travel to a world
Beyond time
Where I have known you for eons
Where I have never known you
Yet, you are myself.
Then, fearing,
I touch you, grope for you
You become flesh again
I return from the realms of angels
And my tears come
At leaving the place that is so beautiful
At sadness that we are separate again.
During those moments together
When we make love
We become
Light.

You

We have stripped each other's souls bare
I have seen your nakedness
Body and soul
And it is beautiful.
I have seen your soul
Shining through your eyes
I have seen the love
You hold sheltered deep inside you
I have seen your fear
And I am not afraid
I have seen your passion
And in passion you become a god
Worshipping the goddess
I have seen what you are
And caught glimpses of what you could be
I have seen your shadow
But I have also seen your light
And it is so beautiful
It hurts my eyes to look.

I wanted to share my words, my thoughts, everything with him. But I held back. I had learned that if I pushed too hard for anything, for time, for intimacy, he would back off. I wanted to share my poetry, but I was afraid to spook him. For I had learned that Ian spooked easily.

Although he would look at me with love and desire in his eyes, he would not always share his innermost thoughts. Sometimes we would talk for hours, but other times he would clam up and I would feel that I was looking for a key to open a door that was stuck solidly shut. Then he would get irritable with me if I kept pushing, so I would try to back off. I wrote in my journal:

February 9

I don't have any expectations. At least I'm trying not to. I just enjoy his company and know that (most of the time) he enjoys mine. And if he gets rejecting, I will let him know that I perceive it as a challenge, that his pushing me away isn't working, that he doesn't bore me as most other men do. That he isn't discouraging me. I want to let him know that.

I saw him last weekend and we made love. It was magical as always. He is so intense, so focused on me. It seems as though he loves me, though he doesn't say it. I'm afraid to say it to him. I stayed the night, but in the morning, he seemed distracted and said he had things to do. He didn't make plans to see me again. He frightens me and challenges me. Over and over again.

I felt nervous over the lack of contact with him. I argued with myself not to call him and won. I tried to read to distract myself but couldn't focus so I went to visit my mother, who lived in a town nearby. She had been alone since my dad had passed away some years ago when my sister was in college and I was in my last year of high school, his liver shot. My mom was doing ok now, she had created a life for herself. She had made new friends, even dated a little. She was not depressed as she had been when my sister and I were growing up. We had lunch together and she asked me about what was going on in my life.

"Are you seeing anyone, honey?" came her usual question after she had made lunch and we sat down to eat. She wanted to see me safely married like my older sister Tina.

"Yes. Kind of," I answered, not sure how to answer.

She laughed. "What exactly does that mean?"

I wasn't sure how to answer. "I have been seeing someone but… well, I'm not sure what the relationship is. How to define it."

"What's his name? What does he do?" That latter question was important to her. My dad never had a career, he kept losing jobs over his drinking. She'd had to be the responsible one, working hard to keep up with the bills. She wanted me to be with someone more settled.

"Ian. He does construction work. He works for different companies when they have work for him."

"Oh. That doesn't sound very secure."

"Mom…."

"Well, I'm just saying." She took a bite of her sandwich.

"I'm not engaged to him or anything." I felt a bit defensive. "We just started seeing each other a couple of months ago."

She raised her eyebrows. "And I'm just hearing about this now?"

"I told you, I'm not sure how to define it. I wasn't sure what to even tell you."

"Are you happy?"

That question took me aback. I hadn't considered it before. Did Ian make me happy? He made me many things. He made me feel beautiful and desirable when we made love. He made me feel frustrated and angry when he backed away. He made me laugh when he was in a good mood. But happy? If I was honest with myself, the answer was no, not really. He was too erratic. He kept me guessing, kept me on my toes. I was never sure where I stood. But should I say that to my mother, who worried about me?

"I guess so. Sometimes. But I'm not sure where the relationship is going. Or if it's going anywhere. Not yet."

She gazed at me for a time, then patted my hand. "Ok. But be careful. You don't want to end up with someone like…" her voice faded but my mind filled in the words, "your father."

I left my mother's place feeling disturbed. When I got home, I called Ginny.

"What's up?" she asked.

"Ginny, I don't know what to do. He backed off

again. I don't even know when I'll see him again."

"Can't you call and ask?"

"But he gets so skittish. He's like a deer in the headlights sometimes. I don't know what to do."

There was a moment of silence on the line. "Ginny?"

"Really, Dana, what do you want me to tell you? This guy is not that stable, ok? I know that's not what you want to hear...."

It was my turn to be silent for a moment. "I guess it's the truth. But..."

"But what?"

"I think I'm in love with him!" I burst out. "I'm crazy about him! I can't stop thinking about him. The sex is so amazing. It appears he loves me then I don't see or hear from him all week. It's driving me crazy!"

Her voice was softer when she responded. "I know. I know you care a lot for him. I just want to see you happy." She sounded like my mother. She continued, "Do you want to stop over? Derek is going to play basketball with his friends, I'll be here this afternoon alone."

"Ok, maybe I will." It was better than sitting here alone brooding.

I spent the afternoon with Ginny but felt restless again as soon as I left. I didn't want to go home. I wondered what the hell Ian was doing. It was Saturday, why were we not getting together, to go out, to make love? What the hell was he doing?

Then the thought came to me; I could drive past his house.

No.

Yes. Why not? Why the hell not?

Instead of turning my car toward my apartment, I headed in the opposite direction.

Ian lived in a small city about a half hour away. As I drove down the road, I argued with myself. This was stupid, this was childish, I am a grown woman of 34, what am I doing? This was like something one of the teenage kids that I worked with would do. But I kept on driving.

It was dark when I got to Ian's neighborhood. My heart was beating so loudly it was throbbing in my head. I slowed the car and drove past his driveway. I could see his black Toyota parked there.

And another car behind it.

Someone else was there. Someone else was there! Oh my God.

I didn't know what to do. I couldn't just knock on the door. I couldn't peek in the window. Oh, why did I even think of that? Wouldn't it just be great if I got caught and the headlines read, "Caseworker for Troubled Teens Arrested as Peeping Tom?"

So, I pulled my car over and parked on the street to wait. I could see lights on in the house. At least it wasn't dark. That would mean… could mean… that he was in bed with someone else. But the lights stayed on.

I waited. I waited. I had to pee. But I still waited.

After about an hour I thought maybe I should go home. What was the purpose of this? If he didn't want me, he didn't want me. There was nothing I could do about it. I started the car… then I saw his door opening. And a man came out and got into the other car.

My relief was so palpable I gave a great sigh. When the car was gone, without even thinking, I backed up my own car and pulled into his driveway. I was going to find out what was going on. At least I knew he wasn't having an affair. At least not that night.

I went to the door and knocked, operating on pure adrenaline. Ian opened it.

"Doug, did you forget something…" he started to say, then stopped, seeing it was me. "Dana. What are you doing here?" then, "Come in."

Now I was starting to wonder what I had been

doing. How was I going to explain this?

But he leaned over to kiss me and said, "You look great. It's good to see you," and I started to relax. I said, "I missed you. I had to come…. I mean, I was in the neighborhood…."

He pulled me to him and kissed me again. And again. "You look hot," he said. "You're so sexy," he said. And I stopped talking, stopped thinking. I was with him. That was all that mattered.

Chapter 3

Things continued like that; back and forth, up, and down, left, and right. Ian had been happy to see me that night when I stopped by unexpectedly. But there was no explanation for his lack of contact all week. I had stayed the night, and in the morning, he seemed to be in a good mood, bantering and joking with me. I sat and watched while he shaved that day. It was Sunday and neither of us had to work. I wondered if he wanted me to spend the day but was not going to say anything. I didn't want to spoil the mood. It did occur to me that the idea of saying something shouldn't cause such anxiety, but I still did not speak of it.

He finished shaving, gave me a big kiss, and went to the kitchen to make breakfast. He made pancakes, bacon, eggs, and coffee. A feast! He was treating me like a queen. He didn't let me help.

"Sit and relax," he said. "I've got this." I felt a bit guilty but complied. Why did it make me nervous when he was nice? Did I expect it to shift? Of course. That was why. He could be wonderful, then not call for a week. Suddenly it felt like too much.

"Why are you doing this, Ian?"

He turned from the stove to look at me. "Doing what? Cooking for you?"

"I didn't hear from you all week. Then I stopped over because…well, I was in town to… I had missed you…and" I faltered and went on, "It was wonderful last night. And now you're cooking breakfast and I… I just don't know where I stand with you." I finished, almost fearing to meet his eyes.

He turned back to the stove. I thought he wasn't going to answer at first. Then he said without turning around, "Look, Dana. I told you I had been hurt before. I'm struggling with this, ok? I'm trying. But sometimes it seems like…like just too much. You want so much. You want…me, it seems, so much of the time. And I just can't always deal with it."

My heart had started pounding in anxiety. "So, what do you want?" I asked in a small voice.

"I don't know. I'm just not sure. But right now," he turned to look at me this time, "I just want to make you breakfast. Do you think you can just enjoy that? And not always be asking for more?" His voice was tense, and I stiffened. Was I really asking for too much? Wasn't he my boyfriend? Was he? Was it too much to want to spend time with him?

But I answered, "Ok, Ian. I'm glad you're making me breakfast, I appreciate it. I'm sorry," I added, not sure exactly what I had done wrong. Except maybe to stalk him last night, but he had seemed happy to see me.

"Ok. Ok," he said, turning back to finish cooking. After a moment he added, "I was really glad to see you last night."

I felt a bit mollified.

We spent most of that day together, then I went home, feeling a bit better. He called me a couple of times that week. It seemed that he was trying. I started to relax a bit.

Then something happened at work. I went in on Thursday morning to find one of the caseworkers crying. "What happened?" I asked, alarmed.

"There's a meeting," she started and wiped her eyes, "There's a meeting at 9:00. One of the kids overdosed."

"Oh my God," I said, "who was it?"

"Jamie."

"Oh no. Is she…"? I could barely say it, "Is she alive?"

"She's in intensive care. They don't know if she'll make it."

Jamie was one of the girls that had been very hard to reach. She was hostile at worst, brittle at best. She was defensive and being nice to her seemed to elicit either verbal abuse or sarcasm. But she had kept coming in and attending activities at the center. She did seem to have a couple of friends among the other kids. My favorite, Pedro, was one of them.

Pedro! "Do the other kids know?" I asked Katie, my co-worker.

Katie sniffled, wiped her nose and said, "I'm not sure. Time for the meeting, the director probably knows more. Let's go in."

After the briefing about how to handle the situation we all went back to our offices, sobered and worried. These kids were volatile. Who knows how they would react when they found out? And we were worried about Jamie herself. Would she survive?

When the kids came in after school that day it was clear that some of them had already heard. Pedro and his friend George came up to me. "What do you know, Ms. Taggert? Do you know how she is?"

"No, sorry boys, I only know she is in the hospital and getting the best care. We can only hope and pray that she is ok."

"What's the point?" George said. "Even if she's ok, she'll only do it again."

I was taken aback. I had thought this was an accidental overdose. But George was implying that it had been purposeful. "George, why do you say that?"

He and Pedro looked at each other. It seemed that a silent message went between them. Pedro nodded slightly. George took a deep breath and looked back at me. "Her stepfather… he abuses her. You know. Touches her. She tried to kill herself."

I tried not to react with shock. This was not an uncommon story. But for some reason I did feel shocked. Shocked to the core. And scared. Because this one…. this hit too close to home. I tried to control my runaway emotions.

"Ok, well. You know we must report that kind of thing, boys. We have to take some action."

They both nodded. "We know. We weren't sure we should say anything," Pedro said, "But we thought we should. We want her to be ok. We want her away from that son of a bitch. If she's ok," he added.

I brought them to the director to report what they had said and to obtain more details, and then contacted Child Protective Services. I let them know that the girl in question was hospitalized. Later that day Jamie's caseworker called the hospital as we all waited on pins and needles to hear the latest news. She got off the phone with tears running down her cheeks. Fearing the worst, we waited to hear but she said, "She's out of the ICU. She's going to make it!" We all breathed a sigh of relief. I went out to the group of kids who were sitting more quietly than usual in the rec room. "It looks like she's going to be ok," I said. Some of the girls cried and hugged each other. Pedro and George looked at each other and then at me. "Thanks, Ms. Taggert," they said.

"Thanks to both of you," I said quietly. I didn't want the other kids to know what they had told me. Jamie was going to have a long road ahead of her, but we had reported the abuse and when she was better, we would get her some help. She would know that she wasn't alone. Unlike…

Unlike me.

Chapter 4

Ok, I haven't talked about it yet. Because I can barely stand to remember. Because it's just too painful. Because I have never in all these years fully come to terms with what happened.

It was my father. My beloved, fun loving father. My drunken fool of a father. My monstrous horrible father.

For he was all of these.

I had been twelve years old. My sister Tina was fourteen and had just gotten her own bedroom. She had been begging and begging, saying that she was too old to have to sleep with her annoying younger sister. So finally, my mother had made over a small room she used for sewing into a bedroom for me. My sister got the bigger room that had been ours to share until then.

I was excited about getting my own room. Money was short, as always, because my dad was always losing his jobs, but my mom worked hard, and she was frugal. She bought a cheap mattress and box spring and a secondhand dresser. She let me pick out a new bedspread and curtains. So, I moved into my new room.

My parent's bedroom was on the other side of the house. But my father often did not sleep there. He would come in drunk late at night sometimes, so he had taken to crashing on the couch, so he did not wake up my mother. I don't really think she was asleep on those nights, but he still stayed on the couch. Maybe he did not want to face her wrath. She wouldn't yell at him in the living room because it would have woken us up.

I was in my new bedroom one night when I heard him come in. I heard the door shut, then I heard him curse. I didn't like it when he did that. Sometimes he would just go right to sleep, but sometimes he was angry after drinking. This appeared to be one of those times. But I never would have guessed what would come next.

He came into my room.

At first, I thought he was confused. Maybe he meant to go into the bathroom next door. Maybe he had forgotten that I had moved into this room.

But he kept coming. To the bed. And got in. "Sweetheart," he said. And his hand started groping me. Groping my body. Finding my just budding breasts. Sliding down to my crotch. Slipping inside my panties.

At that point I was frozen for a moment. I thought I was dreaming. I thought it was a nightmare and I would wake up.

Then I came unfrozen and screamed.

Suddenly he pulled away, jumped up and ran out of my room. Just as my mother came running, with my sister behind her.

"What the heck?" said my sister, clearly angry with me. "You brat, you just woke me up, what are you screaming about?"

But my mother just looked at me. I will never forget the look on her face. She knew. She knew what had just happened.

My mother turned and went to find my father. He was sitting on the couch. She turned on him and slapped him hard on the face. And then she slapped him again.

Tina looked shocked. She had no idea what was happening. Now when she looked at me, she was no longer angry, but had a question in her eyes. A question she clearly feared the answer to.

"Get out of this house," my mother said. "Get out."

My father did not say a word. He got to his feet and walked out the door.

My mother did not say another word either. She glanced at me, looking more defeated than she had ever looked before, and she went back to her room.

Tina started to cry. Then she hugged me, and we just held each other for a minute. I didn't want to tell her what had happened. She didn't really want to know. She just knew it had been bad. "Do you want to come and sleep with me?" she whispered. I nodded. I stayed with her all night, but though she fell back to sleep, I did not. I lay awake all night.

My father came back. He came back a few days later. He was not drunk that day. He never said anything about that night. Neither did my mother. No one ever spoke of it again. He continued his drinking, but he never stayed out late again. He went back to sleeping in the bedroom with my mother. A few years later he became sick. Even when he was sick, he never said he was sorry. He never said anything at all. He treated me like I was not there most of the time after that. And sometimes I felt invisible.

When he died, my mother tried to commit suicide. She went home and took a bottle of tranquilizers that the doctor had given her to help her sleep when my father had gotten sick. Tina was living at college by then and had left to go back after the funeral, so I was the one who found my mother. I called 911 and she was rushed to the hospital. They had saved her. After that, she had rallied and gotten help. She had gone to counseling for a long time. Somehow, she had come to terms with herself because she had gotten better, gotten a new job, sold the house and moved to an apartment, and started a new life. She and I got along well now, and she was close to Tina too, who was the mother of her only grandchild. But we had never talked about any of what had happened. Ever.

And it still lived inside me, that frightened little girl whose father had betrayed her. And maybe that was why I kept seeking out men. I wanted a man to heal me. I had never been able to heal myself. But the men I fell for were often like my father. Unreliable. Frightened men who could not face reality and who could not be adults. Who hid behind drugs or drink or who ran away and never faced themselves. Those were the men I was attracted to. Men like my dad.

Men like Ian.

Chapter 5

Ian was not much of a drinker. But he did like to smoke weed. I didn't know that at first. I had learned gradually. Sometimes he would light up after sex. Sometimes when I stayed the night, he would light up in the morning "just to relax." I didn't really like it. Working with teens had opened my eyes to drug use and abuse, and I had never really done drugs myself, though I had tried weed when I was younger. Now, with Jamie's overdose, I was thinking about it more than ever, and feeling that maybe it was time to say something to Ian.

I also wanted support. I had been so shaken, not only by the overdose but by the revelation that Jamie was being sexually abused. After my initial shock I found myself going into a state of rage. I wanted to get that SOB who had done that to her! That angry brittle girl, whose defenses were so high she couldn't let anyone be good to her, she had been violated, she had been harmed, I was not going to let someone get away with that! Her stepfather would be charged and prosecuted. But I knew that it was not going to be easy and for Jamie, the road would be long and hard, though she would have the full support of the agency where I worked and of her friends. But I was upset. I was afraid. This event had triggered my own trauma. I wanted help. I wanted Ian's help. I wanted to hear his voice. I wanted to know he cared.

I called him.

It was early evening and I had gotten home late that

day. I heard the phone ring and ring. Where was he? I thought he would have been finished with work by now.

He didn't answer. I didn't bother to leave a voicemail. He could see that I had called by his call log.

In an hour and a half, he had not called back. I had taken a long bath, tried to relax but the events of the day had me too angry and upset. And now of course I was upset that I had not heard back from Ian. I needed him today! I needed him, where was he?

Finally, I called back. This time he answered.

"Ian!" I burst out. "I'm so upset! I have to tell you what happened today!"

But rather than be supportive, his voice sounded rather cold. "What?" he said shortly. I started to explain. But he cut me off.

"Look, Dana, I don't think I'm up for this right now. It was a rough day."

He had a rough day? He had a rough day?? But I needed him, I needed his support, I needed his caring. Before I could answer, though, I realized he was no longer there. He had hung up.

I was stunned. He was my boyfriend; he was supposed to be supportive of me. He was supposed to be there for me. He had said he would be there for me. I had never really asked him to help me before. This was big! This was important! How could he just cut me off?

I felt helpless and alone. I went to my couch, curled up in a ball and started to cry. I lay like that for most of the night, dozing on and off. I couldn't think about it, I couldn't do anything. I felt like that helpless little girl whose father had violated her trust, sending the world into a spin that never quite stopped. I wanted someone to be there for me. I had wanted Ian. But there was no one there.

Chapter 6

I am not sure how I dragged myself to work the next day, but I did. I was responsible, like my mother. No matter how I felt I did what I had to do. After my father did what he had done, I still went to school. I still studied and made decent grades. I graduated and went to college, then to grad school. I did what I had to do. I would do that now too.

But I felt devastated. By everything that had happened to Jamie. By my own trauma that had been triggered. And by Ian.

I didn't want to tell Ginny. When we met at lunchtime all we talked about was Jamie and how to proceed with what we had to do. I didn't mention Ian's response to my need. I knew what she would say. What did she know of it? She had a supportive boyfriend. Derek had come to pick her up the day before when she had called him and said she was too upset to drive home. He had brought her in this morning. He was there for her, he cared. But Ian didn't. And I knew what Ginny would say. I could picture the look on her face, I could hear her words in my mind. "Dana," she would say. "You deserve better. What are you doing with this guy?" And I would have no answer. Because despite everything, I wanted him. I wanted him terribly. I wanted to hear his voice, feel his touch. I felt I could not survive without it.

I went through my day as best I could, but it felt like sledging through mud. But I didn't even want to go home.

What would I do there? Just be alone, no one to call, no one to help. Helpless. Scared. Just alone.

I did go home eventually. I tried to eat but picked at my food. I tried to watch something on TV but couldn't concentrate. I tried to sleep but dozed, then woke up startled.

The next day was Saturday, which really scared me. What would I do with myself all day? And all night? I still didn't want to tell anyone how Ian had reacted. And I still felt helpless and scared, thinking about what had happened to Jamie and what had happened to me.

I decided to go out that night.

There was a bar with dancing where I used to go with a couple of girlfriends. These were casual friends, not anyone to talk to about serious things, but they enjoyed going out, having a few drinks, and meeting men. I went sometimes before I had met Ian. And where was Ian now? Not there for me. I would call up Bonnie and see if she was planning to go out tonight.

Bonnie was surprised but delighted to hear from me. "Lacy and I are going to the Bird's Nest," she said. "You're certainly welcome to meet us there. I thought you were seeing someone?" she added. "I haven't seen you out lately."

I tried to swallow my pain at her words. "I was but it isn't working out."

"Oh, sorry to hear that. Well, we'll see you tonight." We hung up and I felt a slight relief. At least I had something to do. I would go out, have a couple of drinks, dance and maybe flirt with some guys, and forget about everything for one night. Especially Ian.

I dressed carefully. I wore my usual costume of a short skirt, tight top, stockings, and heels. I was slender and could pull off this outfit. I put on heavier makeup than usual on my dark eyes, mascara, eyeliner, and dark eye shadow. I blushed my cheeks and put on pink lip gloss. I put on dangly earrings and brushed out my hair. I looked good. I was primed. I was ready.

I drove to the Bird's Nest and shortly found Bonnie and Lacy at the bar, flirting with the cute bartender. I ordered my drink and sat, chatting with my friends, trying to keep things light. When the music started a man came up to Lacy and asked her to dance. Lacy was a redhead, short, busty, and cute, and she often got asked first. Bonnie was a tall blonde, with long straight hair and full lips. She wrinkled her nose as Lacy walked off. "Why do they always go for her? She can be such a bitch." She laughed, taking the sting out of her words. Lacy was her best friend. "But I do love her." I just smiled.

It didn't take long for men to come up and ask us to dance as well. Soon I was shaking my booty on the dance floor, swinging my hips seductively against the tall thin man with an adorable smile who had asked me to dance. He had freckles and shaggy hair, and he seemed quite taken with me. When the music turned slow, he held out his arms and I went into them.

I was in full flirt mode. I pressed up against him. I looked up at him coyly (he was quite tall). He smelled good. He was cute. I was in the moment. I didn't know his name. But it didn't matter.

When the music had stopped, he asked if I wanted a drink. Another drink? I didn't hold my liquor well. But I said ok.

We went to the bar and he ordered my drink, as well as a beer for himself. He turned to me. "What's your name?" he shouted. The music had started again, and it was hard to hear. "Dana," I shouted back

"I'm Jerry."

"Nice to meet you."

He kept trying to talk to me, but it was difficult over the noise so when our drinks were finished, we started to dance again. I saw Bonnie dancing with a new guy for each song. Lacy was still with the first man who had asked her. I looked over at her, looked at Bonnie, and shook my head. I saw her laugh and nod.

I turned back to Jerry and snuggled up to him for a slow dance. It felt good. I had a buzz on, and I wasn't thinking about any of the problems in my life.

The dancing, the grinding, the snuggling led to the logical conclusion. He asked me to come home with him.

I was tempted. I wanted to forget all that was going on. I wanted to forget Ian.

"I'm not sure," I said. "But let's go out to your car." It was a clear invitation. We were soon making out like mad dogs in his car. He knew how to kiss. He really knew how to kiss. But when he touched my breasts and asked again if I would go home with him, I hesitated.

I would have done, once. But it didn't feel right. It just didn't feel right. He was cute, he was smart (during a break in the music he told me he was a computer tech), he was younger (30), he had an adorable smile.

But he wasn't Ian.

He wasn't Ian.

I suddenly pulled away. "I can't," I said. "I'm sorry."

To his credit, Jerry looked disappointed, but not angry. "Well, can I see you again then? Maybe take you to dinner?"

I thought, why not? Why not let this nice guy take me out? I don't have to have sex with him. Not if I don't want to. But maybe things will change, maybe he'll grow on me. I do think he's cute.

"Ok, I can do that," I told him. We exchanged phone numbers and I got out of his car. He got out too, and walked me to my car, which seemed like a nice gesture. He gave me a quick kiss on the cheek as I got in. "It was really nice to meet you, Dana. I'll call you," he said. And I knew that he would call. He would do what he said he would do. I could tell.

When I got home, I started to crash. Everything started to come back, and the pleasant feelings of the evening started to fade. I had a spasm of wanting Ian so deep I grabbed my stomach and bent over in pain. My eyes burned with tears. My longing for him, my desire for him, was desperate, it was raw and primal. It burned me from inside out. And I got out my notebook and wrote a poem. Another poem that he would never see.

Full Circle
M
I want to swallow you
To feel you slide down my throat
To take you into my womb
Then give birth to you
Squeezing the pain out of your head
With my contractions
Putting you to my breast and giving suck
Until you are a man
And your penis fills me
We come full circle.

Chapter 7

Ian called.

I hadn't expected it. The call came a week later. It had been, predictably, a very tough week at work. Jamie was out of the hospital and had been placed in a foster home with a very kind couple who specialized in working with abused kids. We were working on getting help for her and her stepfather had been arrested. Her mother was crazily angry that her husband had been accused. But the indictment would go forward; the evidence against him was clear. And Jamie had talked. She had talked about the abuse, finally, and was on the mend. It would take a long time, but she was on the mend. Pedro and George had gone to see her, as had some of the girls from our program, and they were encouraged by her attitude. She had realized that she really wanted to live, she said. She wanted to get better. She wanted to get on with her life.

And me?

I wanted to do that too.

Jerry had called, two days after we had met. He asked me out for Friday night. I had agreed. He seemed kind and stable.

But the longing for Ian, while l pushed hard against it, had not abated. It sat in my gut, coiled like a dark serpent, a deep primal wound, weighing me down.

I went out with Jerry on Friday. I met him at the restaurant he had chosen and was pleasantly surprised. The restaurant was a very nice one. He ordered a bottle of wine, told me to choose whatever I wanted to eat. He seemed nervous, which I found endearing. I really did like him. The date was pleasant and when it ended, he walked me to my car and kissed me gently goodnight. He did not ask me over to his house again. I was grateful for that. He promised to call soon, and I went home. I tried to concentrate on the date with Jerry, but thoughts of Ian assailed me. Ian had gotten to the core of me. He lived in my mind, in my body, even though I had known him for such a short time. He seemed to be in my sinews, in my blood.

I slept and dreamed of him. He was larger than life, he was naked and beautiful. Then he turned slowly into a snake, a huge serpent, writhing and strange. I awoke, frightened. The image took a long time to fade. In the middle of the night, unable to sleep, I wrote another poem:

In the Garden

We coil around each other
Like snakes
In the dark night
The earth breathes
Living scents
Around us
Our bodies slither wetly
Together
Into each other
We breathe each other's breaths
Think each other's thoughts
Become each other's
Flesh.

The next night he had called.

I had grabbed the phone without looking at the number, expecting that it would be Jerry. Then I heard that dark deep voice. "Dana." It was all he said. It was enough.

My heart caught in my throat. I could barely speak. He said again,

"Dana?" This time it was a question.

"I'm here," I choked out.

"So am I," Ian said. "I'm still here." He didn't say he was sorry. He didn't reference not being there for me. Not specifically. But I knew what he meant.

"Ok," I said softly.

"Can I come over?"

"Yes. Yes."

He was at my apartment an hour later. The moment he walked in, we grabbed each other as though we would never let go. We sucked at each other's mouths as though we were taking the breath from each other's lungs. We tore our clothes off, not making it as far as the bedroom. We had sunk onto the floor, grabbing at each other, clawing, grasping, as though if we let go one of us would sink into an abyss and never be found again.

Finally, we lay side by side, breathing heavily. I felt bruised and battered. I felt healed and whole. We finally went to the bed and he stayed the night, holding onto me.

The next morning the light of day caught us and made us a bit shy with each other. He got up, said he had to leave. But he lingered for a time, told me he would call. Then he said, "I was scared. I'm still scared. But you've gotten to me, Dana. You've gotten into my soul. I don't know how; I don't know why. But I missed you. I had to see you."

"Me too," I said. "Ian, I know you're scared, so am I. But we have something good, something rare. Don't..." I stopped, feeling tears well up, "Don't throw it away. Don't let it go. I won't let it go. You're too important to me."

He looked at me, gazing with those deep blue eyes. "I know," he said. He hugged me, kissed me goodbye, and was gone.

But this time I felt, I knew, he would be back.

Chapter 8

It took me days to realize that we had not even talked about anything. Not about what had happened at my work, not about Ian's drug use, not about anything. For some reason, we both seemed to feel a primitive need for each other, a body hunger, a desperate grasping need that only our physical union could satisfy. It had seemed all I craved in life. But now I thought with a start, what about talking things out? What about sharing the things that are going on in my life, having someone to lean on, to support me, to be supported by me? A relationship was more than just physical satiation. When I had met him, he had told me he would be there for me, that he wouldn't turn away. But when I needed him that was exactly what he had done.

Yet my hunger for him was so deep, so desperate, the intense passionate connecting sex had seemed like enough at the time.

He hadn't called since then but this time I was not worried. I felt the connection on a psychic level. But I knew we needed to talk. I would call him after work that night, I decided.

Work had finally been settling down, after the crisis. I was teaching another poetry class and some of the kids were getting skillful at putting their feelings into their writing. I was teaching them a new way of expression and it meant something to them. I could see it in their faces. It felt good.

That night after dinner, I sat down with my phone. I felt a little nervous, but it was more like nervous anticipation. I wanted to hear Ian's voice. I wanted to tell him I missed him. I wanted to fill him in on all that had been happening in my life.

He answered after two rings. I was happy to hear his voice. "Ian," I said, "I want to talk to you. I want to tell you what's been happening."

This time he did not shut me out. He listened. I told him about work, I told him about Jamie (without naming names of course), I told him about the poetry class, I bragged a bit about the kids I worked with. He listened. I felt so connected to him, so close. Maybe we had turned a corner. Maybe he had worked out some of those fears and we were on an upswing. Maybe he would not cut me off again. We said our goodnights warmly and I slept better than I had in weeks.

I was hoping to see him that weekend and I was not disappointed. He called, and when he didn't ask me over, I asked him. He told me to come on Friday night.

I arrived bearing gifts, a bottle of the zinfandel I knew he liked and a candle. He seemed glad, opening the wine, and pouring us both a glass. "To you," he said as he raised his glass in a toast. Then he smiled. "To us." That pleased me so much.

We sat and talked for a time and it seemed easy this time, being with him. The crude passion was quiet for the moment, the tension was gone.

Then he got up and lit the candle, saying, "Come on." He walked into the bedroom, holding the lit candle in his hands.

And we made love. We made love for a long time. How can I describe it? It was like traveling to another dimension. It was like a suspension in time. I didn't know if hours have passed, or only a moment. It was magical. Every cell in my skin felt alive with him.

He knew exactly what to do, exactly what I like. It was rough and intense, then it became slower, sweet, and tender. At one point he raised his head up and looked at me, looked into my eyes. It was like drowning in blue crystal. I put my hands up to his face and he kissed my face, my eyes. It felt like love. Not just lust. It felt like love. We never spoke the words. But it was there, between us, like a golden thread. It was there.

But morning comes. It has to come.

It seemed like a fragile balance between us had shifted. It felt more grounded, more solid. We parted tenderly, holding each other, kissing softly, sucking at each other's lips. I drove home with a smile on my lips that lasted for most of the day.

Chapter 9

I wrote another poem:

Desire

I want to taste you
I want to lick you to the very last drop
I want to smell your musk
I want to suck you
Down to the bones.

Ian. Ian. I knew now that I was in love with him. No doubt at all.

And was he in love with me? He didn't say it in words. But he said it with his eyes, with his body. I could see through to his soul when he gazed at me like that.

I went through my days in a daze of emotion, floating on a cloud, feeling little pain or exhaustion or tension. At night I called him, or he called me, and we talked, about nothing important, just connecting. He had taken to sending me short little texts while I was at work, just to say hello.

One day at lunchtime my phone buzzed with a text. I looked at it and smiled. Ginny, sitting across from me, noticed. "Who was that?" she asked nosily.

"Ian," I said.

"So now he's texting you at work?"

"Yes, sometimes."

"What does it say?" she leaned over to try to read

the screen.

"Stop it!" I laughed, moving the phone away. "It's private!"

"Oh, a little text sex," she said, amused by the line.

"Maybe," I prevaricated.

She got serious. "So, things are going better then, Dana?"

"They seem to be. Yes."

"I'm glad. I want you to be happy. I wasn't sure at first... but maybe it just took some time."

"Maybe." I didn't want her to burst the bubble I had been floating around in. But she didn't say any more and we went on to speak of other things.

But then he did it again.

The weekend was approaching. It was now April and spring was in the air. It was warmer and flowers were blooming. My favorite time of year. I wanted to share it with Ian. I wanted to share everything with him.

I was hoping we could go to a flower show that Saturday. When I called that evening after work, he seemed distracted, a bit distant. I could feel a flutter of nerves in my stomach. But I forged ahead. "I thought we could go to the flower show this weekend, Ian. It's really beautiful and..."

He interrupted me. "Dana, I can't go this weekend. I'm busy."

I was flabbergasted. He was busy? With what? We had been seeing each other every weekend for over a month now with no breaks.

"What do you mean?"

"I made other plans. With a friend."

"But...with what friend?"

Ian seemed annoyed. "I do have friends, Dana. I do have a life, you know."

"I didn't mean...I know you have friends. I know you have a life! But we've been together so much lately, we've been having so much fun. I love being with you. Why…" I broke off, feeling hot tears start to burn my eyes.

His patience broke. "Oh, for God's sake, Dana. I made plans with a friend. So what? I have the right to do what I want. We're not married. I don't owe you an explanation for everything I do. I'm ending this conversation. Do something else, call your friends. I'm busy. Bye." He was gone.

I sat frozen in my chair. Things had been going so well, now this? I wanted to call back immediately, to hear his voice saying kind things, to hear him tell me he didn't mean it, he wanted to see me, he loved being with me. But I didn't redial the phone and it remained silent. My stomach was in knots again, and I remembered how this had felt the last time he cut me off. I didn't think it would happen again, I thought we had gotten past that. But we had not. He had not.

Well, maybe I would do as he had said. Maybe I would call some friends. In fact, maybe I would call Jerry.

For Jerry and I had become friends of a sort.

He had never stopped calling me, but when Ian and I had started seeing each other again, I had come clean with Jerry and told him about it. I knew he liked me still, but he was willing to be just friends. We would talk on the phone regularly, and a few times had gone out for coffee or pizza. I had been right about him. He was a kind and decent man I gathered myself together and called him. I told him what had happened.

Jerry was good for me. He told me that Ian was a fool, that he did not appreciate me, that I was casting my pearls before swine. He asked me if I wanted to hang out with him the next day and I said I would. I hung up feeling a little better. Ian, you are not the only fish in the sea! You are not the only man around! In fact, you are a jerk of the first order!

But his unkind words burned inside me.

I wrote:

Words

Your words burn like white ice
Ripping at my soul
Your words are harsh and cold
Like the icicles that hung from your roof
Last winter.
Sometimes warmth bursts inside you and melts
them
But only for a moment.
Then they grow cold again
And hang in the air, frozen, above your head
I can feel them
Frostbitten
In my heart.

Chapter 10

From my journal:

April 8
I miss him so intensely. How can he not miss me? How could I have meant so little? I need to know this. I am obsessed with knowing this. If I meant nothing, if I was just a fling, then a pursuit is not worth it. But if I did mean something, if those feelings were real between us, if that's what he's running away from, then it makes more sense. I can understand the fear and anxiety of getting into something that heavy or serious, that intense. It's either that- or I didn't matter at all. I need to know.

But how was I going to find out. Reach out again? And possibly be rejected again?

I finally told Ginny what was happening. She said, "Don't pursue him, Dana. You're worth more than that. Why don't you go out with Jerry? He really likes you and he's a nice guy. He doesn't play head games."

Was that was Ian was doing? Playing head games? Fucking with my mind? And my body and soul? For he had reached within the depths of me, the deepest darkest depths of me, the parts I never shared with anyone else ever. The parts I had buried deep. Somehow, he had reached inside, shone a light on those parts, even gave me hope. How could he just leave?

A week, two weeks went by, then three. No word from Ian. I went about my days, I worked. I spent time with Jerry, but as a friend. I tried to take my mind off Ian.

But he came to me. He came in dreams. He came in waking thoughts. He came to me larger than life, in feelings so deep they felt like wounds, jabbing into my heart, into my soul. I knew that no matter what my friends told me I would have to act. Soon.

I planned how to do it. Call? Stop over? I went back and forth, tormenting myself. I told myself that I would ask my questions, that I just needed to know what had happened. Then I would be able to move on.

I decided to wait until Sunday. I was afraid to call on Friday or Saturday night, afraid he would be out- or maybe be with someone else. Sunday seemed safer.

So, I steeled myself on Sunday evening to dial Ian's number. I felt terrified. Did I really want to know the answers? Would he even talk to me? Would he even answer? Would he be cruel? Would he…

He answered.

"Ian," I said.

"Hello, Dana." So, he wasn't going to reject me right off.

"I just needed…I just wanted… to ask you something."

"Ok." His voice sounded neutral, not warm, but not cold either.

"Did I mean anything at all to you?" I blurted out. He didn't answer right away.

"Ian? I just want to know. I need to know that. It seemed like we had something so special, so… then it was just gone. You were so cold. I don't know why. I want to know. Was I just someone to have a quick fling with, or did I mean something to you? I won't bother you again, I just need to know."

"Dana. Don't you know you did mean something to me?" he said softly. "You still do."

I was surprised by his last words. And angered.

"I still do! I still do? But you blew me off a few weeks ago, you told me to call friends, you wouldn't tell me where you were going. You were so cold! And you haven't called. It's been three weeks! How can you say I still mean something, Ian, how can you?"

"I know, I know. I didn't handle it very well."

"Handle what?"

"Look, Dana. I'm…interested in you. You do mean something to me. I enjoy what we have together. But I… it seemed to be going too fast. I feel…claustrophobic sometimes. I know I can't always give you what you need. I pull away to get a breather. Then you freak. It's too much sometimes. I can't deal with you like that."

I was upset but tried to keep the anger out of my voice. At least he was talking to me, giving me some explanation. And he did say I meant something to him.

"Ok, Ian, then what is it you want? I never seem to really understand what it is you want."

"I'm not sure," he said slowly.

"Do you miss me at all?" I asked bluntly.

"Yes," he said, "I do miss you."

My voice softened, "I miss you too. So- are we going to see each other at all?" I asked that with trepidation, but it was time for a reckoning. I needed to know.

"Yes, I would say so." But no plans were offered.

"When?"

"Please don't push, Dana. Please don't push. We will see each other soon. Just give me a little more time."

Time for WHAT? I wanted to yell, but I didn't. I said, "Ok. Ok, fine."

He knew I wasn't happy. "Dana…"

"What?"

"Dana… I do care about you," he said. I guess I had to accept that. I guess it had to be enough. For now.

"Ok," I said again. "Maybe we can talk again soon." I would have to leave it at that. We said our goodbyes and hung up.

I would have to leave it at that. I would have to accept the crumbs he offered if I ever wanted to be with him.

But that was really hard. Because I wanted the whole loaf.

Chapter 11

My birthday was coming up soon in early May. Every year my mother and sister threw a little family party for me at my sister's house. She lived about two hours away in a small town in Vermont. I usually drove there with my mom. My sister was a teacher at an elementary school and was happily married to Lenny, who managed a hardware store. They had one son, my nephew Collin, who was now a sophomore in high school.

I was looking forward to seeing my family, but I was also sad. I thought about how nice it would be to have a boyfriend who would be coming with me to celebrate with my family. A boyfriend who was kind and caring, a boyfriend who was there for me. Instead, what did I have? Did I even have a boyfriend? Ian was... what to me? Just a lover? Right now, he wasn't even that.

I was quiet on the trip to my sister's. My mother didn't push. She could tell I was upset and didn't want to talk. I tried to put on a happy face when we got there. I didn't want Tina to start wondering if there was something wrong. We were close enough, but we didn't usually talk about deep or difficult issues. Since that terrible incident in my childhood, we seemed to have come to a mutual agreement not to discuss such things, as though talking about anything difficult would lead us back to that time that we both wanted to forget.

I hugged my sister, and my nephew, and my brother-in-law. I exclaimed over the decorations they had put up for my birthday, and the delicious meal and cake. Lenny was the baker, and he was very good at it. My sister burned anything she tried to bake. Collin caught me up about his life, what he was doing in school, his soccer team. My gifts were opened. One was a book of poetry by e.e. Cummings, whom I admired greatly. The other was a slim silver necklace from my mom. I thanked them for the party and the gifts, putting on the necklace. It was a very pleasant time and I put Ian out of my mind for a while.

On the drive back, my mom finally spoke up. "Dana, I didn't want to ask before but…are you ok?"

I didn't really want to talk about it, but she went on.

"What about that man you were seeing? I haven't heard you say anything lately about him.

"We broke up. I think."

She looked at me. "What do you mean, you think? Don't you know?"

I pondered this question for a moment. It was a logical question. How could I not know whether we were broken up or not? It sounded ridiculous. But it felt like the truth. I didn't know. I didn't really know at all.

"It's complicated, Mom. I mean… I guess we're taking a break, see what happens."

"Oh. Why?"

Why? That was a really good question. Why the hell were we taking a break? Because he was freaked out by closeness, by intimacy, by whatever it was that we had between us.

"I guess Ian has problems, Mom. He's a bit skittish." I wasn't sure how else to explain it to my mother.

"That doesn't sound good," she said, looking worried. "It doesn't bode well."

I didn't really want to hear this. "Can we talk about something else?" I said shortly.

"What about that other guy you told me about? What's his name? Jeff?"

"You mean Jerry?" I had mentioned that I had met someone named Jerry and he seemed nice. She had latched onto that. I wished I hadn't told her.

"Jerry, yes. You said he was a nice person."

"He is."

"Why don't you go out with him?"

"Mom! We're just friends!" I was getting a bit aggravated by this conversation. "Come on, Mom, it's my birthday, can you let up?"

"Ok, ok, sorry. I just want you to be happy, dear." She was silent after that and I felt guilty for snapping at her.

After a few moments I said, "I know you do. I'm ok."

. She gave me a small smile but said nothing more. I dropped her off at home. We hugged and I told her I would see her soon. I went home feeling frustrated with myself and my reaction to her questions. This is what Ian did to me. My feelings were in turmoil, I was snapping at my mother, I was nervous and scared. Was this all worth it? Why couldn't I just let go? Why the hell couldn't I just let go of him?

But that thought frightened the hell out of me.

Chapter 12

Maybe I would try.

I awoke with that resolve in my mind.

Maybe I would try to let go of Ian. Maybe I should give Jerry a chance.

I went to work. There was a surprise that day. Jamie had come back. Everyone was so happy to see her. She looked pale and wan, but she was ok. Her sarcasm was alive and well, but the surliness was gone. She came over to me with her friends, Pedro and George and another girl, Amy. "Hi Ms. Taggert," she said, then with a nudge from Pedro, "Thanks for helping me." I couldn't help it, I reached out and gave her a quick hug. After looking a bit taken aback, she hugged me too then pulled away. Pedro gave her one of his big grins, then looked at me.

"You ok, Ms. Taggert, you ok." They walked away. Tears came into my eyes. This was what it was all about, helping these kids. This was what gave my life meaning.

That evening I gave Jerry a call. We hadn't talked in almost a week and he seemed surprised to hear from me. We talked about what had been going on in our lives then decided to get together the next day. Before we hung up, he said, "Glad you called. I was going to call you anyway, there's something I wanted to tell you."

"What?"

"Let's wait until tomorrow."

"Ok." I didn't think much more of it.

The next night we met at the local pizza place for

dinner. I got there first and smiled when I saw his tall lanky form come through the door. It was good to see him. I gave him a big hug. We had worked out that we would take turns paying. That way there was no tension about who would pay for dinner. It was his turn this time.

We talked for a while, and he didn't bring up what it was that he wanted to tell me. I finally asked. "Jerry, you said you wanted to talk to me about something. What is it?"

He looked nervous for a moment then said, "I wanted to tell you that I met someone." He looked me directly in the eyes, waiting.

And for some reason, instead of being happy for him I was upset. I tried not to show it.

"Oh, that's…nice. Where did you meet her?"

"I had an ad out. She responded. We went out a couple of times and…she's cute, we hit it off."

"Oh, that's…" I started to say again, but he cut me off.

"You're upset, aren't you, Dana?"

I got defensive. "Why would I be? We're just friends."

"Because you depend on me. You depend on me to be there when you need me." Jerry was insightful. Too much so sometimes.

"Jerry," I said, "Isn't that what friends do for each other?"

"Yes, Dana, I know that but what I mean is…you depend on me when Ian isn't around."

I felt a bit stung. I really liked Jerry as a friend. I thought of myself as a good friend to him too.

"I would be there if you needed me, Jerry!"

"I didn't mean that you wouldn't but…if Ian beckoned, you would go running no matter what."

I started to protest, then shut my mouth. How could I get angry about what Jerry had said? It was the truth.

But wait. Wasn't I going to give up on Ian? And start dating Jerry? This was all wrong. What a time for him to meet someone else!

"Jerry, look. I know I've been, well, obsessed with Ian. I really cared for him. But he isn't there for me and you have been and... well, I thought maybe we should start dating. Each other."

He looked at me, surprised. "When did you decide that Dana? Just now when I told you I met Sandy?"

"No!" I felt hurt again. "I've been thinking about it. You're good to me and we get along. I know I don't always go out with the best of men. I seem to be attracted to the bad boys. But I do like you, and... maybe it would work out."

He just gazed at me for a moment. "Dana," he said softly, "You know I really like you. And I'm really attracted to you. I was from the minute I saw you at the Bird's Nest. I wanted to go out with you. But you were... elusive."

That word surprised me. Me elusive? I wasn't the one who was elusive! Ian was the one who was elusive! But I realized with a start that Jerry was right. I wasn't elusive with Ian because he was the one who always pulled away. But with Jerry, with some of the other men who had liked me, I was the one pulling away, I was the one who ran.

Jerry was right.

"I'm sorry, Jerry."

"I understand. I know that you care for Ian." Then he said, "Are you sure about this, Dana? Because you know I'm still really attracted to you."

Was I sure? Was I? Jerry and I had become good friends. I didn't want to mess that up. But my birthday lunch had made me realize that I wanted so much to have someone who would be around, that I could make plans with, who would come with me to flower shows and birthday lunches, who would talk to me when I got upset and hold me when I cried. Jerry would be the type of boyfriend who would do those things.

"Yes," I told him. "But if you like this woman, Sandy, well…"

"It's ok. There were no promises made," he said. "I like her, but I like you better."

It seemed that it was decided.

I went home with Jerry that night.

As I said, he was a good kisser, as I had learned that night when we made out in his car.

He wasn't only a good kisser. He was good in bed. He made sure I was satisfied. He cared about what I needed. The physical part was good.

So why did I cry after?

I tried to stop the tears, but as I lay in bed with Jerry, all I could think of was Ian. And the tears started, and they flowed down my cheeks, and they just would not stop.

Jerry didn't turn away. He may have understood why I was crying, but he didn't turn away. He held me and made soothing sounds and stroked my hair until the tears finally stopped and I started to doze. I should have felt safe with Jerry. I did feel safe with Jerry. But I didn't feel safe. I still longed for what I couldn't have. I longed and longed for Ian.

Chapter 13

It had been over a month since I started dating Jerry. We had gotten into a routine. A few times a week I would stay at his house. I didn't want him to stay at my place. It had too many associations with Ian. Jerry had a small ranch style house that was close to his work. He would bike to work in good weather. About once a week we would go to dinner, usually at our favorite pizza place. He had taken to paying now that we were dating. Sometimes we went to a fancier restaurant as a treat. Other times he would cook. He was a good cook, creative, much better than me. He was always generous and caring.

I had even brought him to lunch at my mother's. Excited to meet my new boyfriend, she had made quite a spread. Jerry was pleasant and charming. She had called me later and said, "He's so nice, Dana, I really like him. He has a good job, he's pleasant, he's good-looking. I hope…" she trailed off and I waited for a criticism. Of me, not him. "I hope you stay with him," she finished. She knew that I usually went for the bad boys.

"I like him too, Mom," was my neutral answer. I did like Jerry. In fact, I was very fond of him.

But I wasn't in love with him.

I had been spending all this time at his house but had started to resist the sex. We would have dinner, then curl up on the couch to watch TV or a movie together. He was easy to talk to and I felt comfortable and safe cuddling with him.

But I just didn't want to have sex with him. And it was starting to cause a problem.

The first time I resisted, he didn't say much. We went to bed and he held me, maybe thinking I was just not in the mood that night.

But it happened again. And again. Finally, he had to speak. I had been waiting for it.

"Dana?" he said one evening, after we had finished watching a movie, "What's going on?"

"What do you mean?"

He was straightforward. "We don't have sex anymore."

"We just did…. I mean we did it…." I realized that it had been over a week ago, even though I saw him multiple times a week.

"Dana," he said again. His voice was not harsh, and I felt the tears welling up. He was such a good man, a good person. Why couldn't I love him the way he wanted to be loved? But it wasn't there. Those feelings were just not there.

Because I was still madly, crazily, wildly in love with Ian.

I didn't want to tell him that. "I'm sorry, Jerry. I have just been… well, I've been down lately, just not in the mood, but…I know you're good to me and I really like spending time with you…" I was stumbling, not sure what to say. Then I rallied. "Let's go to bed."

He looked at me, then said, "You sure?"

"Let's go," I repeated.

I took the initiative that night, trying to put Ian out of my mind. I wasn't going to screw this up! This relationship was a good one. Jerry was supportive and kind. He was everything a boyfriend should be. I needed to try harder.

It wasn't so bad, I told myself. I was really fond of him. I enjoyed his company. We could talk without arguing. I knew exactly where I stood with him. He was clearly in love with me. He gave me tender looks, listened to me talk about my kids from work, made pertinent comments if I had a problem. The only fault he seemed to have was working too much. He would get caught up and sometimes forget anything else. But he didn't get angry when I told him that. He would laugh a bit self-consciously and tell me how much he loved what he did, but he would try to do better, and if I needed his attention to just let him know.

My friend Ginny was thrilled that I was seeing Jerry. We had gone on a double date with her, and Derek and she was full of approval. She too urged me, in a less nice way than my mom, to "not fuck this up."

We even went to visit his parents, who lived in a small town in nearby Vermont. It was a beautiful drive. I was a bit nervous, but not very. They were both retired college professors. He had one sister, who had moved to California, but they stayed in touch regularly. His parents were lovely, greeting me happily. They gave their son big hugs, then both hugged me. They seemed very pleased that he had found someone.

I felt guilty.

I wasn't sure I could keep this up. But I kept on.

Another month went by.

Then the inevitable happened.

Did I know it would happen? On some level, maybe I did. Because I started to feel him. I started to sense him around me. Ian.

His voice, his face would pop into my mind and I would have the overpowering sense that he was thinking of me in just that moment. A current would run through my whole body, as though he had touched me from afar.

I didn't go to Jerry's every night. We were seeing each other about three or four times a week. He sometimes had work meetings, or projects that he had to finish. And I had to admit to myself, it was sometimes a relief not to be with him. It could be difficult hiding the fact that I didn't want to jump his bones, that what I felt for him was more like friendship than love.

One night I had fallen asleep early, being exhausted from the day. We had held a sports competition for the kids at a local gym and track and it had gone very well, though was a lot of work to pull together. I had been especially pleased that Jamie had won the racing competition. She was doing so well now, considering what she had been through.

I startled awake, my heart pounding. I sat up.

I heard a knock.

I heard it again.

I glanced at my bedside clock. It was almost midnight! What had happened? Why was someone knocking on my door at this hour?

Alarmed, I grabbed my robe and went slowly to the front door without turning on any lights. The knock came again, making me jump. Then I heard his voice, "Dana?"

Ian.

Ian was at my door.

I took a deep breath. I could just pretend I wasn't there. No, he would have seen my Honda in the parking lot. I could pretend I was asleep. What right did he have to come knocking on my door this late at night, scaring the hell out of me? What right did he have at all? I was with Jerry now. I was settled. I was…

I missed him. I wanted to see him. No power on earth could have made me keep that door shut.

I opened the door.

He just stood looking at me for a moment. His hair was longer, falling in his face. He hadn't shaved and his face was rough. He looked exhausted and disheveled.

He was the most beautiful thing I'd ever seen.

He stepped inside my apartment and I closed the

door. And turned to him. "What the hell are you doing?"

"Dana, I'm sorry, I'm sorry for all of it. I had to see you. I tried to forget you, but…I couldn't. I was wrong. I had to see you."

"You couldn't have called at a reasonable hour like a normal person? Oh, wait. You're not normal. You're special. The world has to cater to your demands." I wasn't going to let up on him. He had hurt me so badly, then he just showed up? Months later? In the middle of the night??

But I had let him in.

"Dana, you're right," he said "You're right about everything. I haven't been sleeping well, I haven't been… things haven't been good. I started wondering why I did what I did. You know I was scared…but that's no excuse. I should have talked to you; I should have explained. I can't… I can't forget you."

My heart was softening toward him. He sounded so contrite, so sincere. And I felt the familiar pull, the desire, I wanted to touch him, to feel his skin against mine, to climb inside him, to ravish him, to…

He held out his arms. And I went into them.

After that there were no more words.

Chapter 14

And so, it began again.

He stayed all night, holding me, whispering words in my ear. We made love again that morning, even though I had to get up for work.

I was late to work.

We had finally parted. He had kissed me; told me he would call. I believed him.

At work I tried to avoid Ginny. She knew me too well; I was afraid she would see that something was up. I even went out for lunch, grabbing a sandwich at a local deli, rather than have lunch in the usual lunchroom at work. Of course, she would notice that too, but I could just say I had to run errands.

But I couldn't avoid her forever.

And I couldn't avoid Jerry.

Jerry and I spoke nightly on the phone when I wasn't at his house. I was grateful that tonight was not a night when I would be going over there. He had to work late and was supposed to call when he got home. I wasn't sure what I would say to him.

But all I could think about was Ian. His voice, his body next to mine, his heat, his warm words in my ear, his smell, his touch… everything.

He felt like everything to me. The reason for living, the pleasure in life, the sun, the moon, the stars, everything.

This was what it felt like to be in love. Madly,

passionately, deeply in love. It was worth more than anything.

What was I going to do?

I have a conscience. I don't want to hurt people. I care for others and try to treat them well. That was why I worked in the profession I was in. I certainly didn't want to hurt that wonderful soul who was Jerry, who had been so kind and good to me. But how could I not hurt him?

Because I couldn't go back to him now.

Jerry called when he said he would. He always did.

I was on pins and needles, of course, because Ian hadn't called yet. It was only about 8:00 but this was my usual response to Ian. Nervousness, fear, worry, excitement, terror, passion, love…my usual response. All over the map.

But what would I say to Jerry?

He called, and we talked of nothing. Casual chit chat how was your day. If he sensed me holding back, he didn't mention it. At the end of the conversation, he said, "See you tomorrow? Regular time?" and I realized with a pang that it was one of my usual nights to stay over. But how could I? How could I stay with Jerry now, sleep in his bed, have sex with him? How, when I felt that I belonged, body, mind, and soul, to Ian?

But what could I say? "I'll see you," I said, and we hung up.

It took Ian until almost 9:00 to call. I had been so nervous waiting for the call that I was holding my cell phone in my hand and jumped when it rang. He sounded wound up. He was talking very fast.

"Dana, I got held up, I was going to call earlier." I didn't ask him what had held him up.

"That's ok," I told him, holding the phone like a lifeline, just so happy to hear that deep dark voice. We talked, we bantered, he told me I had looked so hot the night before, all rumpled from sleep, with no makeup on.

"You're organically sexy," he said. That thrilled me down to my toes. "I want to fuck you again," he said. "Soon."

We made plans for Friday. I hung up glowing, and did not think of Jerry, or anything else at all. Ian was the only one who existed for me. Only Ian.

When I went to Ian's and walked into the small house that he rented I was surprised to see boxes full of his things. Some of his furniture was gone. I turned to him. "What's going on? Are you moving?"

"Yes, I have to move."

I felt a knot in my stomach. "Where are you moving to? Is it nearby?" I was afraid he was planning to move far away. No, no, not after we had just gotten back together, just gotten started again.

He named a town that was not far. I breathed a sigh of relief. He said, "I rented a cabin over there. It's rural, near a lake, it's really beautiful."

"Sounds nice. Why are you moving? I thought you liked it here."

Ian hesitated. A dark look passed over his face. I saw it.

"What, Ian? Tell me," I urged.

"Well, I've been having some money issues," he said. "Problems at the job site. The construction manager is a jerk. We had an argument." He stopped.

"Did you lose your job?"

"He wanted me off the site." Ian saw my face. "Don't worry, I know some other guys who will hire me, they have a project coming up, but work is slow right at the moment."

"You can't just stay here?"

"It costs too much; I rented a cheaper place." Then, "Dana, what's the big deal? What difference does it make? It's only a little further away from where you live. I like the rural setting, it suits me. I'll start working again soon. It's not that big a deal."

I wasn't sure why I didn't fully believe him. He had looked disheveled and disturbed when he showed up late at my apartment the other night.

But maybe it had just been because of me. Because he had been upset with himself over how he treated me. That's what I told myself anyway.

"Ok, I just worry about you," I told him. "But it's ok."

"I didn't ask you over here to argue. Or to talk about moving." He came toward me. "Or to talk about anything." His voice had softened. He put his hands around my head, pulled my face to his, kissed my lips. He pulled off my coat, started to unbutton my shirt. He stopped, but only to slide his own shirt off, then his jeans. He wasn't wearing underwear. He never wore underwear. I gasped with pleasure as he continued to undress me. And then I thought of nothing else but him.

And Jerry?

Usually Jerry and I got together on Friday. I had called him today and made up an excuse. The silliest one in the world. My mom was not feeling well, and I had to go and take care of her.

Of course, when I called to cancel with Jerry, he had been solicitous. He offered to come with me. He offered to pick up chicken soup and Kleenex. I put him off, saying she didn't like seeing people when she was sick. He seemed a bit hurt, as though he had thought of himself as not just "people" but family. But he backed off, and said, "Of course, Dana. Let me know how she's doing." So of course, I would have to call him on Saturday to maintain the fiction.

I left Ian's house in a glow of sex and passion, but also worry. Worry about him and his financial situation. Worry about what I would say to Jerry. Worry about my lies, and how in the world was I going to keep them up? The truth was, I couldn't. I had to come clean with Jerry.

I had offered to help Ian move that day, but he said he was fine. He had a friend coming to help with the heavier items and he had sold off a lot of furniture because the new place was smaller. He would be fine.

I didn't realize until later that he had never given me his new address. But I would get it from him when we spoke.

I thought about how I would tell Jerry I couldn't see him anymore, at least as a boyfriend and lover. I still liked him so much. I chastised myself for dating him. I should have just kept him as a friend. He had been such a good friend! Why had I been so selfish as to date him? He could have dated that woman he had met, Sandy, and probably would be much happier. Because now I was going to break his heart.

But I hadn't been thinking of him. I had just been trying to find a way to get over Ian.

As though that was possible.

I wanted to call Jerry but chickened out. Eventually he called me.

"Dana," he said when I answered, "How's your mom?"

Oh my God. The sick mom excuse. "She's fine," I faltered, "Feeling better."

Jerry said nothing for a moment, then, "Dana? Is something else going on?"

I'd been caught out. Jerry had always been perceptive.

"Dana? Be honest with me."

I still said nothing, and he said, "Is it Ian?"

I had to tell the truth, at least partially. "He contacted me."

"And? Are you going to see him again?"

I didn't tell Jerry that I already had. "I still care for him, Jerry," I said softly. "I'm sorry, Jerry, I care about you so much. I really do, but…. I still have feelings for Ian. I…"

I heard his intake of breath over the phone. "I knew

that you did. I knew you still loved him. But he was so mean, I thought if I was good to you, you would…that maybe you would start to forget about him. He seemed so unstable, so… well, so cruel at times, I couldn't believe how he treated you…. you seemed so unhappy with him, I thought… I thought I could make you happy, Dana. I wanted to make you happy. This other guy didn't seem to do that for you," he said, apparently not even wanting to use Ian's name. He added, "You know I love you, Dana."

Oh my God. Did he have to say that now? And I didn't want to hear about how badly Ian had treated me. I wanted to focus on how much Ian had missed me, that he still wanted me. I felt the tears start. "Jerry, I care for you very much, but I just…I still love Ian."

"You were selfish, Dana," he said, sounding a bit angry. I had never heard that tone in his voice before. "You could have told me how you felt. You could have told me when we started going out that you were still in love with him."

This seemed unfair. Jerry had known how vulnerable and sad I'd been. He knew that I had really loved Ian. Did he really think I would have gotten over it so soon?

But maybe he was right. I had thought the same thing myself- that I had been selfish.

"Jerry, I'm sorry. I'm sorry."

"I guess I knew it might not last with someone like you."

I wasn't sure what that meant. But he told me.

"I mean, I'm not really your type. I'm stable. I'm not exciting. I don't drink or use drugs or blow you off."

"Come on, Jerry. I like that about you."

"No, you want to like that. But it just doesn't turn you on. You need someone way more exciting than me. You don't get turned on by kindness or stability."

He was right. Jerry had hit the nail on the head. I

didn't get turned on by those things. I may like them; I may appreciate them; but I didn't want to have sex with men like that or have a relationship with a man like that.

"Jerry…"

"I'm going now, Dana. I have to go." And he hung up.

I sat holding my phone for a long time. I had hurt Jerry so much. He hadn't said very kind things about me. He had said things I found hard to face, didn't want to face about myself.

But his words had the ring of truth. I couldn't deny that.

Chapter 15

I sat alone that night.

I knew Ian was moving. I had broken up with Jerry. I was back with Ian, but I was still alone.

I had hoped that Ian would call when he had gotten moved in, at least to tell me how it had gone. But the phone was silent. I thought about texting, but decided not to, I didn't want to bother him. The thought crossed my mind that if it had been Jerry I wouldn't have hesitated to text. But with Ian I just couldn't be sure of his reaction.

But didn't we just get back together? Hadn't he said he missed me, that he had been sorry for how he behaved before? Didn't that bode well for our future?

I wanted to believe that, but when I went to bed that night it was hard to fall asleep, and my dreams, while I didn't remember their content, were troubled.

On Sunday I awoke and made a light breakfast but found it hard to eat. The same thoughts from the night before were roiling in my head. Guilt about Jerry. Worry about Ian. Worry about the fact that he lost his job, worry that he didn't have enough money, worry that he wouldn't call or text. It seemed that after that initial burst of faith in him, that I was right back to where I had been a few months ago. Nerves knotting the pit of my stomach, anxiety about what to do, fear that he wouldn't contact me. This was ridiculous.

I finally called Ginny when the morning was late

enough. I knew she liked to sleep in on Sunday.

"What's up, Dana?" she asked. She sounded a bit surprised. I normally didn't call her on Sunday since that was hers and Derek's designated day to spend together.

I told her everything.

When I was finished, she said, "I can't say that this makes me happy, Dana. And the reason is because I don't think it's going to make you happy. You're miserable already!"

"I'm not miserable," I protested, "What are you talking about? I'm glad I'm back with Ian, I'm happy about that!"

"Ok, so you're sitting alone on a Sunday, he hasn't called, you don't know what to do. You broke poor Jerry's heart, a man who was so good to you! You're a nervous wreck. Yes," she finished sarcastically, "You just sound ecstatic to me."

Leave it to Ginny. She always told me what she really thought, didn't mince words. I was beginning to wish I hadn't called her.

"Ginny, can you just give me some support? I just need support right now. I feel badly about Jerry, but did you want me to just keep leading him on? I care for him very much, but I just couldn't be in that relationship anymore, not when I feel like this about Ian." I added, "Look, I can't help what I feel for Ian. I didn't plan it. But I just do feel that way. I can't help it."

Ginny sighed. "I know, I know, it's just so frustrating. You know I want the best for you."

"I know."

"Listen, can we change the subject. I have some news."

"Ok."

"Dana, this is big. Derek and I," she paused then finished, "Derek and I are getting married! He proposed last night!"

"What? Wow, that's wonderful!" I said, taken out of my own head for just a moment. They had been living together for so long I hadn't thought it would ever happen.

"I'm so happy!" Ginny exclaimed. "I thought he would never ask," she went on, echoing my thoughts.

"When is the wedding?"

"We thought in the fall. Maybe November or early December if we can pull it together by then. But we don't want anything too big so it should work out."

"I'm happy for you, Ginny," I said. Just because my relationships went nowhere didn't mean I couldn't be happy for my best friend.

"Listen, I have to go now, but call me if you want to talk more, Dana," she said. "You know I'm here for you."

We hung up and I sat for a moment. Other women's lives were going on. My sister, only two years older than me, had been married for sixteen years, having met Lenny her second year of college, and she had her son, my wonderful nephew. Now Ginny, who was 35, was getting married for the first time to a man who treated her well. She had a run of not-so-nice boyfriends herself in her twenties when I had first met her. But then she had met Derek and that part of her life was over. She settled down. Now she would enter a new phase of her life. Many of the women I worked with were settled and married, with families. What was wrong with me?

But I knew the answer to that. Deep down, I knew.

Chapter 16

I still didn't know where Ian lived.

He had texted me on Sunday night, saying that he was still unpacking and getting settled. I answered ok, talk to you soon. I felt let down that he didn't call, but told myself at least he had texted, he had thought of me. I held back from calling and he finally did call on Tuesday after I got home from work. I smiled to see his name come up on my phone. "Hi, Ian. Have you gotten settled in?"

"Yes, pretty much. It's been hectic. What are you doing tonight?"

My heart started pounding. Did he want to see me? Oh, how I wanted to see him!

"I just got home from work. I was going to have dinner and.... that's it really, I must work in the morning.

"What about if I come over and we go out to dinner?"

Wow. He didn't usually offer that. I was excited. "That would be awesome!"

"Ok, I'll leave in a few minutes. It will take me a little longer to get to your place from here. About an hour?"

"That's fine, I'll be waiting."

We hung up and I did a little dance around my living room. He was coming! He had just been getting settled in his new place, he hadn't forgotten me! And we were going out!

It was as though he had handed me a bar of gold. Time with him was the most precious thing I knew.

When he got there, I threw my arms around him, hugging him tightly, kissing him passionately. He laughed. "Dana, if you keep doing that, we're never going to make it to dinner!"

I laughed too, feeling so happy. "Ok, ok, we'll wait until later. Let's go."

We went to a little Italian restaurant nearby. After we had ordered, he said, "Listen, Dana, I'm short on cash and my card is kind of maxed out. You wouldn't mind paying this time, would you? I should have asked on the phone but I... I just really wanted to see you. I didn't want you to think I was using you or..."

"Ian!" I interrupted. "It's no problem. I know you're waiting to start your other job, you just moved. I mean, you usually pay when we go out, I don't mind at all."

He smiled, a slow smile that lit up his craggy face and made his blue eyes crinkle. "You're really great, you know that? I'm lucky."

Ian's words made my whole body warm up. He was finally learning to appreciate me! Things were taking a turn for the better.

Again, as before, we laughed and talked and bantered and flirted. When we got back to my house I turned and kissed him, seriously this time. We were in my bed two minutes later.

And it was as always, incredible. He hovered above me, kissing me slowly, then more intensely. He ran his hands along my body, making me shiver in delight. He pressed against me, then raised himself up again and just gazed at me with those blue eyes. When he finally entered me, I burst with pleasure. I felt our bodies melt into each other.

At last, it was over. He turned and held me for a time, then said, "I have to go."

The bubble started to burst. "You're not staying?" I asked incredulously.

"No, I have too much to do in the new place, I want to get an early start."

"Can't you just leave early in the morning?"

"Not really, I need to…" he looked down at me in the dim light. Then he said, "Ok, Dana. I'll stay. But I have to get up early."

I set the alarm for him and we curled up against each other. I slept peacefully all night with him beside me.

When I got home from work the next day I was bursting with inspiration. I wrote a new poem:

Come to me and
Sear me with your heat
Kiss my mouth with kisses that melt like wax
Molding your lips to mine
Gaze at me with
Eyes like blue water
Bathing me in crystalline desire
Pierce my body with yours
Flooding me with pleasure
Let me hear your heart
Beat like thunder
Along with mine
As we join
Making sparks fly like lightning
Come with me
On a visit to
Infinity.

Chapter 17

Things continued like this for the next few weeks, into July. Ian would come over sometimes after work, or on the weekend. Sometimes I would buy groceries and we would cook together, sometimes we went out. Ian's problems with money had continued, so I was just quietly paying for everything. I was starting to wonder when this would change, but I was afraid to make waves by bringing it up. The sex continued to be explosive. I also wondered when I was going to get to see his new place. He had lived there for three weeks and I hadn't yet been invited. I told myself to not say anything, to not argue with him over such a minor thing. After all, he was making the effort to see me. But finally, I had to say something.

It was a Saturday. We had just had dinner, which I had cooked, and we had gone for a walk in the warm evening, enjoying the weather, holding hands as we walked in the nearby park. When we got back to my apartment I hesitated, but then said, hoping to sound casual, "It must be beautiful up at your new place," I started. He had told me that it was close to a lake. "Maybe next week I can come there instead of you coming here." Then I added hastily, "Not that I don't want you to come here, Ian, you know how happy it makes me when you're here."

Ian looked at me, and I could see that dark look

start to shadow his features like a cloud. "Are you kidding, Dana? First you say you want me to come here, you're glad when I'm here, then you start demanding more?"

I didn't think I'd been *demanding*. But I continued, "Well, I just meant I'd like to see your new place. You've been living there for almost a month now, I used to go to your old place…" I trailed off. My voice was starting to rise, I was getting upset. Then I burst out, "God, Ian, we're dating, you're my boyfriend! Why the hell can't I come to your house?"

The cloud over his face was getting darker. "Fuck," he said. Then he turned away and went over to the window. "Fuck it."

"What, Ian? What's wrong?"

He turned again to me. "Look. I didn't want to tell you; I knew you'd flip out."

Fear coiled in my stomach. "What?" I asked again.

"Dana, you remember Patty right?"

"Your ex?"

"Yeah, well, she…. she had a relapse. Drugs. She was in rehab and when she got out, she didn't have a place to live. She was evicted from her apartment and…"

I interrupted. "What does this have to do with anything?" Light had not yet dawned.

"She's staying with me."

I was stunned. I had not expected this. Not in a million years.

"You're…..living together?"

"No, no, it's not like that. She called me up, begged me, cried, said she had no other place to go. She doesn't get along with her parents, they gave up on her years ago. What was I supposed to do?"

He spread his hands, as though he were a sacrificing hero.

"I had to help." Then he added, "I like to help my friends."

I thought of the time he had refused to help me, had refused to even speak to me when I had been upset over Jamie's overdose at work. Times when he had cut me off.

But maybe he only did that to me. Other people he was willing to help. Even his drug addict ex-girlfriend.

"There's nothing between us," he said.

"Where does she sleep?" I asked coldly.

"On the couch, Dana." He was cold too. "You really don't trust me, do you?"

Trust him? Trust him! He had bailed on our relationship over and over, refused to let me know his new address, not said a word about his ex-living there, had not been there for me when I needed him. Trust him?

"I don't know what your problem is, Dana," he was getting irritated. "I come here; I take you out..." I didn't correct him. But after all, I was the one paying for everything when we went out. He went on, "I sleep here with you, I have sex with you, not her." He stopped then added angrily, "You know what, Dana? You're broken. You're a broken person. You're always the victim, you think that you can't trust any man. You've been hurt, so you project that onto any man you meet. Well don't do it to me!"

My head was reeling. I was broken? I was projecting? He was the one who had lied, albeit by omission. He was the one who had bailed on me before. I had been there for him, helped him when he said he had no money. Had he been there for me? But now, somehow, I was the one who was broken. Somehow it was all my fault.

Maybe somehow it was. Maybe it had been my fault that my father had come into my room that night. After all, he hadn't bothered my sister. Maybe there was just something about me. I felt tears burn.

"Oh, yes, cry now, that's going to make it all better," Ian said sarcastically. "Maybe I should just go."

"No!" I yelled, "No, please don't go, Ian." Suddenly I couldn't bear the argument, all I wanted was for him to hold me. "Can we just talk about this?"

"What do you want me to do? Kick her out?"

Well, yes, I thought, but didn't say it.

"When is she supposed to leave?" I said, wiping my eyes with the back of my hand.

"I don't know, don't give me the third degree about this, Dana."

"I…" I tried to find a way to say it, "I don't feel…. comfortable about this, Ian."

He gave a quick bark of laughter. "Comfortable? Are you channeling some new age self-help book now?"

"Ian! Why are you being so nasty?" My anger was rising again. "What the hell! You just dropped a bomb on me, ok? How would you like it if I did this?" I was yelling now. "How would you like it if I brought an ex-boyfriend to live here with me? How would you like it if I did the same thing you're doing?"

That seemed to stop him for a moment. He looked at me, then said in a quieter voice, "I wouldn't." He stepped up closer to me. "I wouldn't. Because you're mine, Dana. You belong to me." He was very close. His voice was soft, his eyes intense. Then he was holding me, kissing me, almost with violence, biting at my lips, grabbing my breasts, sliding his hands between my legs. He whispered, "You're mine."

I went limp. I couldn't resist him. I held onto him as though he was a lifeline. We fell on the couch, ripping off each other's clothes and there was nothing more to say.

Chapter 18

When the glow of the lovemaking faded, I started to feel like a fool. I had a legitimate issue with Ian's ex living at his place. He had gotten angry, had been sarcastic, had deflected my concerns, had insulted me, calling me "broken." Then he had distracted me with sex. Hot, raw, passionate, crazy sex. Then he left, with nothing resolved. I felt a crawling feeling in my gut. He had left… and had gone home to another woman. I wrote in my journal:

July 15

How can I believe that nothing's going on? His ex is a troubled and fucked up woman and he dated her for over a year. He's not with me every night. He could be having sex with her and how would I know? Is he lying to me? But how could he have sex with another woman when what we have is so profound, so intimate, so intense? How? What is going on?

And what is wrong with me? He didn't tell me she was there. He got angry when I questioned him. He wasn't kind or reassuring. He called me broken. He twisted things around, making it my fault for being upset, like there's something wrong with me. He's mean and cruel to me. So why do I hang on like I can't survive without him?

I had no answers to my own questions.

I didn't know what to do. I felt like I was crawling out of my skin. I could only focus on Ian. What were they doing right now? I thought, as I made dinner that evening. Were they cooking together? Were they talking about old times, at least the good parts, and laughing?

What were they doing now, I thought as I sat down to read a book (at least to try to read). Were they cuddling on the couch watching TV? Were they cuddling on the couch making out?

And at bedtime my thoughts raced like a racecar speeding down a track. Were they going to bed together? Was he undressing her slowly, were they…? Stop! I told myself. This was crazy. He had been coming here, he stayed over two or three times a week. He clearly wanted me still. If he wanted to be with her, why come to be with me at all?

I had to believe him. If I wanted this relationship to continue, I had to believe what he had told me.

I called him the next morning to apologize. I was afraid as I pressed his number on my phone, but I knew I had to take the first step. He didn't answer.

I started again. What were they doing? Were they having sex? Were they taking a shower together? What…

I was driving myself crazy. But he called back about an hour later.

I couldn't help myself. "What were you doing?" I said when he answered.

"Hello to you too," he said.

I backtracked. "It's just that… I called earlier…" I stumbled, then went on, "I wanted to say I'm sorry. I'm sorry for not believing you, Ian."

I heard nothing for a moment then I heard a voice in the background, "Who's that, babe?"

Babe?

Ian didn't answer her. He said to me, "Ok, Dana. I appreciate that. I want you to believe me. I wasn't lying…" He broke off, and I heard him say, "Shut up, Patty, I'm on the phone."

It sounded harsh. Part of me was glad he was telling her off, but his tone was sharp, nasty. A frisson of fear went through me. He had used that tone with me the night before.

But why was she calling him "babe?" Who the hell did she think she was?

How could I ask him that now? He was softening toward me. He had cut her off to talk to me.

He said, "Listen, I can't talk now, she won't stop bugging me but I'm going to get rid of her soon, I just don't want her to hear me, ok? I can't really talk now," his voice had lowered.

"Well, when can you come and talk?" I felt a bit emboldened by his words.

"Not sure. I'll call you." Then he said, "Look, Dana, she knows all about you, she knows I've got a girlfriend. I'm at your place all the time. She obviously knows where I am when I'm not home at night. I'm not with her anymore. Don't worry," he finished. I did feel some relief at his words. Before I could respond he said, "Gotta go, bye," and hung up.

It had been a bit abrupt, but I tried to accept what he had said. What else could I do?

Because there was no way I could let go of him now. I was in far too deep.

Chapter 19

I had no peace in my life. I was nervous and jumpy. I tried to avoid talking to my family. If my mother or sister called, I would talk for a few minutes, then say I had to do something, I had to go shopping, I had to do laundry, whatever. I'm sure they wondered why suddenly I couldn't put laundry in while talking on the phone. I'd done it before. But so far neither of them had pressed the point.

Three days after the last conversation, I finally called Ian again. He had texted me the day before, but said only, "Miss you." If he missed me, why the hell didn't he come over? But he hadn't made plans, hadn't showed up.

When I called him after work that evening, he picked up right away, saying, "Dana," in that slow deep voice. A zing went all the way down to my toes.

"Ian. When are you coming here? I want to see you." I hadn't planned on being so direct, but it had just come out. He didn't answer for a moment.

Then he said, "I can come tonight if you want."

If I wanted! All I wanted was to see him, touch him, bury my face in his hair, smell his smell, taste him…." Yes, ok. What time?"

"About 8:00, will that work?"

"Ok."

I couldn't help but feel a thrill. He was coming! He hadn't broken up with me! I knew he had texted that he missed me, though that hadn't been quite enough. But now he was coming over!

I bathed and put on a silky top and tight pants. I wanted to look sexy for him. I wanted to seduce him.

But there were also other thoughts in the back of my mind. He had his ex, living with him. He hadn't been coming over as much since I had confronted him. I still wasn't sure what was going on between him and his ex.

I did not trust him.

But I wanted to see him anyway. I seemed to have no pride when it came to him. I couldn't see past my feelings for him, my love, my desire. I didn't want to set boundaries. I wanted to immerse myself in him.

He showed up, a bit late as usual, but I didn't say anything. I just grabbed and held onto him. It was he who pulled away first.

"Dana, listen, sit down," he gestured toward the kitchen. I poured some wine and we sat. "I know you have a reason to be upset," he started. "Maybe I shouldn't have let Patty stay with me. I felt sorry for her, I knew what she'd been through but…I should have at least told you. Anyway, she's gone."

I felt a thrill at his words. "She's gone?"

"I told her I couldn't do it anymore. She was getting on my nerves big time and she was stealing my beer, she found my stash of weed…"

"I thought she just went to rehab."

"She's hardcore, she uses whatever drugs she can get, and if she can't get the drugs, she drinks. Whatever she can get her hands on. I told her to leave. She went to stay with some friend. I think he's a drug addict too but… well, I just can't be responsible for her anymore." Then his voice softened, and he said, "I missed you, Dana."

My heart jumped at those words. I ignored the fact that he could have come over anytime he wanted. I ignored the fact that he could have been calling, that he could have reassured me when I got upset. Because now he was coming around, he had kicked her out, he was here.

"And I want you to come to my place," he was saying. "It's cute, you'll like it."

Hadn't I suggested that before? Hadn't he become really angry when I had suggested that? Oh, that's right. He had been hiding something. Someone. But I pushed that thought away too.

Because this was Ian. Ian. I couldn't resist him. And all I wanted was to...

I leaned over and kissed him, and we went to the bedroom.

I saw stars, I saw dragons, swirling in bright colors. I heard angels singing. I loved him, I loved him. My heart felt full, my body satisfied. He was it for me. He was the one. I loved him, loved him, loved him. I wanted to climb inside his skin, have my heartbeat inside his. I never wanted him to leave.

He didn't leave until the morning.

I got ready for work, went around in a glow. I smiled at the kids, at my co-workers, at Ginny. At lunchtime, she remarked on it. "You look happy, Dana."

Of course, I had not told Ginny anything. I had not told her about Patty. I had not told her any of my troubles. I had avoided her questions about how things were going. I knew she had her suspicions, but she hadn't pushed too hard.

Now she leaned in and whispered so our colleagues wouldn't hear, "Did you get laid last night?"

I grinned. She had her answer. "So, things are good, Dana? He's treating you right?"

For some reason that question took me aback. Was he treating me right?

I was afraid of the answer. The glow faded. I was suddenly struck with the reality of it.

Because the truth was, Ian didn't treat me right. Not at all. Even though he had kicked Patty out. Even though he had come over last night and we had the kind of sex that transported me to another dimension.

Ginny must have seen my smile fade because she peered at me intently. "Dana, why don't we meet up after work and talk about this. You haven't said much lately. You know I'm here for you."

"No, it's ok, it's fine, I did see him last night, we're…"

"Well, if you want to. It's up to you." She got her meal out and sat down, started chatting with another caseworker. I sat down too but was quiet for the rest of the meal.

What could I say? What could I tell her? What would she say if I told her the whole story? I didn't want to be judged. I knew she loved me, but she would judge. She couldn't really understand why I wanted a man like Ian.

Sometimes neither could I. But then I would remember that horrible episode of my childhood.

Chapter 20

I did go over to Ian's new place. I went that Saturday.

He had come over the evening before and stayed over. The plan was that I would follow him to his place in my car the next day.

After breakfast we drove over. I was surprised when we got to the cabin. It was cute, but very small. It bordered a grove of trees, and past the trees you could see the lake. There was a woodshed to the side because the cabin had a wood stove and no other heat. It had a tiny kitchen and living room combined and a tiny bedroom off the living room. The bathroom had no tub, just a shower stall. But what could I say?

"It's cute," I said.

"I like it," he said. He pulled out a joint.

"Oh, Ian, do you have to…" I started, then stopped. Let him smoke if he liked. I didn't want to argue. Not now.

But I was thinking of him and Patty living together in this small space for all those weeks. And I was feeling angry and upset. He criticized her then he used drugs himself. And why had he let her stay here? How could I believe that nothing had happened between them? This space was so tiny, they would have been so close together all the time.

I tried to push the thoughts away. He gave me a look, not a happy one, then continued to light up his joint.

I took a deep breath. I had been so happy about seeing him, about coming to his new place. This had to stop.

"It's really cute," I said again. "Do you want to take a walk down to the lake?"

We walked in the sunshine and I tried to let go of my tension. We went back to the cabin and he made sandwiches, then we went outside to eat them. He said, "Are you staying over?"

"Do you want me to?"

"Sure, yes," he said. It was a bit stilted, but we left it at that. He clearly did not want to argue either. He did not want me to talk about Patty or his drug use, or anything of those tense topics. He just wanted to enjoy the day.

Ian smoked a lot of weed that day and I could see him relaxing. My tension stayed. I didn't like drugs and refused when he offered me a hit.

"Come on, Dana," he said. "You're too uptight, look at you. Take a hit, relax."

"No, Ian, you know how I feel about drugs."

"But it's just weed."

"No, I don't want to, ok?" I got up.

"Where are you going?"

"I just have to use the bathroom, be right back."

We had been sitting outside at the picnic table. I went inside to the small bathroom and closed the door.

And took a deep breath. Again. I couldn't pretend to myself. My emotions were roiling. I had so many questions about what had happened when Patty was there, I was getting irritated that he was smoking so much when he knew how I felt about it. He usually didn't do it when he was at my place. But he was in his own space now and he was in control.

But wasn't he always in control? Of my mind and heart?

I didn't know what to do. I was having trouble hiding my feelings, but I didn't want to leave.

I took out my phone, peeked to see whether Ian was still outside and called Ginny.

When she answered I said in a low voice, "It's me."

"Dana? I can hardly hear you," she said.

"I know, I'm…" I raised my voice slightly, "I'm at Ian's and he's…I'm kind of upset."

"What did he do?" she asked, worry in her voice.

"Oh, nothing, it's just that…. well, I never told you the whole thing," I finished. "But he finally let me come here and…"

"Let you come? What do you mean, let you come?"

"Well, I never saw his new place until today. Look, Ginny, I can't tell you everything now, I'm hiding in his bathroom, I don't want him to hear me. But I just need some support. I'm upset. I don't know what to do. I don't want to fight with him, he wants me to stay over…"

"Ok look," she said, "Why don't we get together tomorrow, and you can tell me what's going on."

"But tomorrow is your day with Derek."

"Doesn't mean I can't take some time for my best friend when she needs me."

This was a true friend. "Ok," I said, "I'll call you when I leave here."

"Take care, Dana," she said. I could hear the concern in her voice.

"I will." I felt tears sting my eyes. I washed my face and went back out.

That was one positive effect of Ian smoking so much weed. He didn't question what I had been doing, why I had taken so long. He was too laid back.

The day progressed into night. We went to bed. But for once we didn't have sex. He started snoring almost as soon as we lay down.

I lay awake for a long time.

Chapter 21

I called Ginny as soon as I drove away the next morning.

I had finally fallen into a restless sleep. I awoke with a start in the morning. Things were a bit tense as we got up. Ian said little, didn't ask me to stay for breakfast, and gave me a peck on the cheek when I left.

I knew it was early to call my best friend, but I just couldn't wait.

She sounded sleepy when she answered the phone.

"What's wrong?" she said right away. I burst into tears.

"Where are you," she said.

"D...driving," I stuttered. "Going home."

"Oh my God, don't drive like that. Pull over." She sounded worried.

I heard her mumbling something to Derek.

"Let me go in the other room, Derek's still trying to sleep. Pull over."

I wiped my eyes, trying to stop the tears so I could see the road. "No, I'm ok," I said. "I just want to get home."

"What happened?"

"Ginny, it's a long story, I haven't told you everything."

"Do you want me to come over?"

"Yes, can you? I mean, I know you and Derek usually do something together on Sunday." I added bitterly, "It must be nice to have a steady relationship."

She didn't remind me that I'd had such a relationship with Jerry.

"It's ok, we can do something later. We didn't have any special plans for today. Let me know when you're home. I'll get ready now."

Ginny was such a good friend, the best. I was lucky in my friendships, but not in my love choices.

But whose fault was that? I had given up a kind steady man for Ian.

I had given up a lot for Ian. My peace of mind, my pride, my well-being. A lot.

I called Ginny after I had taken a quick shower. I made some eggs and toast so I could feed her. She liked to eat a good breakfast in the morning. I made coffee and had it all ready when she arrived.

She gave me a big hug, hanging on to me for a long time. I started to cry again.

We sat down to breakfast, but I could barely eat. I told her everything that had been going on. I told her about Patty. I told her about Ian's drug use.

Ginny did not speak at all while I was talking. She had refrained from her usual sarcasm and outbursts of opinion. She knew this was serious; she knew how upset I was.

Finally, she said, "Dana, I know you care for this man very much. He has you all twisted up like I've never seen you before. Even after Miguel left, you were really upset and depressed, but you got over it eventually. You weren't all caught up in craziness. But this is crazy, Dana. This man is up and down, back and forth. He doesn't know what he wants. And you are being driven crazy along with him."

"I don't know why he's like that!" I burst out. "When it's good, it's amazing, it's…. "I searched for the word, "Transcending. But then he gets cold, or he smokes weed and almost disappears, or…"

"Or has his ex- come to live with him," she added wryly.

I looked at her and almost whispered, "Do you think they were sleeping together? Having sex?"

"I don't know, Dana. With his erratic behavior it certainly is possible. He seems to have fluid boundaries; he uses drugs himself. He wouldn't tell you what was going on for weeks. It is very possible."

My stomach dropped. I had not wanted to hear that. I had hoped she would praise him for helping someone through a hard time. But that was hardly likely. Ginny was very honest; she would not prevaricate. I knew she was right.

"I'm an idiot," I said, "I'm such an idiot."

"Dana!"

"No, I am. I give him the benefit of the doubt. I believe his stupid stories. But I thought you were supposed to give people you love the benefit of the doubt. I thought that was the right thing to do."

"Well, it can be if the person is usually honest and forthright. If you know that they have your best interests at heart. Dana, does Ian have your best interests at heart? Does he care about how you feel?"

The answer to that question was at best, "Sometimes he seems to."

"Is that enough?"

"I don't know," I said slowly.

Now she was beginning to get irritated. "Dana, why are you valuing yourself so lightly?"

"Because I feel…" I hesitated, not really wanting to put into words how I felt about Ian. "I feel I can't survive without him. Like I can't breathe without him. Like I'm drowning without him."

Ginny was silent. Then she said softly, "You feel like that. But you know that isn't really true." Then she added, "Look, Dana, maybe I'm too close to this. I'm your friend, I love you. Maybe you should talk to someone, a professional counselor."

For a moment I felt horrified. Tell my deepest secrets to some stranger, someone who could look into my heart, who could tell that something had happened to me when I was a child? I had never told anyone about that. I had never told Ginny.

"I don't know," I started slowly, "I don't like that idea. I mean, I can tell you, I know you, I don't want to talk to some stranger..."

"It was just an idea. I think it might help."

"Well, if you don't want to talk to me..."

"Dana!" she exclaimed, cutting me off. "Of course, I want to talk to you, I'm here for you. But I don't always know the answers. I'm not sure how to help you. Also," she sighed, "I don't know if you listen to me. I mean, I've told you before what I think but you just keep running back to this guy. It gets frustrating to see you like this."

I looked up at her. "I guess I can see that, but...it's like I can't help myself, he does something that hurts me, and I tell myself it's no good, but then he calls, and I just go running, or even worse, I call him because I can't stand the silence between us. I just can't seem to help it. I feel powerless..." I trailed off, realizing that this was the primary feeling I had in this relationship with Ian. Powerlessness.

Just like I had been with my father. My breath caught for a moment as a piece of the puzzle of my own behavior slid into place.

But I didn't say that to Ginny. "Ginny, you're a wonderful friend, I appreciate you being there for me. I just don't think I can stop right now with him. I just can't."

She gazed at me and said, "At least think about seeing a counselor to talk about this. Just think about it. Our insurance at work covers it, I think there would just be a co-pay. You could try it and if it didn't help, you could stop. Can you think about that, please?"

"Ok," I had to agree, I had to appease her. She was trying hard to help me. "I will think about it.

"I'll check and see who takes our insurance for you if you like."

"Ok, sure, check it out," I told her. I didn't want to do this, but I felt I had to give in. She had come running when I needed her, but I couldn't do this to her all the time. She had her own life; she was planning to get married.

"Listen, Dana, maybe you shouldn't be alone today. Do you want to come over and spend the day with us?"

Oh, yes, be with her and Derek all day, be the third wheel. That's all I needed to make me feel better.

But I knew she was trying to help me.

"No, that's ok, you and Derek need your time together. I'll be ok," I told her.

When she left I curled up on the couch and cried. And tried to sleep. I didn't want to be conscious right now. It hurt too much.

Chapter 22

At work on Monday morning, I tried to concentrate. I had paperwork to do, and I tried to focus my brain on the words. I also needed to plan activities for the upcoming week. The kids would arrive early today, as they usually did in the summer when there was no school.

A little later that morning I got a call from Pedro.

"Ms. Taggert?" I knew his voice.

"Pedro? What is it? Are you coming in today?" The kids were due before lunch.

"Don't know, listen, I need your help."

I was immediately alert. "What's wrong?"

"George got arrested last night. He's in jail."

"What?"

"He's in jail," Pedro repeated.

I took a deep breath. I was the adult, I was the professional, I had to stay calm, though my nerves were already on edge because of Ian.

"Tell me what happened."

Pedro explained that they had been at the park. They had been doing drugs. He hesitated then added, "Coke."

"Who was there, just you and George?"

"No, we were with Johnny and his big brother. He got us the coke."

"Pedro, I thought you didn't do drugs. Especially not coke," I felt I had to say.

"I don't, Ms. Taggert," he hurried to assure me,

"But Johnny's brother, he's so cool and he had some and we just thought we'd try it." His voice trailed off. He was smart and he knew he'd done something stupid. He went on, "But then the cops came. We started running. Me and Johnny and his brother, we got away, but they caught George. He doesn't run so fast."

"Ok," I had to take charge. "He's in jail?"

"Yeah."

I knew that it was likely that George was in the youth detention center, not the city jail, but it was similar enough that I could see why Pedro called it that. I would call and find out.

"You come in today, Pedro, as usual. I'll call our lawyer and go down there." The agency worked with a lawyer who assisted in these types of cases. It hadn't been the first time we had to use him.

"Ok, Ms. Taggert, I will. Thanks," he added. "George is my best friend."

"I know, Pedro, try not to worry."

"Ok."

We hung up and I swung into action. This type of thing I knew how to deal with. It had happened before in my job and would again. I could exert some control over this, I could call the lawyer, I could make sure George got justice. It was a first offense. They were young and had been stupid. The real culprit was Johnny's brother, a young man of 19 who was bad news. I would see that the police knew that.

This I could handle. It was Ian and my own emotions that I couldn't deal with.

I met the lawyer at the detention center, and we saw George. He was crying his eyes out, terrified. We talked to him and got him calmed down. We planned our strategy and I contacted George's parents. They knew what had happened, the police had called them because George was only 16. But they were both alcoholic and did not work.

They seemed concerned but didn't seem willing to take much action on behalf of their son, which was typical. That was why George was in our program in the first place.

This crisis helped pull me out of my own head and into full helper mode. By the end of that day, I was exhausted. I only wanted to go home and sleep.

Ian called me just as I lay down.

I answered with some trepidation. I didn't know if he would berate me for the weekend or if he just wanted to connect. But he sounded fine at first, even apologized for smoking so much weed when I had been there. Then he went on, "I just felt uptight, Dana. You know, you're not always easy to be with. You want so much. You always think you're right. You can be demanding. It's like you're insatiable."

I was getting irritated by this. I hadn't been demanding at all. I didn't think I was always right. I didn't think I was insatiable. I had said nothing about his smoking, nothing about Patty. In fact, I had held my feelings back all weekend! But he went on, "I want to please you, I really do, but you make it hard sometimes."

I wasn't sure what to say. I didn't want an argument, but he was being blatantly unfair, blaming his tension on me. I burst out, "Look, Ian, I don't need to hear how demanding I am, how awful I am. I had a hard day at work." Then it came bursting out, "Speaking of work, are you working yet? What's going on with that job you talked about?"

That had turned the tables. He got defensive. "It's in the works. It's starting soon. What the hell! Why are you asking me about that? Don't you believe me? I'm not a slacker, I work hard."

Ok. But he wasn't working hard now. I didn't even know how he managed to buy weed.

"Never mind, Ian, I'm just tired. We had a kid get arrested last night. For drugs," I added, to get a dig in.

He was silent for a moment, then said, "Yeah, so?"

"What do you mean, so? It's a big deal. This is my job, Ian. I care about these kids. This kid was so scared, he's never done anything like this before. And his parents are alcoholic, they won't bestir themselves to do anything. I will, though. I got him a lawyer and we're going to make a deal. Hopefully he'll just get community service, maybe probation."

He was silent for a moment then said, "Ok, well, that's good." He added, "I know you're good at your job, Dana. I know you care and that's a good thing. But you don't have to rub it in that I'm not working yet, ok? It wasn't my fault I lost my last job."

Really? I thought it was, you had a fight with the boss, I was thinking, but didn't say it.

"Ok, Ian, I know. Look, I'm tired and…"

"Do you want to come over?"

I was surprised. "I do want to see you but I'm so tired, I just explained…"

"I felt bad about the weekend. I wanted you to see my place and then… it wasn't exactly how I'd planned. Then I fell asleep, and we didn't even have sex. Sorry about that, Dana."

Wow. He was apologizing. That seemed big. I was becoming more awake. I did want to see him. I always wanted to see him.

"Why can't you come over here? I'd love to see you."

"Uh, well, I ran out of cash."

"What?"

"I don't have enough to gas up my car, ok?" He sounded embarrassed.

"But you can use your credit card."

"It's maxed out."

"Oh my God, Ian. What are you going to do?"

"I didn't want to tell you about it. But you always

push, Dana."

I was quiet for a moment then said, "Do you need some help?"

"It would be nice. But I wasn't going to ask, that's for sure." Then he added in a voice that had become soft, seductive, "Dana, I just want to see you. I don't want to argue. I'm hungry for you, Dana. I'm starving for you."

I felt something hot and melting deep in the core of my body. I said, "I'll come over."

When we hung up all my exhaustion had disappeared. He had called, he had reached out. He had admitted he needed help. He had also blamed me for the problems on the weekend, but he had admitted he was wrong too. And he didn't ask me for money, I had offered. And I would do anything to help him. I loved him, if I didn't help him, who would? I kept the running dialogue of justifications in my head as I got ready. Because I wanted to see him. Despite everything, I wanted to see him.

And he wanted me. He was hungry, starving for me.

As I was for him. As always. Forgetting everything else.

Chapter 23

I gave Ian money to tide him over. I loved him. I had to help him. I had to be there for him. That was how I justified it.

Because all that really mattered was that we were together.

As soon as I arrived that night, he had met me at the door. Then instead of going inside, he grabbed my hand and almost ran with me down to a grassy area at the edge of the lake. He laid down a blanket and there under the stars in the warm summer night he pulled me to him and starting yanking off my clothes. We clutched at each other, pulled, and clawed, bit at each other's lips, violently, hungrily. I couldn't get enough of him, nor he of me. It lasted a long time. I felt my whole-body humming, humming a song that said his name, over and over. I was so in love with him I could hardly breathe. He was my food, my drink. He was my savior, my god. He was my life.

Later, we lay together for a time, satiated, then made our way back to the cabin to his bed. I stayed the night even though I had to go to work the next day. In the morning before I left I gave him the cash that I had stopped to get at an ATM before I had gone to his cabin the previous night. "Thanks," he had said, kissing me. "I really appreciate this, it's a huge help. You know I'll pay you back."

"It's ok, Ian, pay me back whenever you can." I

stood in the doorway ready to leave. I wanted so much to say I love you. It was on the tip of my tongue. But I wanted him to say it first. Because what if I said it and he didn't say it back?

We kissed and I left, saying merely, "I'll talk to you later."

Work was hectic. I was still dealing with George's arrest, talking to the lawyer and the police. I would be going to court with him when it was scheduled. I was confident he would get a good deal since it was his first arrest.

I had to deal with Johnny and his brother too. After consulting with my boss, I set up a meeting with Johnny's mother. She was a single parent and was having trouble controlling her boys. Johnny wasn't a bad kid. He participated in our program and was well liked, but when he followed his brother's lead he got in trouble. The police were now aware that the older boy had been the one to procure the cocaine and they were pursuing that. I wanted to talk to his mother to see if there was a way she could try to keep her younger son away from his big brother, though there was a chance now that the older boy would go to jail. It seemed that he had been selling drugs as well as using them and had been giving them to his younger brother and his friends.

Johnny's mother was a pleasant woman and eager to help her son, unlike George's parents. We talked about the situation and planned on how to support him. She told me that the arrest of his friend George had scared him, and he didn't want to get into trouble like his brother. Pedro had also talked to him and had told him that they had all been stupid to try coke and they shouldn't be doing things like that if they wanted to make something of themselves in life. Pedro was such a good kid. The other kids really listened to him.

"Johnny wants to be a cop," his mother told me.

"Now he's afraid he won't be able to do that."

"I'll talk to him," I said. "He wasn't arrested, and it seems he might have learned something from what happened."

"I tried so hard with my older boy, Ray," she said, sounding discouraged. "But he got in with this crowd and he just wouldn't listen to me anymore. He's been living with this older guy and I think he sells drugs. Ray wants to be like him. I don't want..." she started to tear up, and I handed her a tissue, "I don't want Johnny to go down that road, you know?"

"That's why we're here, Mrs. Torres. We're trying to help Johnny. And he's a good kid. I think he's going to be ok."

We spoke a little longer and when she left she seemed a bit more encouraged about Johnny, though she was still full of worry about her older son. I felt gratified. Here was a parent who was really trying. And the fact that I could help her, and her younger son was another thing I really loved about my job.

At work I felt competent, capable, professional, in charge. But with Ian I was never in control. He had the control all the way.

I put that thought aside and went on with my day.

August had come. High summer. Ian and I had been spending time together regularly, though not always without problems. He would get tense, smoke weed, and I would get angry. He didn't always call when he said he would. He did finally start working but didn't work a lot of hours and hadn't yet paid me back. I tried not to worry about it, but deep down I felt some resentment.

Ginny had asked me numerous times how things were going. She had, true to her word, found a few counselors in the local area who would accept the insurance that I had through work. I thanked her but told her that I was ok just now, and I would hang onto the information in case I ever needed it. She didn't push, thankfully.

I decided to spend some family time. I took a much-needed vacation day on Monday, picked up my mother, and we drove over to see my sister and her family. Being a teacher, my sister was off for the summer, and we all went to the beach. We spent a lovely day sitting in the sun, swimming, talking, and laughing. They both knew I was seeing Ian but didn't ask me about how things were going, and I was glad for that. Even though things had been ok, I was afraid to talk about it much, afraid to jinx it. For one day I wanted to forget about Ian and just enjoy myself. No problems, no worries, just my mother, my sister and my nephew, the sun, and the water. I felt a modicum of peace come over me that day. If only I could hang onto it.

The following weekend Ian and I were planning to go out on the lake. As always, I was excited to be with him. We had gone out Tuesday night to a movie, and I was so happy just to be close to him, holding his hand in the movie theater. True, he had not called me afterward. This was typical of him. But when I finally called him on Thursday, he told me he had borrowed a neighbor's rowboat and asked if I wanted to go out on the lake on Saturday.

That morning I approached his cabin. The door was unlocked so I went in, but he wasn't inside. I went back outside. Looking toward the lake I could see him down by the water. "Ian!" I called. He turned and gave a half wave. I went down to the water's edge and moved in to kiss him, but he pulled away, turning to pull the boat further in. He said, "Ok, get in." I clambered into the boat and he followed me. He was quiet. He got like that sometimes. It made me nervous. I started to feel tense.

Ian launched the boat into the water with an oar then started to row. He clearly was not a master at this since the boat started moving forward at first then went sideways. He struggled with it and righted it. "Do you want help?" I asked.

"I've got this, Dana." He sounded abrupt. He pulled too hard on one oar and the boat slid sideways again. "Clumsy!" I said, trying to joke him out of his mood.

"What?" He turned to glare at me. "What did you call me?"

"I was joking!" I cried. He kept glaring then suddenly he turned nasty. "Get out," he said.

"Ian! I was joking!"

"Get out."

"But I just got here! We're out on the water!"

Saying nothing, he pulled the boat around and approached the shore again. As we neared it, he repeated, "Get out. Now." The look on his face was icy, his voice matching. I felt tears burn my eyes as I clambered out of the boat, getting my sneakers and shorts soaked as I sloshed to the shore. I got in my car then looked back at him. He was rowing out again, seemingly more smoothly this time. What had that been about? What the hell had happened? My stomach was in knots and tears rolled down my face as I drove back home. What had happened? Things had been going well! Why had he turned on me?

Chapter 24

I didn't know what to do. I felt shattered. Just when I had started to feel that the relationship was more solid, when I started to feel that I could depend on it, Ian had shattered me again, attacking me out of the blue. I sat curled up on the couch all day. I couldn't move, I couldn't eat. I finally got out my notebook and wrote a poem.

Not the Night

The fire in me is stilled, quietened
I feel a cold wind upon me
But it is not the wind
It is the harsh chill in your heart.
I see the darkness descend upon me
Like a black cloak that hides the sky
But it is not the night.
It is the darkness in your soul.

I argued with myself. He was bad for me. But he had been trying. We had been spending time together. The sex was phenomenal. He had reached out to me more regularly. He had been coming to see me, I had been going to see him at his place. But then he would push me away. This time he had been really nasty. What was I doing with him? But he had been trying. Back and forth went the argument in my head, back and forth.

But there was one fact I couldn't deny it any longer. Ian was not good for me. Having a boyfriend who pushed me away, hurt me, tore apart my heart on a regular basis was clearly not good for me. What kind of a fool was I to not admit that to myself? Just when things had seemed good, he became destructive. There was some darkness in him that I didn't understand and instead of me bringing him up out of the darkness he kept pulling me down into it too.

What was it inside Ian that caused him to do that? I knew he had been hurt by his ex-girlfriend's addiction, but was that enough to cause this type of horrible behavior, this push-pull come close, go away behavior that had me reeling? And this time his pushing away had been brutal.

I suddenly became obsessed with knowing. What was the darkness in his soul that caused him to behave this way?

I thought about the kids I worked with. Some of them had a lot of anger inside them. Many of these kids had been sexually abused, as had Jamie. Some had been physically abused. Some had family members who had abandoned them. Some did not come into our program willingly, but through the court system. It could take a lot to get through to those kids. At times we failed. But at times we could see them blossom as they spent time with people who cared about them, as they saw that they had someone they could talk to. It helped for them to find other kids with similar issues, and work on their problems together. Yes, we failed at times. But we also succeeded. Look at Pedro, look at Jamie.

Had something like that happened to Ian? Something he had never told me?

Somehow this thought helped me get through that miserable day. Somehow I would find out. I wasn't sure how, but I would find out.

I was getting ready for bed when my cell phone rang.

I had finally managed to choke down a bit of food

and had turned on the TV to watch some mindless program. I didn't think I would sleep much, but I had to try.

When I heard the ring, my heart started pounding. Ian! Was he calling to apologize? It must be him. Who else would call at this hour?

I almost didn't recognize the voice when I heard it. A quiver of shock went through me.

"Hello, Dana," said a voice. A very familiar voice. A voice I had not heard in quite some time.

Miguel's voice. Miguel, with his slight Spanish accent.

"Dana?" I heard him again.

"Hello," I said faintly.

"I know you're probably surprised to hear from me," he said.

"Uh, yes, I…yes."

"Listen, Dana, I know we didn't break up in the best of circumstances. I know you were hurt. I cared about you a lot, but it was hard for me to make a commitment. I just wasn't ready. And I think you were."

I wasn't sure what to say. Why was he calling me now to tell me this? A year later? Really?

"Dana, are you there?"

"I'm here. I'm not sure what to say, Miguel. I mean, I haven't heard from you in all this time and…" my voice trailed off.

"I know, I know. Lo siento," he said, "I'm sorry. I thought about calling, but I didn't want to upset you."

So why was he calling now? I didn't say it out loud, but he seemed to hear my thoughts.

"I hope you're not angry that it took me so long to call. But I called for a reason," he went on. "I'm coming upstate on business and I hoped I could see you. Take you out."

I was shocked. I couldn't think what to say. He

wanted to see me? After all this time?

I found my voice, "Why, Miguel? I mean, what would be the purpose?"

"I've missed you, Dana. I did care for you, you know."

He missed me? For a whole year?

"Dana, I know it's been a long time. I moved, you know, back to New York City. I have a new job; I work for a clothing manufacturer. I have to come up to your area to service some stores up there and I thought we could get together."

I heard a new note in his voice. He was nervous! He really wanted me to say yes.

Shaking off my surprise, I found myself thinking, why not? Why the hell not? I was over Miguel. Any remnant of feelings that I had for him had been washed away in the tide of emotions evoked by my feelings for Ian. Miguel was now safe. With Miguel, I would be the one in control.

"I guess that would be ok," I said slowly.

"Are you seeing anyone?" he asked, perhaps wondering if there would be any complications to our getting together.

"I have been," I answered cautiously, "But I can meet you."

He went over the details of his visit upstate and said he would call me when he got settled at the hotel. We planned to meet later that week.

I hung up feeling a myriad of feelings, excited and confused and gratified, but upset as well. Would I have said yes to Miguel if Ian hadn't hurt me so? But it was nice, really nice, to know that I had not just been a blip in Miguel's life, that even after a year he would call and say he had missed me, he wanted to see me. Perhaps I had more of an impact on him than it had seemed when he left me.

And I had made a date to see him. Again, I thought, why not? I was a free woman; I was not in a committed relationship. I had thought I was, but I wasn't. Why not go out with my attractive ex-boyfriend? I could do what I wanted to.

I slipped beneath the bedcovers and closed my eyes, but my mind was racing with thoughts. Of Miguel and how it had felt when he left. And how he had said he missed me.

And I thought of Ian. And how he had broken my heart. Again.

Chapter 25

At work the next day I told Ginny about Miguel's call. I wanted to hear her opinion. She was cautious.

"I think it's ok to see him," she said slowly. "I mean, I realize he really hurt you, but you do seem to be over him. Unless you think you might get caught up again?" her voice rose in a question.

"Ginny, I really don't think so. I mean, I was a bit shocked to hear from him, but I didn't have any of those old feelings. I think," I added bitterly, "that someone else has taken all of those feelings in me and battered me with them."

Ginny knew what I was talking about. I had told her that Ian had rejected my company on Saturday, though I hadn't told her all the ugly details, just that when I had gotten there, he'd been in a bad mood and had asked me to leave. She was angry.

"I'd rather you dated Miguel than the other one," she said contemptuously.

"Ok, well, I am going out with him. He's going to call me when he settles in his hotel up here, so it will be either Thursday or Friday."

"I wish," she started, then stopped.

"You wish what? What, Ginny?"

"I wish you were still seeing Jerry, that's what. He was so good to you! Have you heard from him at all?"

I felt a pang. I had hurt Jerry and he hadn't deserved that.

"No." I added, "He's probably going out with that woman he met before I interfered. I hope for his sake anyway. Or maybe with someone else he met online."

"I hope so too," Ginny said, "But I really wish you hadn't blown him off, Dana."

"Ok, I know, please don't beat me up over it. I feel bad about that. But you know how I felt about..." My voice trailed off, but she knew what I was saying.

"It's destructive, Dana."

"Yes, I know that too."

"Please go see a counselor," she said. I had never followed up on that.

"Maybe this time I will," I told her. What could it hurt? I did feel a need to talk to someone and I couldn't always dump my feelings on Ginny. I didn't talk to my mother or sister for fear of upsetting them too much. So maybe a neutral party would be a good thing. After all, we encouraged the kids we worked with to discuss their feelings with someone.

"Ok fine, I'll go see someone."

She looked relieved. "That's good, Dana, it will be good for you."

I did follow up the next day. I found the list she had given me and called the first person on it. She was a licensed social worker, and her office was not too far from my apartment. She wasn't taking new patients, however, so I called the next name on the list. She was a licensed psychologist, and she was taking new patients. I made an appointment for an intake and sighed. At least that would make Ginny happy. I texted her to let her know that I had done it. She texted back,
"Great! I think it will help."

I tried not to think about Ian that week. I was thinking about Miguel. How he had left so abruptly, yes, but also how much fun we had together during that whirlwind six months. He had met my mother and sister and her family, and everyone had liked him. He was upbeat most of the time, and he was funny, though a bit moody at times. We had done everything together during that time, which was why it was so hard when he left, and I had to learn to be alone again.

And now he had told me he had cared for me; he had missed me.

I wasn't sure if I wanted to start up an affair with him again. As he had said, he wasn't ready to commit to a relationship. But I could have fun with him again. Perhaps in his company I could feel like an attractive and desirable woman again. A feeling that I used to have with Ian until he battered it- and me- into the ground.

Miguel called me on Thursday afternoon. I was still at work, getting my paperwork organized to be ready the next morning. I saw it was him and answered quickly.

"Dana," he said, "I'm here in town, just got in. I have to get settled now, but would you like to have dinner with me tomorrow?"

"Yes, that would be nice."

We made plans. I still lived in the same apartment, so he knew where I lived. He said he had a rental car and would pick me up at 7:00.

I was excited. It would be good to see him.

And with Miguel now I was the one in control.

When Friday evening came I dressed carefully. I wanted to look sexy, but not too obvious. I chose a blush-colored dress that was not one of my tight dresses, it had a slight flair to the skirt. It was low cut, but not too low. I put dangly silver earrings in my ears and brushed out my wavy hair until it shone. I put on the necklace my mother had given me for my birthday. I put on low heels that matched the dress and sprayed on light perfume. I looked in the mirror. I looked good.

Miguel picked me up right on time. He came to the

door and when I opened it, he looked me up and down appreciatively. "You look great, Dana, you look beautiful." He gave me a quick hug and a kiss on the cheek. "It's great to see you."

"You too, Miguel." God, he was good-looking, I had almost forgotten how good-looking he was. He had straight black hair, cut short, and smoldering dark eyes. He was clean-shaven and had a sharp jawline and nicely shaped lips. He was tall, about six feet. He had always made me feel dainty, since I was only five foot four. It was good to see him. I felt a warmth inside being around him again.

He took my arm and escorted me to the car, politely opening the door for me. We went to a very nice restaurant; one I had never been to before. He must have found it online. He ordered white wine, my favorite brand, which he had remembered, and we talked. The talk flowed easily, surprisingly so. He kept saying how good I looked, how he had missed me.

I finally asked, after about three glasses of wine, "Why did you leave, Miguel?"

I wasn't sure he would answer at first. Perhaps I had upset him. But he said, "Dana, I was getting in too deep. I got scared. I really cared for you and I got scared. I know it wasn't right. I know I hurt you. I was starting to think that… well, I could see myself with you for the long term. But then I started feeling overwhelmed, I couldn't handle it. You know what happened with my parents."

I nodded. I did know. He had told me early on that his parents had gone through a very bitter divorce when he was only thirteen and it had traumatized him and his younger brother. His brother had married young and divorced only three years later and now had to pay child support for his two children. He got to see them only occasionally and it was an ongoing battle with his ex-wife, just as Miguel's parents had battled over custody and visitation when they had been divorced. Miguel did not want to repeat the pattern.

"So, I left before it could go any further," he continued. "And I have to admit, I got involved with other women right away. I was playing the field, having fun, trying not to get too attached to any one of them."

"And?" I asked when he stopped talking.

"Well, I didn't get too attached. But I still thought about you."

"Oh." I wasn't sure what else to say.

"I know I waited too long to call. I wasn't sure what you would say, how you would react. We had so much fun together, but…I really didn't mean to hurt you, Dana," he finished.

I had drunk too much to prevaricate. "You did hurt me; I was really hurt. I really cared for you, Miguel."

"I am so sorry. And now?"

"Now what?"

His voice softened. "Do you still care for me?"

I wasn't sure what to say. He seemed so familiar, even dear in a way. He was so attractive. Though he had hurt me, he had been kinder than Ian, less erratic. But how did I feel now about Miguel?

An unwelcome thought came into my head.

He was not Ian. No one else was Ian. And I loved Ian. Still, despite his horrific behavior, I loved him.

Miguel saw my hesitation. He asked, "I don't mean to push, Dana, but is there someone else?" When I didn't answer right away, he said, "You said you had been seeing someone."

I decided to come clean. "Yes," I said, "But it appears we are not seeing each other now. I did… I do care for him. Even though we …. we're not together now."

"Can I help you forget?" Miguel said softly.

I looked at him steadily. "I don't know," I said.

We continued with our dinner. He changed the

subject, asking me about my work. He had always admired what I did for a living. He had attended a social event at my job once and had met some of the kids. They had liked him, and he had liked them. He told me about his new job and his apartment in the city. "You can visit me if you like," he said. I didn't comment.

When dinner was over, we walked to the car and he drove me home. He turned to me when we pulled up to my building and said, "Do you want me to come in, Dana? I'd like to."

Did I? I felt conflicting emotions. I was certainly still attracted to Miguel. Yes, I loved Ian, but Ian wasn't there, and Miguel was. What could it hurt? Would it hurt?

But I was already hurting.

"Ok," I said. And we walked into my apartment together.

Chapter 26

I sat on the couch with Miguel. We talked and flirted for a few minutes, then he kissed me. His taste, his feel, his smell, were familiar to me. I felt a momentary pang, remembering Ian, then I willed myself to forget. This was Miguel. I knew him. I felt comfortable with him.

I wasn't in love with him anymore. So, he was safe.

We kissed for some time and we were both getting aroused. Then Miguel pulled back and said, "Dana?" with a question in his voice. I knew what he meant. I nodded.

He arose from the couch, then bent down and picked me up in his arms. I felt a thrill down to my toes. He was so big, so masculine! He carried me into the bedroom, lay me gently on the bed and undressed me.

Afterward he curled up around me. I lay next to him, unsure of my feelings. The sex had been exciting, as it always was with Miguel. He knew what he was doing, and he knew me, what I liked. He had always been warm and affectionate after sex. I felt physically satiated. I felt excited, as though I had done something forbidden. I felt desirable again.

I missed Ian.

But I pushed that thought away.

I awoke the next morning with Miguel still curled up next to me, his arm around me. I slowly pulled away and got out of bed. I used the bathroom, washed my face, and put on a little makeup. I felt a bit self-conscious and didn't want to look like a mess when Miguel got up.

I went to the kitchen and started to make breakfast when I heard his voice. "Buenas días, querida."

I smiled, turning. This seemed so familiar. Miguel had often spoken words of endearment to me in Spanish. He came up to me and kissed me on the lips. "It was magnifico to be with you last night," he said into my ear.

I smiled at him again. "I'm making breakfast. How long can you stay?"

"I have to leave around noon," he said. "But let's enjoy the morning."

We ate, we talked, we laughed. It felt so comfortable, so normal, being with Miguel. I was over the hurt he had inflicted when he left me. I understood it better now. And being with him was making me feel like a woman again, someone valued, attractive and worthwhile.

Finally, noon approached. Miguel said that he had to go to his hotel to gather his belongings and get back to the city. He hugged me tightly at the door and kissed me again. "Come visit me in the city," he said. "I have an apartment in Brooklyn, near where my brother lives."

"Maybe I will," I said, looking up into his dark eyes. "Why not?"

I watched him drive away then went back inside, feeling better than I had in some time. Miguel still wanted me, he still desired me, he wanted to see me. I had no particular expectations from him. It had been very good for me to be with him.

Though it had not made me forget Ian.

Nothing could do that.

I had planned to go shopping that afternoon. Tina's birthday was coming up in late August and I always got her an item of clothing that she, with her practical nature, wouldn't buy for herself. My mother and I were planning to drive there tomorrow to celebrate with Tina and her family.

I didn't feel like going shopping alone, so I called

Ginny, but she and Derek were going to her parent's house to do some wedding planning with her mother. On a whim I called Bonnie.

"Hi Dana," she said when she answered. "Do you want to go out with me and Lacy tonight? We're going to that new place over on Monroe Street."

I thought about it. I wasn't really in the mood. I wanted to just stay home that night and process the time with Miguel. "I don't think so, but would you like to go to the mall with me today?"

She agreed, and we set up a time to meet. After lunch I drove to the mall and met Bonnie at the coffee shop. We chatted over cappuccinos then went to Macy's. Bonnie said she was going to buy a new outfit for that night.

I chose a beautiful top for Tina. Bonnie found a svelte blue dress that set off her blonde hair. We paid for our purchases and started to walk out of the store.

As we passed menswear, I saw a form that looked familiar, a tall form with shaggy brown hair. A short slightly plump woman stood beside him. He must have felt my stare because he turned. It was Jerry.

I couldn't hide now; he had seen us. I walked up to him.

"Hi Jerry," I said. I felt embarrassed. He looked a bit startled, but said "Hello, Dana." He nodded to Bonnie. A short awkward moment passed. Then Jerry said, "Oh, this is Marcy," turning to the woman next to him. She had straight dark hair to her chin and round glasses. She smiled tentatively and said in a shy voice, "Hi."

I introduced Bonnie and Jerry said, "Yes, I remember you, you were at the …" his voice trailed off. Perhaps he didn't want Marcy to know where he had met me, or what we had been to each other.

We said self-conscious goodbyes, then left. Bonnie turned to me.

"That was the guy you met at the dance, right?"

"Yes, Jerry," I said.

"So, what's the deal?"

"We dated for a while, but then we broke up." I added, "I broke up with him. I liked him a lot, but I wasn't... well, it was more of a friendship feeling on my part."

"I know what you mean," Bonnie said. "I was going out with a guy I met about a month ago, and he was really into me, but I just didn't feel the same. I tried, but it just wasn't there." She looked at me with a rueful smile, "You love who you love, right? You don't choose who you love. It just happens."

For some reason that statement struck my heart. You love who you love.

And I loved Ian. It wasn't my fault; it wasn't something terrible. It just was.

I wasn't sure if that made me feel better or worse.

I hugged Bonnie as we left to go to our separate cars. She asked, "Are you sure you don't want to come out with us tonight? Lacy would love to see you," but I declined and drove home.

Later that night I felt restless. I had wrapped Tina's present, called my mom to plan when I would pick her up the next day then tried to read a book, but I couldn't concentrate. Maybe I should have gone out with Bonnie and Lacy. I thought about Miguel. He had texted me when he got back to Brooklyn, saying what a wonderful time he had with me, calling me, "mi amor." My love.

But it wasn't Miguel who I loved. It was Ian.

I suddenly had a thought. I could drive over there. To Ian's.

I tried to talk myself out of it. I had done that before when he had lived in his other place. That time it had worked out, but this time, could I expect the same? He had chased me away from him, he had treated me very badly.

Why would I expect that he would welcome me?

How did I know he was even alone there?

I tried to concentrate on other things, I turned on the TV, but the words just sounded like droning, and I turned it back off. I threw on jeans and a top, got my purse and keys, and walked out the door.

This compulsion wasn't going away. I started the car and headed toward Ian's.

It took some time to get there. It was getting late, and it was dark. I wasn't sure what I was going to do when I got there. When I had done this before, when he lived in his old place, there had been a place to park on the street. Now he lived in a cabin along a rural road. There was no place to park. The driveway was rather long, but if I pulled in he might see my car. Did I want to pull in? Did I want him to know I was there? Should I just go and knock on his door? What reception would I get?

I couldn't believe I was doing this again. Driving over on a Saturday night, uninvited, with the bad feelings from his rejection lingering like a dark cloud. And after that wonderful night with Miguel.

But maybe that was what had triggered this. Miguel had been kind, sexy, hot, gorgeous. I had enjoyed my time with him.

But he wasn't Ian. And Ian was the one I loved. I wanted Ian.

My heart was pounding as I approached his home. I wanted to drive by slowly at first, without pulling into the driveway. As I did, I looked over at the cabin. There were lights on. I could see Ian's Toyota, but I also realized there was another car there.

I froze inside.

Someone was with him. I had to know. I had to know if he was with another woman.

I drove a short distance down the road and turned around in someone's driveway. I drove slowly back to

Ian's. Luckily there was very little traffic on this rural road.

I realized I could not really see enough from the road. I would have to pull into the driveway. Because it was a long one, it was possible that I could pull in without anyone seeing me.

I turned off my headlights and pulled in. I drove a short way down then stopped the car and turned it off.

There were no curtains on the windows, and I could see people moving about inside. I saw a man's shape, then my heart sunk as I saw a smaller obviously female shape pass in front of the window.

But then I saw another man, someone taller, someone heavier than Ian.

So, was he having some kind of a party? I could hear faint music coming from the cabin.

I slowly and quietly got out of my car after turning off the light inside that would have given me away if anyone was looking out the window. I shut the door very quietly and walked a bit closer to the cabin.

The music was louder, and I could see the cars more clearly now. The car that wasn't Ian's looked familiar though I wasn't that good with identifying the make of cars. I realized it looked the same as the car I had seen in his driveway that first time I had stalked him, back at his other house.

So maybe the woman inside was this man's girlfriend or wife. Maybe she had nothing to do with Ian.

I could hear laughter coming from inside. I needed to get out of there.

I went slowly back to my car, got in carefully and backed out. As I turned to look at the cabin one last time, I thought I saw someone looking out the window. I caught my breath, hoping whoever it was hadn't seen me. I didn't turn the headlights on until I pulled out into the road. My heart was pounding so hard I could feel it in my head, pulsing and throbbing. I drove back home.

What the hell was I doing? I was going crazy. I was losing it.

I couldn't tell anyone what I had done. I had been lucky to have not gotten caught.

What would Ian do if he knew? Would he have laughed it off? Would he have called the police?

I had no idea. This had to stop. I had to focus on my life and let Ian go.

But when I finally went to bed I dreamed of him, of his body on mine, his voice in my ear, over and over, all night long. I awoke craving him and I knew my obsession with him was not going away.

It was stronger than ever.

Chapter 27

I had to put thoughts of Ian aside as much as I could the next day because I was picking up my mom and going to Tina's for her birthday party. I did the best I could, focusing on the day, wanting to make it happy for my family. I didn't want them to know the torment I was going through.

Luckily my mom didn't question me much that day. She was full of her own plans. She was planning to go on a cruise with some friends and was happily telling me about it as we drove to Tina's then back again after the party.

It had been a good day. When I had dropped my mom off and got home, however, I started to obsess about Ian again.

I either had to contact him or I had to forget him.

I picked up my cell. I hesitated, put it down, then picked it up again.

Then I thought, maybe I should just go see Miguel next week, if he wants me. Let go of Ian and this craziness. Spend time with someone else. Start going out with Bonnie and Lacy again. See if I can meet someone new.

As though that would make a difference. But I had to try.

I went to bed without calling.

I had an appointment with the psychologist later that week, after work. I wasn't sure I wanted to go but I had promised Ginny. I also realized that I needed help. It had been stupid for me to go over there the other night and risk so much. I had never acted so crazy over a man before, ever. Did I want to talk to anyone about it? No! But I knew I had to be honest, I had to come clean, if I was going to get any help.

I fell into a light sleep but startled awake. I sat up groggily, my heart pounding, and looked at the bedside clock. It was 11:30 at night. I wasn't sure what had awoken me. Then I noticed that my cell phone, which sat on the small dresser next to my bed, was lit up. It dinged and I realized that the ding was what had woken me up. But who would be texting me at this hour? Miguel?

Ian?

I grabbed the phone and checked the message.

Ian.

It said only, "Hi."

Oh my God, he had texted me. At first I felt a happy thrill go through me, then I thought, oh no, what if he saw me outside his house that night? What if he was angry?

But I thought that he would not have texted a "hi" if he was angry.

Maybe he felt lonely. Maybe he missed me. Should I answer?

Probably not, but I found myself pressing 'reply.'

"Hi," I wrote back.

"Can I come over?"

What?? After all this, he wanted to come over? At this hour? He was so crazy. I knew I should say no. I couldn't live like this.

I couldn't live without him either.

Still, there had to be some boundaries. I had to have an ounce of self-respect.

"It's too late," I wrote back, "I have to work tomorrow." I hesitated. Should I mention that the last time I had seen him he had brutally chased me away?

"And you didn't want to see me last time I was

over," I wrote. "What changed?" I pressed 'send' before I could change my mind.

I waited, heart pounding for his answer. For a moment nothing happened, and I started to regret what I had written. But then "I'm sorry. I know I was wrong."

Hadn't I heard those words from him before?

But he had apologized. And I was only too ready to forgive.

"Ok," I wrote.

The phone pinged again, "I miss u."

I wrote, "I miss you too."

Then nothing more. I finally lay back down and tried to sleep, but I kept waking up, my mind racing. What now? Would he contact me again? I had actually refused to see him! Maybe I was getting stronger.

What now?

Chapter 28

The next day I went to work feeling a bit righteous. I had done the right thing. I had not just let Ian come over at midnight after weeks of complete silence on his part. I had not given in!

But there was a small voice in my head that was telling me I had made the wrong move, that he would never come back now, that I had lost him. And that voice was scaring me. Because I didn't want to lose him, not for good. Even after all that he had done.

I tried to focus on work that day and succeeded for the most part. Summer was ending and so was our summer program. I had to work on helping to plan the fall program and I threw myself into that as best I could. I did keep surreptitiously checking my phone but there were no more texts from Ian. Maybe my rejection had scared him away. After all, he was the one who was supposed to be rejecting. I was not supposed to reject him!

After work that day I had my first appointment with the therapist.
She worked out of a big Victorian house that she apparently shared with other therapists, since there were four names on the sign inside the door. I parked my car, took a deep breath, and went in.

I let the receptionist know I was there and was instructed to wait. I sat nervously for about five minutes then a matronly looking woman came and said, "Ms. Taggert?"

I stood and followed her. She had short graying hair and a billowy dress on. She wore large square shaped glasses. She looked kind. I felt reassured. Her name was Dr. Clarkson.

We sat in comfortable chairs that faced each other. She asked me some basic intake questions about my living situation, my family, my work. She took notes on a notepad as we talked. Then she asked why I had come for help.

"My boyfriend," I started. "I mean, the guy I was dating….my friend thought it might help if I talked to someone. He was not really treating me very well and I haven't seen him lately…"

Dr. Clarkson wrote something on her pad and asked, "In what way was he not treating you well?"

How to describe Ian? "He kept leaving," I said, and then the words poured out of me. "Things would be good, great, and then suddenly he would freak out, and he would push me away and I didn't even know what I had done wrong. I even lent him money…" my voice trailed off, I felt stupid. Ian had not paid me back the money I had lent him, despite his reassurances that it had just been a temporary loan.

I went on, "I was so upset so much of the time with him. But I really had feelings for him." I looked down at my lap, mortified to feel tears pricking my eyes.

"And do you still have these feelings?" Dr. Clarkson asked.

"I still love him."

The hour was drawing to a close. She asked me what my goals for therapy were. What did I want to do? Did I want to explore why I had been drawn to someone like Ian? Did I want to move on?

I suddenly thought of my father. I wasn't sure I wanted to disclose my childhood trauma to Dr. Clarkson. I had never told anyone. But wasn't that her job, wasn't that why I was coming to her? Maybe Ginny thought I needed to talk about Ian and how badly he treated me, and how I could stop jumping to see him whenever he walked back into my life. But wasn't the deeper issue what had happened with my father?

I just wasn't ready to tell my new therapist about that yet. I told her I wasn't sure, but I wanted to work on feeling better. She looked at me kindly for a moment and said, "Why don't we plan on you coming in weekly for the next four weeks then we can reevaluate? We can plan for therapy when you come in next time. Think about what you would like to get out of this."

I agreed and left. I wasn't sure therapy could help me, but I would give it a try.

When I got home and walked up to my door, I saw a small pink bag on the steps. Confused, I bent down and picked it up. It said "DANA" in block letters.

I brought it inside and opened it. There was a rock with beautiful purple crystals inside, a small geode. And there was a piece of folded paper. I opened it and read.

You are my rock
You are the beautiful crystals
That reach to the heavens
You are the anchor that keeps me
Close to the earth
I'm sorry I hurt you
Come back to me.
Ian

My breath caught and tears filled my eyes and spilled down my face. He wanted me back!

Ian didn't call or text that night, but it didn't matter. The next step was really up to me, he had placed it in my hands. I put the geode on the dresser next to my bed and the note under it. I cherished it. It was from him, it had magic. I fell asleep early that night and slept more soundly that I had in some time.

Chapter 29

I called Ian when I got home from work the next day. He answered, and his voice was warm. "Thanks for the poem and gift," I said. "They're so beautiful."

"I really missed you, Dana," he said. Of course, an unwelcome thought crossed my mind- he always says that after he blows me off. But I pushed this thought away like a puff of wind and focused on the moment.

"I know," I said. "Ian, I want to be with you, only you."

"What does that mean?" he said, and his voice suddenly sounded suspicious. "Were you with someone else?"

How had the conversation turned so quickly? I thought of Miguel and felt a guilty pang. But why should I? Ian had rejected me. I didn't know whether he would come back or not at the time.

"Ian, why are you asking me that?"

"I don't know, sorry, I just…I think of you as mine, Dana."

For some reason a thrill went through me at that remark. His voice had softened, deepened, as he said it. He had told me this before.

"If I'm yours, Ian," I told him, "then we have to be together. You can't keep pushing me away."

"I know, I know. It's hard for me, Dana," he said then added, "You don't know everything about me. You don't know the whole story."

No, I didn't. I didn't know a lot about his life because he would never talk much about it. When we had met and were sharing about our families, our histories, he said that his mother was deceased and that he wasn't close to his father. He didn't share details and knowing how prickly he could get, I didn't push. I said, "No, you don't like to talk about things, Ian, that's why I don't know. You never would tell me much."

"Maybe it's time I did."

"Yes, that would be good," I said cautiously.

"I want to see you," he said.

"Ok."

He asked me to come over on Friday night and I agreed. I hung up feeling excited, but also feeling some annoyance and dissatisfaction. I was getting tired of this come close go away game. I was getting tired of being jerked around, having my heart trampled on over and over. Yet I knew I would be there on Friday. I couldn't resist Ian. When he pulled me back, I was always there, running to him.

On Friday I drove to his place, feeling excited, but feeling trepidation too. After all, the last time I had been there he had told me to leave in such a cruel way.

But he wasn't cruel this time. He was waiting for me by the open door. He pulled me into his arms and kissed me deeply as soon as I reached him.

"I've been so hungry for this," he murmured in my ear.

But for once we didn't go straight to bed. "Sit down, we'll talk," he said. I sat at his table. He poured me a glass of wine and sat down too.

"I know I've been skittish," he said. You know something about my last relationship. I stayed in it always hoping, always reaching for something. I knew what she was, but I kept thinking I could change that, make it better. She was always one or two steps away from me, the drugs were more important to her. I guess when you came along..." he looked at me intently, "and you were always there for me, I guess maybe I didn't value it as much as I should have. I mean, how much could something be worth if it was right there in front of me, if I didn't have to keep striving for it. There was nothing to pursue. You were right there. And it felt uncomfortable to me."

I had been listening to him. What he said made some sense, but it wasn't enough. I couldn't believe that one difficult relationship that had only lasted for a year had completely damaged his ability to love.

"Ian, I get that, but that's something I already knew about. There's got to be more."

He took a deep breath and got up. He went to the cupboard and took out a bong.

"Ian…" I started to say.

"Look, Dana, this is hard for me, let me take a hit." He did so then put the bong back. He sat down again.

"Ok, well, I know I didn't say much about my family. That's because they were really bad. My mother…" he stopped, then went on, "My mother was a big time alcoholic. She used to beat me with a belt for anything, anything I did wrong. Or even when I didn't really do anything wrong. She would hit me when she thought I did something, even if I hadn't. When she was sober, she could be affectionate, but when she was drinking she was a holy terror."

I felt appalled. I had a feeling there was something bad in his childhood, and I felt such compassion for the younger Ian. "I'm so sorry, Ian." When he didn't say more, I asked gently, "And your dad? Was he around?"

"He was at first, when I was really young. She wasn't as bad then. But as I got older, she got worse. He would come home from work and she would be drinking and ranting and raving. They would get into these raging fights. Then he started hitting her. It was so awful. I would try to hide in my room, but I would hear them. Sometimes he would leave and then she would take it out on me."

"Oh my God," I said, not able to hold back. "That's

terrible, Ian."

"He finally moved out. He couldn't take it anymore. He tried to stay in touch with me for a little while, but the calls slowed down, he got his life together, met someone else. He married her. I only met her once when I was about 17. By then my mother was getting pretty sick and ever since I had gotten bigger, she wasn't hitting me anymore. She didn't last too long after that, about a year. Then I sold the house and moved on."

"Ok, so I understand more about you, Ian. Thank you for telling me." I got up and put my arms around him. He stiffened for a moment then relaxed into me.

I heard him say, "There's more."

"Ok, tell me," I said. I sat back down.

"I was, well, I was kind of lost when I left. I was pretty young and didn't know where to go. My dad certainly didn't want me living with him and his new wife. I didn't have any brothers or sisters. I had just graduated high school that spring and I had to work, so I got a job working construction and a cheap apartment. I had a few girlfriends along the way, girls seemed to like me, but nothing serious, just to fool around with. But one of them... she got pregnant."

I looked up at him, my eyes wide.

"When she told me, I freaked out. I was only 18 and I sure as hell didn't want to be a father. I told her to get an abortion."

He didn't speak for a moment, and I finally said, "Well, that's not the worst thing. She must have been young too, and that was probably the best thing to do at the time."

"No, Dana, you don't understand. She refused. She had the baby. I have a daughter. She's nine now, she'll be ten soon."

It took me a minute for that to sink in. Ian had a daughter? A child he had never even mentioned to me? I felt shocked. I didn't know what to say.

"She's nine and I don't even see her. Her mother doesn't want me to see her. She doesn't think I'm a good influence. I mean, I tried at first, but it was so hard. My ex's mother was so angry with me. Julie wanted to get married, she thought I would marry her. But she went ahead and had the baby, and they lived with her parents. I left her. I left after she told me she wouldn't have an abortion. I didn't want to deal with the whole thing, I just couldn't handle it. But I did try to see the baby after she was born. I tried."

I wasn't sure what to say. So many questions were popping into my brain. I wasn't sure where to start. I finally said, "Well, did you see her?"

"I did get to see her when she was about a month old. Julie's mother called me and told me I could come. I went to their house. It was pretty awful, but the baby- she named her Emily- was beautiful. I held her and I realized I did want to be part of her life. But they kept pushing me away. So, I don't see her. I mean, I saw her a few more times. The last time was when she was six. I don't even know if she understood who I was." Ian was suddenly overcome with emotion. He put his head into his hands. He spoke from beneath them in a muffled voice, "So do you understand why I'm so fucking scared to get too involved now, Dana?"

I rushed to reassure him. "Yes, I do, I do, I'm so sorry all that happened to you, Ian." I said. I wanted to go and hold him again, but I wasn't sure I should. He sat quiet for a few minutes and I just waited. Then he lifted his head, wiping his eyes with his sleeve.

"I know, I'm a mess," he said. "I guess I'm bitter about relationships. And women," he added. "I don't really trust women. My own mother was a drunk and she hit me. My ex-girlfriend had a baby and then pushed me out of my daughter's life. Why should I trust any woman?"

"But women aren't all the same, Ian!" I protested. "Everyone is different. Just as men are."

"I just can't trust anyone. I find it very hard." He looked into my eyes, "Then you came along, Dana, and there's…. a purity about you. You work with troubled kids, you still seem to, well, believe in people. And I know you care for me…" he gazed at me for a moment, then said, "I know you love me."

We had never used the word love between us before. It hung there in the air as we looked at each other. "And you know what, Dana? I love you too. I fell for you. That's why I keep getting so scared, why I keep running away."

He loved me. Ian loved me!

"I do get it, Ian. But I'm not like your ex-girlfriends. I would never keep the father of any child of mine away. And I don't even do drugs. I don't even drink that much!" I raised my glass. I was still on my first glass of wine and I usually stopped after just one or two. "I've seen what it can do. My father…" I stopped. How much should I tell him? "My father was alcoholic too. He …" I couldn't go on, not just yet. I finished, "He could be pretty awful when he was drunk too."

"We have something in common, don't we, Dana? We're both broken. Broken people with fucked up families."

Something about that didn't sound right to me. Even with all of my problems, I didn't feel broken! And my current family, my mother and sister, were fine. My mom had overcome her problems. She and my sister lived decent lives; they weren't fucked up. But I didn't want to contradict him and ruin the moment.

We sat quiet for a time then he got up and held out his hand. We went to the couch and he held me, just held me close, for a long time. We talked a bit, of superficial things. The words of love still hovered between us. When the night grew late and we went to bed, we made love softly, gently, gazing into each other's eyes. Something had shifted between us now and I had never felt closer to Ian.

Chapter 30

I stayed the night and the next day with Ian. Things were subdued between us. He was affectionate, a bit quiet, but I didn't feel the tension in him that I sometimes felt. It was as though the air was clear now between us. He had told me things he had been afraid to tell me before and there was a new connection between us, a deeper intimacy.

We had breakfast together then went for a walk by the water. The season was turning into fall and there was a mild crispness in the air that morning. We held hands as we walked and talked only intermittently. It felt peaceful, which was something I had rarely felt with Ian. I stayed that day and into the next. Finally on Sunday afternoon, I kissed him goodbye and drove home.

I had to process everything. He had told me so much and we had been so close. But what he told me was bothering me too. I needed clarity and I couldn't really process when I was with him. Being with him, even in quiet times, impacted all of my senses, pulled me into his orbit, fogged my brain. When I was with him I wasn't just myself, I was Dana/Ian. I was part of him as well as myself.

When I got home I made dinner, laid out my clothes for work the next day and thought about what Ian had told me. I could accept that he had a daughter. At least he had attempted to be part of her life, he hadn't just ignored her. He had been so young when she was born. And after the trauma he had endured I could understand better why he was so skittish about being in a relationship. In fact, that was likely the reason he had chosen someone like Patty, a drug addict who could never get too close.

But somehow I had gotten to him. I got too close. So, he left and kept leaving.

Yet he kept coming back too. There was something inside him that wanted that closeness while he also feared it, so it went on, the come close go away game, back and forth, up and down. It was exhausting for me, but it must have been for him too, to be inside his head with all of that going on.

I felt an enormous compassion for him. I loved him. And he had not only acknowledged that, but admitted he loved me too!

But what did that love mean for us if he continued to be so afraid?
And why did he say we were both broken? What did that mean?

I tried to go to bed but the thoughts kept churning around and around in my head. At some point we would have to talk again. I wanted to know more, I wanted to stay as close to him as I felt right now. I knew that bringing these issues up with him was risky, but I didn't feel I could ignore them either.

I fell into sleep finally. I thought I dreamed about Ian, his image was so strongly in my mind when I awoke, but the dream images were scattered and fragmentary. I couldn't quite capture them, but it had seemed as though he was me and I was him and we had swirled and blended into each other. In the morning before getting ready for work I grabbed my notebook and wrote a poem.

Dreams

I feel you

Sometimes
In the dark of night
Your desire arises
And you want me
I am there
With my passion
Drinking the sweat on your skin
As though it is wine
Tasting your mouth
Flesh to flesh
Becoming you
Not knowing
In those moments
Where you stop
And I begin.

The next day at work I looked for Ginny at lunchtime. "Let's go out to eat, I want to talk to you," I told her. We went to the deli down the street and ordered sandwiches. When we sat down to eat, she said, "Ok, what's up?"

"I spent the weekend with Ian," I told her. "He told me a lot about his childhood. Ginny, I get now why he is the way he is. He had an awful childhood! I really want to show him that I can help him, make his life better."

"Can you do that, Dana?" she seemed skeptical.

"At least I understand more about him now. Don't you think it's a good sign that he is opening up? That he's trusting me more?"

"Maybe," she said cautiously. "Was there something you wanted to tell me?"

"He told me he loved me, Ginny."

"Really?" her voice was cool. I was feeling a bit annoyed. This was a huge thing for me!

"Yes, he loves me! You know I love him so much, but I wasn't sure how he felt about me."

Ginny looked at me and I saw compassion in her eyes. "Dana, I'm glad you're happy about that. But…" she hesitated, then went on, "Love isn't just something you say, it's something you show. It's actions as well as words."

I was starting to wish I hadn't told her anything, as usual. "You just don't like him, Ginny."

"I don't like how he's treated you," she said carefully, "But I know how much you care for him. I hope he treats you better from now on."

"But I understand why he's so afraid. It took a lot for him to tell me that you know. He's like one of the kids at our agency. He was hurt badly as a kid himself, and you know how hard it is for them to trust. Well, Ian's like that too. But he is starting to trust me."

"He should. You've really been there for him."

"I know, I have, and maybe now it's paying off."

"I just don't want to see you hurt, Dana. You're my best friend."

"Thanks, Ginny. I wanted you to know. He is so important to me and so are you." I was starting to feel a bit better about what she was saying. "I wish you could meet him, Ginny. Would you if I can set it up?"

"I guess so."

"I'll see if he'll do it. He's kind of shy, actually."

"Ok." She didn't sound overly enthusiastic, but I thought if she could meet Ian she would come around. I thought I would approach him about it soon.

That night I was thinking again about the weekend and the things Ian had told me. I found that something was bothering me that I hadn't told Ginny. Ian had said that we were both 'broken.' Why did Ian feel that way? What did that mean to him? Was it something that could be fixed? Wouldn't being in a loving relationship help to heal that?

And maybe that was part of what had drawn me so

to someone like Ian. The fact that he was so difficult to get close to, the fact that he gave me intermittent reinforcement but was not always there for me? Because who else had not been there for me in my childhood? What kind of template did I have for the way a man should behave? Not a good one. Was I modeling my adult relationships on that? Was I drawn to men who were not available, like my father? Maybe Ian and I fit together at the broken places.

I realized too that while Ian had opened up to me, I had not told him about that significant event that had traumatized my own childhood. I had not opened up completely to him. And I wasn't sure I was ready. But maybe I had to trust him as he had trusted me. Wasn't that a way to bring us even closer?

I called him later to say goodnight. I wasn't ready to bring all of this up just yet. I wanted to bask in the warmth of the feelings we had just disclosed to each other. We spoke briefly and said warm goodnights. I took a deep breath and said, "I love you." I waited. Ian didn't speak at first then he said, "Love you too." I sighed in relief. For a moment I'd been afraid he wouldn't reciprocate. But he had! We had turned a corner.

Or so I thought.

Chapter 31

For a time, things were ok between us.

Sex was still a huge part of our relationship, but we also started to talk more about so many things. We didn't stray too much to the topics of his daughter or the painful times in our lives, but talked about things that made up our days, interests that we had. I talked about my love of poetry, told him of my favorite poet, e.e. Cummings, and I gave him a poem that I had written. I had written it after we had made love by the lake that summer night.

> *Milk-hot white summer night*
> *We danced on the waves of the sun*
> *Kissed our fingers and threw stars into the sky*
> *Turned silver as the moon melted on our heads*
> *We lay in full bloom on the grass*
> *And made love with the world.*

I felt a bit shy as I showed Ian my poem, but he read it and looked up at me with an almost awed expression. "That's beautiful, Dana," he said, and reached forward to kiss me. He took the poem and put it up on the refrigerator with a magnet. "I'll frame it when I get a chance to buy a frame." I was very pleased at his response.

Ian told me that his ancestors had come from England and he liked to watch documentaries and read about English history. He especially enjoyed the Tudors and their colorful and dramatic times. I hadn't known that about him before. I was thrilled to learn more and more about Ian. He was demonstrating more sensitivity than before.

Ian was also working more hours with his friends who did construction and had paid me back the money he owed me. I felt there was a new flow between us, a comfort zone that had not been there previously. The bond between us was getting tighter, drawing us together.

One Friday evening I drove over to Ian's and found him in a playful mood. "Hello, Milady," he said, bowing. I laughed. "We are going to sport together tonight." He went to the bedroom and pulled something from the closet. He turned and presented it to me with a flourish. "Your gown, Milady."

"What?" I said, laughing. It was a green gown, but it was a style of centuries ago, I could see.

"Put it on," he said. "Go into your chamber, Milady, strip, and put it on."

I felt a sexual thrill go through me. I did as he asked, going into the bedroom, and shutting the door. I stripped off my regular clothes and put the gown on. It took a while to get into the unfamiliar garb but when I did I looked in the mirror, fascinated. I looked as though I had stepped out of the sixteenth century. The gown fit me well, tightly at the top, then swelling out to a voluminous skirt. I twirled and my dark hair flung out and swung around my shoulders. I thought that maybe I should put it up but left it as it was. It was sexier that way. I went out to the living room.

Ian had stripped off his shirt and was wearing only shorts. He looked at me, looked up and down with a lustful eye, as though he could see through the dress. Again, I felt a thrill go down to my toes. This was exciting! What game was he playing now?

Then I noticed his hands. By his side he held a knife.

Now the thrill I felt was one of fear. What was he doing?

He came toward me. He spoke softly, "When Elizabeth was young- as you are young, Milady-her guardian, Thomas Seymour, came after her in the gardens and ripped her dress to shreds with a knife. His wife, who had been Henry VIII's widowed queen, held her while he did it. She didn't know that he had sexual feelings for Elizabeth. She didn't know what he really wanted to do with Elizabeth."

I realized that he was speaking of Elizabeth I, before she had become Queen.

Ian had come close while he was talking. He reached the knife up and I gasped, trying to pull away, not knowing if he was going to hurt me. He grabbed my arm with one hand and slashed with the other. Part of the bodice of the dress ripped away.

He slashed again and again. The knife came close to my skin but did not touch me. I felt that I was in a dream, that there was only Ian's closeness and the knife in his hand. He slashed and the skirt fell about my feet. He slashed and my breasts were exposed. He slashed and the dress was in shreds around me, and I was naked.

Ian dropped the knife and picked me up in his arms. I was trembling with fear and arousal. "I'm going to ravish you," he whispered. And he carried me to the bed.

I could hardly believe it afterward. Had he really done that, had he really enacted a scene from centuries ago? And yet it had been so exciting, so thrilling so... dangerous. What if the knife had slipped? I could have been hurt.

But I hadn't.

Ian was warm and loving the next morning. But he did not speak of what he had done the night before.

When I went home after the weekend was over I wondered about it. I had been frightened, but so excited too. Did I relate sexual excitement to danger? Was that why I got such a thrill over men who behaved erratically, over sexual experiences that were possibly somewhat perilous? Was there something wrong with me?

I knew the answer. I knew deep down that it was related to my father's abuse of me. Something I had not yet told anyone. Not the therapist, not Ian, not Ginny.

But was it time? Could I have been hurt last night? What if the knife had slipped?

It hadn't... but what about next time?

Maybe it was time to talk to someone.

Chapter 32

I was still seeing the therapist. I felt like I was bumbling along, not really disclosing everything. But while the reenactment of the sexual episode of long ago had been extremely erotic and exciting, I felt disturbed by it too. I could have been hurt. At first I hadn't been sure that Ian was not going to harm me. Why was I with someone I couldn't trust not to harm me? Why would I be with a man like that?

I vowed to talk to Dr. Clarkson the next time I saw her.

The day of my appointment I drove to Dr. Clarkson's office with trepidation. What in the world would she think of me, participating in a crazy scenario like the one Ian had enacted? Should I even tell her?

But I felt afraid. I was feeling afraid of Ian, even as I continued to be so drawn to him.

We settled in our usual seats and I blurted out, "Something happened."

"Yes?" the psychologist said in her calm way.

"When I was with Ian last weekend he… well, he…did something that scared me."

She looked at me. "Do you want to tell me what he did?"

I really didn't want to but… "It was a sex game. He used a knife."

I saw Dr. Clarkson's eyebrows rise. "Did he hurt you?"

"No, but I was afraid he would."

"Did you try to stop him, Dana?"

I looked down at my lap. "No."

She was gazing at me with some concern when I looked back up.

"Is there a reason you didn't try to stop him?"

"I don't know, I… when I'm with him I don't feel in control. I feel like I have to do what he says in some ways," I started, fumbling to articulate how I felt with Ian. It was hard to put into words. "I felt scared but excited too, you know…" I trailed off.

"Did it occur to you to try to stop it if you wanted to?"

"No. No it didn't."

"Can you think about why that might be?"

I thought. "As I said, I feel…almost helpless with him sometimes, maybe because I feel like I need him so much. And he can get so angry, I want to please him." As I spoke, I realized that what I was saying was true, and it didn't make me feel good about myself. I was a strong woman, a professional who did a good job working with troubled kids. Why was I a helpless little girl at times when it came to Ian?

I thought I knew why.

"Something happened when I was young," I started. I looked down again. I felt shame, not really knowing why I would feel that way. I suddenly thought of Jamie. She had been abused, not just once but over and over, and yet she was healing, she was doing so well now. She was coming out of her shell and learning to trust others. Her friends were all happy for her and they had been so supportive. All of the kids in the program had learned something from Jamie. They had learned that they could overcome abuse and adversity and create better lives for themselves with help from others.

And here was Dr. Clarkson, ready to help me. Was I

going to be less courageous than a teenage girl?

"I was abused when I was a kid." I said bluntly.

"I'm sorry that happened to you," she said. "Can you tell me more about it?"

"I never told anyone," I said quietly. Then I told her the story, in bits and pieces. She probed gently when I stopped, and I continued. Most of the time I looked down but when I was finished, I looked up at her. Tears were stinging my eyes, and I grabbed the ever-ready tissue from the box she had sitting on the end table next to my chair.

"That sounds terrible, Dana. You were very brave to tell me about it. I know it was difficult for you."

"Dr. Clarkson, do you think it's related to my problems now? Why am I so drawn to men like Ian?"

"I do," she said. "As a social worker yourself, you know that sometimes we reenact things that happened to us when we were young. Not necessarily in the exact same way but I do think you have become so attached to Ian in order to recreate a dynamic that you had as a child. Your father drank; Ian uses drugs. Your father could be charming but distant too; Ian is great, then he disappears. Your father abused you; Ian can be abusive toward you; he frightens you sometimes. And he doesn't seem to consider your feelings the way he should, as your father certainly did not."

Put that way it made so much sense. Emotionally I felt like a truck had hit me, but there was a sense of relief too. Dr. Clarkson hadn't rejected me as someone "broken." She had accepted and helped to explain why I was the way I was, why I was drawn to men like Ian. As I had known in my heart, but it was good to share my deepest pain with someone else and to have her understand. My tears started up again, and I dabbed my eyes with the tissue.

"You've done good work here today, Dana," Dr. Clarkson said.

"Let's continue next week." I realized that my time was up.

I thanked her and left.

When I got home I called Ginny.

I had never told Ginny what had happened to me as a child, but I owed her. She was the one who had pushed me to see a therapist. I felt that a burden had been lifted from me by telling Dr. Clarkson my secret.

"Ginny," I said when she answered.

"Dana, what's up?" She seemed a bit surprised to hear from me. After all, I had just seen her at work that day.

"I saw the therapist just now and, well, I told her some things I didn't tell her before. About when I was a kid."

She was silent for a moment. "What things?"

"Ginny, I had some things happen that I never told you, or anyone. I don't know that I can get into it now, but I wanted to say thank you. Thanks for pushing me to see someone. I realize it was the right thing to do and… you're such a good friend. Thanks."

"Oh, well," she sounded a bit embarrassed. "I'm glad it's working out for you, Dana," she said. "You know you can talk to me too, anytime. But only if you're ready," she added. I knew she was probably bursting with curiosity now about what I had told Dr. Clarkson, but she was too good a friend to push me about that.

"I will," I promised.

I felt such relief that day that I realized I didn't even want to talk to Ian. His calls were hit or miss; he didn't call every night. Often I was the one to call him. But I just did not want to talk to him that night.

I did something unprecedented; I shut my phone off. And though it made me anxious, I didn't turn it back on until morning. When I checked the next day there were no messages from Ian. I felt a bit upset, but relieved as well. I wanted to process the session with Dr. Clarkson and wasn't sure how I felt about Ian's sex game right now, or his behavior in general.

I had to work that day, but I continued to feel some relief and a lack of desire to speak to Ian. He didn't text me that day, as he sometimes did, but I felt ok with that. By evening, however, I was starting to wonder at the lack of contact.

The next day went by and the next. By this time, it was Friday and I had not heard from him. Of course, I had now gone from feeling relief to anxiety about his failure to even text me, much less call.

I finally texted him that evening, just saying that I texted to say hello. Nothing came back. I waited and waited, getting ever more anxious.

At last, at about 9:00 that night I called his number. It went straight to voicemail.

Now I was really getting worried. What the hell was going on? Was he with someone else? After all we had been through? After things had been going well between us? Was he trying to sabotage our relationship?

It struck me hard how little I trusted him. I did not trust him. He hadn't always proved trustworthy. So why was I with him?

Because I wasn't able to trust my father either.

But wasn't the task before me to break that pattern?

For some reason, I suddenly thought of Jerry. Jerry had been a good man, a good person. So of course, I didn't stay with him. I felt a desire to talk to him, to try to mend fences. Not to get back together, but just to see if it was possible for us to be friends again. He had been a good friend. I missed that.

It occurred to me that I could drive over to see what was going on with Ian, but I pushed that thought away. After that session with Dr. Clarkson, I felt a bit stronger, and I was not going to stalk Ian again. I hadn't told her about the stalking, but I just was not going to go there. I tried to focus back on thoughts of Jerry. Was it too late to call him? On a Friday night? He was probably with his new girlfriend.

What's the worst that could happen, I thought, and pressed his number into my cell. It rang a few times before Jerry answered.

"Hello?"

I hadn't thought about what I would say but I said, "Jerry, it's me, Dana. Sorry to be calling so late."

Jerry did not speak for a second then said, "No, it's not too late. You know I don't go to sleep this early. What's going on, Dana?"

"I just… I felt bad about our break-up, Jerry, and I…. I miss you as a friend. I'm not trying to justify what I did, but I… I just miss our friendship. You were a good friend to me."

"Did Ian blow you off again?" Damn. Jerry was so perceptive, even after not speaking to me for so long. But it was a fair question.

"No, that's not why I'm calling," I said, which of course was not quite the truth. "I mean, things haven't been too bad between us lately, but I was just thinking about you. Are you still seeing that same woman?" I couldn't recall the name of the colorless person he had been with at the mall that day.

"You mean Marcy? Sometimes. She's not here now though." He went on, "I tried with her, I mean, she's nice and really smart but she's well, a bit dull. Not like you," he added. "You were exciting. But I need someone who's kind of in the middle. Not too dull, but not too exciting either."

I laughed. Jerry had always been good for me.

"Do you think it's possible we could be friends again? Just friends."

"I guess that is a possibility," Jerry answered slowly. "I was really upset and angry with you for a while, but… I guess that was a bit unfair. I did know going into it that you were nuts about that crazy guy."

I wasn't going to contradict him. Ian was crazy. And he made me crazy.

"I hope we can be friends again," I said.

"Yes, then you'll have a guy to hang around with when Ian won't see you," Jerry said.

"No!" I protested. I could hear the teasing in his voice. "Not just for that!"

"Ok, Dana, let's try to be friends again."

"Ok, I'm glad you agree. Let's stay in touch and talk again soon."

Jerry agreed and I hung up, feeling better than I had before. I would just try to ignore Ian and the feelings he stirred up for the time being.

Chapter 33

The phone rang late the next morning. It was a number I didn't recognize but something told me to answer it.

"Dana!" I heard Ian's voice.

"What? Where are you calling from?" I was surprised to hear from him.

"My phone was broken; I couldn't call or text you. I'm using a guy's cell phone; somebody I know from work."

I couldn't help but think he could have managed to contact me sooner than this if he really wanted to, but I didn't say so.

"How did your phone break?" I asked.

Ian seemed annoyed. "What difference does it make? I just wanted to let you know why I hadn't called."

"Ok," I said slowly. I wasn't sure what else he wanted to hear.

"Listen, are you coming over this weekend?"

I thought about it. As usual, even though I was upset with him, the pull of Ian was like a magnet to me.

"Do you want me to?"

"Why the hell do you think I'm calling?"

That didn't exactly sound inviting. But while I had some new insights and felt a bit stronger, I wasn't strong enough to resist his pull.

"Ok, fine, when?"

"Today. I wanted to bring you someplace tonight.

My friend Doug's house."

"Doug?"

"He's my friend from way back. I want to introduce you to them. Him and his wife."

That sounded more promising. "Ok, what should I bring to wear?"

"You look good in anything, Dana. But nobody is dressing up, we're just going to their house. They live about an hour south of my place."

"What time?"

"Come over whenever you like, we're not leaving here until about 5:00."

"Ok, I'll see you in about an hour and a half."

"See you, gotta go." He hung up.

I felt a combination of aggravation and excitement. Ian always stirred such mixed emotions in me! He doesn't contact me for days, then calls me on someone else's phone and suddenly invites me to his friend's house. Why hadn't he introduced me to his friends before? But it did seem like a step forward that he was inviting me now. But what had happened to his phone? I thought it had been a logical question to ask, but it had annoyed him. He got annoyed all too readily. But I was going to see him, and that always aroused excitement in me.

I chose a couple of outfits to bring, figuring I was staying over. I put on good jeans and a pretty top with long dangly earrings. I brushed out my hair and put on make-up. I wanted to make a good impression on his friends. Then I drove over to Ian's, wondering if these friends were the ones who had been at his house the time I had driven over there and sat in the driveway. I obviously couldn't ask.

When I got there Ian opened the door quickly. He was clearly happy to see me. He looked me over and said, "You look luscious, as always."

"What happened to your phone? Are you going to

get a new one?" I asked, as I walked inside, giving him a quick kiss. He seemed less aggravated by the question this time.

"It was stupid, I had it on the sink while I was shaving, and I knocked it into the water. I tried to fix it, but it wouldn't work. I ordered another one, it should come any day now. I borrowed one from somebody at work who had an extra one." He pulled a phone out of his pocket. "Keep that number I called you on for now."

"Ok," I said, sitting down. We had some time before we had to leave so I asked him about his friends.

"I've known them both since we were in high school."

I was surprised. I didn't realize he was still in touch with anyone from that difficult time in his life and said so to Ian.

"I know, but I stayed in touch with Doug and with his wife too. Well, of course she wasn't his wife then, but they got married a few years later. She got pregnant. They have two kids, a boy and a girl, twins."

"So why are we going?"

"I told them I was seeing you and they've been bugging me about meeting you."

"What did you tell them about me?"

"Just that we've been together for a while now. They were bugging me, telling me it was time they got to meet this woman who has caught my interest for all this time." He was teasing me, but I thought it hadn't been all that long that we were together. The thought also crossed my mind that for part of the time since I'd met him, he had not been with me at all, he'd blown me off. But as usual, I said nothing.

We sat and talked, and when it was time we got in Ian's car and drove to his friend's house.

I was nervous. It was the first time I was meeting anyone from Ian's life, and I wanted to make a good impression.

When we got there the man called Doug answered the door. He seemed pleased to see Ian and said hello to me when we were introduced. He turned to introduce his wife to me as she came up behind him. "This is Nan," he said, as she reached out to give Ian a big hug. She then turned to say hello to me.

Doug was a bigger man than Ian, a bit wide around the waist, pleasant looking, with dark blonde hair cut short. His wife was about my height but a bit heavier, with straight light brown hair that curved around her chin. She had a pretty enough face but was somewhat nondescript looking.

We went inside to the dining area. They had set out dinner and invited us to sit. Two children came running into the room. "Uncle Ian," they cried, throwing themselves at him. He laughed and hugged them both.

"These are the twins," he said to me. "Brian and Brianna."

"Who's this?" Brianna asked, looking at me with curiosity.

"This is my girlfriend," Ian said. It gave me such a thrill to hear him call me that.

"Oh," she said, looking interested. "I like your hair," she said to me.

"Thanks," I said, laughing. She was adorable. So was her brother, who was just staring at me. They were both blonde and looked alike. Brianna had long pigtails and Brian's hair was shaggy around his ears. They resembled their dad.

"How old are you?" I asked them. They answered in unison, "We're eight." Brianna added, "We just had a birthday! With a unicorn cake and everything!"

"That's nice," I said. At that point their mother said, "Ok, come on, kids, let's go to the playroom, the big people are going to eat. You can watch Incredibles 2 if you want."

"Yay!" they both cried and followed their mother out of the room.

"We fed them earlier so the grown-ups could talk peacefully," their father said with a rueful smile. "Otherwise, we wouldn't have gotten a word in."

"They're so adorable," I told him. I loved children.

"They must have watched that movie about a hundred times, but they never get enough. We try not to let them watch too much TV, but sometimes you have to distract them," Doug said. At that point his wife came back.

"Well, they're settled for now," she said.

We started to eat the meal of salad, roast chicken, and potatoes. Wine was poured. Ian talked to his friends and I said little at first. They spent some time talking about people I didn't know, and I wasn't sure what to say to contribute to the conversation. Then Ian said, looking at me, "Dana works with problem teens, as I told you."

Nan looked at me. I wasn't sure what it was I saw in her eyes, but she said, politely enough, "That must be difficult."

"Oh, not really," I answered, warming to one of my favorite topics. "I love my work. It's so rewarding when I can help a kid who's had a tough life. It's really great to see them make progress."

Nan said nothing, but Doug said, "That does sound great. I'm a bank manager, so I wouldn't know anything about your type of work. But it sounds like a wonderful thing to be doing."

"What do you do, Nan?" I asked.

"Oh, I work part-time at a preschool for developmentally disabled children," she said. "Nothing like what you do."

I thought that was an odd remark to make. Certainly, working with small disabled children was worthwhile and valuable! I wasn't sure what to say. It felt awkward for a moment, then I said, "But that's so worthwhile too. It must be very rewarding." She said nothing in response. Then Doug and Ian started talking about a boat building project that Doug was apparently working on and the moment passed.

After dinner I offered to help clean up. Nan and I carried dishes to the kitchen while Doug brought Ian to the garage to show him the boat he was working on.

"They'll be smoking weed out there," Nan said. "I won't let him smoke in the house because of the kids." She had looked in on her children and said that had finished watching their movie and were playing a game. "They're good kids. They're both smart, they do well in school."

"They seem to be great kids," I said. I felt a bit odd with Nan. She seemed to have a tension in her and I had no idea why. Then she said,
"You know, I was surprised that Ian brought you here."

That confused me. Ian had told me his friends wanted to meet me.

"Why?" I asked.

"Well, he doesn't usually bring his girlfriends around. That's probably because he doesn't last long with any of them. He isn't the type to stay with anyone for long."

I felt a slight jolt go through me. Why was she telling me this? Did that mean I was special because he had brought me? Or was she trying to say that he wasn't going to stay with me?

"He tries for a while," she went on, "But most of the time he ends up breaking up with them. He's very picky. Little things can get to him, then he ends the relationship."

That hit home because I certainly knew that Ian could get incredibly irritated at a moment's notice. Was Nan trying to say that if he got irritated enough with me he would break it off?

She must have noticed my expression because she

gave a quick laugh. "Sorry, I guess I'm just trying to warn you. Women really like Ian, and he usually ends up hurting them."

Again, I wasn't sure what to say. It didn't feel right that she was saying all of this to me. She was supposed to be Ian's long-time friend, along with her husband.

"Well, thanks for the warning," I finally muttered, longing to get away from her company. "If you don't need any more help I'm going to find Ian."

She looked at me for a moment and again, I felt something in her gaze that was unpleasant. But she said, "Go ahead, I'm fine here. I've got to get the kids up to bed in a few minutes."

I left and went outside to the garage. Ian and Doug were smoking weed, she'd been right. Ian jumped a bit when he saw me, as though he'd been caught doing something wrong, but then he smiled and put his arm around me. He said, "Look at this boat, Doug built this himself." I duly admired the boat. They talked for a few minutes longer then Ian said, "Well, we should get going. Let's go inside so we can say goodbye to Nan."

We went inside. She was coming downstairs and said to Ian, "Go say goodnight to the kids, they'll be upset if you don't."

He did so and went upstairs as I stood awkwardly again, waiting for him. Luckily he came back down quickly. Nan gave him another hug goodbye. Doug said to me, "Come again, Dana, it was nice to meet you." Nan said nothing.

I told Ian I would drive, since he'd been smoking weed. He started to protest, but then handed me the keys. As we drove away, I said, "What is up with Nan?"

"What do you mean?"

"She was telling me..." I trailed off. I suddenly wasn't sure I should say anything. Ian was so prickly, things could turn in a minute, and I was grateful that he had brought me to meet his friends. But Ian pushed.

"What did she say, Dana?"

I had to answer. "Well, she said that you usually didn't bring your girlfriends to meet them."

"She's full of it, they've met other women I've dated."

"Why would she say that? And she said that you're picky."

He laughed. "I am picky. That's why I'm with you."

That was a nice thing for him to say, but I went on, "She said that you end your relationships quickly, that you don't stay with anyone."

He was silent for a minute, then said, "You know why, Dana, I explained all of that to you."

"Ok, but why would Nan be telling me that?"

"Who knows?" he said. "Just let's drop it. She can be weird sometimes."

I was uneasy about that answer, but let it go.

When we got back to Ian's he turned to me and said, "Ok, I guess I should tell you."

"Tell me what?"

"Nan's got a crush on me."

"What? She's married to your friend."

"That doesn't preclude her having a crush, does it?"

"I guess not."

"We had sex before," he said. I looked at him, feeling stunned.

"Before what?"

"We had sex when we were younger. She really liked me. I blew her off. I knew Doug liked her. He'd started dating her, but I guess I didn't respect that. I screwed her and he didn't know. But I didn't want to go out with her. She's too needy. I wasn't even all that attracted to her."

I wasn't sure what to say. For some reason I felt shocked that he had brought me to see someone he'd had an affair with. And he had gone behind his friend's back? What kind of man does that?

"Were they married then?" I asked, hoping the answer was no. But Ian hesitated.

"Well, the first time we were just kids," he said. "It was after Julie got pregnant. I was really upset, and Nan was trying to help me. She'd been jealous of Julie. One thing just led to another."

"The first time?"

"Yes, it happened again."

"Were they married then?" I asked again.

"Yeah, they were married but she still had the hots for me."

"So? Did that mean you had to have sex with her?"

"No, but she kept coming onto me and one day it just happened."

"What the hell does that mean?" I was getting angry. "Where was your dear friend Doug when this happened? Why were you with her anyway?"

"Doug had to go out of town to a convention for work. She called me to fix the sink, it wasn't draining, and I know how to fix things like that. The kids were in preschool that day. I went over but fixing the sink wasn't the only thing she had in mind."

"Why are you putting this all on her? You went along! You did it, you could have said no!"

"I could have but I didn't. I guess it was a turn on that she still wanted me so much."

"That is so… being such a scumbag!"

"I guess you're right, you're always right." He was getting angry now too.

"Come on, Ian, you know that was wrong. Did her husband ever find out?"

"No, who was going to tell him? Me? Her? No."

"That's just great. Why did you bring me there?"

Now his voice was raised. "You know what, Dana, I

brought you there to include you! I wanted you to meet my friends! That happened years ago. It's water under the bridge. I've let it go. I know she's still attracted to me; she always has been. But they have kids, and they have a life together, and I'm not going to make that mistake again, ok?"

I took a deep breath. I didn't want this to escalate any more than it had.

"Ok, ok, but I do wish you'd warned me."

"I didn't think she'd start on you."

"It wasn't very pleasant."

"Ok, sorry about that." He was calming down. I suddenly felt a surge of sexual jealousy that had me almost breathless. He'd had sex with Nan! But now he was mine, and I wanted him only for myself.

We drove in silence after that until we arrived at his cabin. When we went inside, I immediately turned to him and put my arms around his neck. I pulled him to me and kissed him deeply, my tongue probing his mouth. He responded, kissing me back, and we stumbled to the bedroom, not letting go of each other. He was mine. I would prove that. Right now.

Chapter 34

I couldn't help it though; I was troubled by Ian's revelations. When I awoke on Sunday I kept wondering what kind of man would have sex with his best friend's wife. I could understand maybe why he had done it when they were all young and Doug and Nan had not been married, but to have sex in the man's own house with his wife when he was out of town and their kids were in school? That seemed like such a lowlife thing to do. So disloyal and unethical. What if Doug had found out? It could have destroyed their marriage and their children's lives in the bargain!

Of course, Nan was also culpable. She clearly had a problem with me and that was why the tension had been there. She didn't really want Ian to have a girlfriend or a life partner. She was still attracted to him. Whether she would now act on it if she had the chance, who knew? At least Ian now seemed to realize that what had happened had been a mistake. But was he so impulsive that he couldn't have stopped himself that day he'd gone there to fix the sink? Really? He'd said he wasn't even that attracted to her.

I thought of something else too. What about the time that his ex, Patty, had been staying with him? If his impulse control was that poor that he would have sex with his best friend's wife in their own house, what about when Patty was staying in his house? I remembered that she had called him "Babe." She was likely still after him at that time and what would have stopped him from having sex with a former girlfriend who wanted him and was conveniently living in his own house?

These thoughts churned in my head. I said nothing to him about it that day, but I went home before lunch, telling Ian I had errands to run and housecleaning and laundry to do. He didn't protest. Things were quiet that morning and he seemed a bit more distant, as though he felt my disappointment in him.

I drove home thinking of all of this. I was afraid to question him, as usual. Questioning him about anything controversial usually led to a confrontation and him getting angry, perhaps even cutting me off for a time. I didn't want that to happen, but my perception of him was shifting and it wasn't for the better. The problem was, would it make any difference? What had my response been last night to his revelations? To make love to him like a wild animal, to put my stamp on him as mine. That had been my response. That always seemed to be my response to Ian. I guess I couldn't blame Nan or any other woman for wanting him. He exuded testosterone. His voice was deep and masculine, his body was chiseled like the statue of a Greek god. He was hot. And women-and likely gay men too-responded.

But he was a disturbed person. His actions were so erratic. He thought of himself as broken. Broken as in fixable? Or broken never to be fixed? Or was that just an excuse he used for his bad behavior, a way to justify it to himself?

Again, I asked myself why I was with a man like that. I knew why I'd been attracted to him. I even knew that his erratic presence in my life actually strengthened the attraction. My therapist and I had discussed the concept of intermittent reinforcement. His come close go away pattern only served to pull me in more deeply, because the pleasure of being with him, having sex with him, when he came back was so intense that it was very reinforcing. But just because I understood more about my reactions to Ian didn't mean I could break it off. Just because I had learned about what I perceived as immoral actions on his part didn't mean I could let him go.

I went through my day in this troubled state of mind, doing my shopping, doing my laundry, cleaning the house, my usual Sunday activities. I wondered whether we would talk that evening.

Evening came and I had not heard from him. This was not unusual. Whenever there was tension he would back off, not wanting to deal with it, or me.

But I didn't anticipate what was coming.

I was getting ready for bed when Ian called. I couldn't help but feel the usual tingle of excitement when I saw his name come up on my cell.

"Hi Ian," I said.

"Listen, Dana, I've been thinking about something," he said. His voice did not sound warm.

"Yes?"

"I think…. listen, you seem to want someone who's not me. I mean, you expect things of me that just aren't me. You get so judgmental about what I've done or what I do. You think you're so damn perfect. Well, I'm sick of it. If you can't accept me for what I am then fuck you."

My heart had started pounding. "That's not true, Ian, I do accept you! That doesn't mean I like everything that you do, but I can live with it. You just took me by surprise, that's all."

But he wasn't really listening. "You don't appreciate anything I do. I brought you to meet my friends and all you did was bitch and complain."

I was stunned by the unfairness of his accusations. That was not true! I had simply questioned Nan's behavior toward me. And I had been shocked when he had told me why she was that way, but I thought I'd handled it well enough.

Ian was on a roll. "You think everything has to be perfect and you want everything your way. Then when it doesn't go your way, you can't take it. Well, I'm done. I can't be your perfect boyfriend and I'm sick of trying to be."

I was so scared now I could barely get the words out. "What are you saying, Ian? Those things are just not true!"

"Oh, sure, don't admit your shortcomings, just blame me for everything."

What? Wasn't that what Ian was doing to me? Was there a bit of projection here?

"Why don't you go and find this perfect boyfriend? And I'm going to find someone who appreciates me for me and doesn't expect me to be this perfect man."

"No, Ian!" I was crying now, but he continued relentlessly.

"Whatever, Dana, I can't keep up with your expectations of me. I'm not perfect and I never will be. It's too much. Go find this perfect man, you're free to do whatever you want."

"But I want you!" I was sobbing now, but he had hung up.

I sat on the bed, stunned. We had been doing so well! I had been so happy that he wanted me to meet his friends; that had seemed like a big step forward. He had told them I was his girlfriend. And now he was breaking up with me? It seemed surreal.

I was crying and couldn't stop. The pain was so intense I didn't know what to do. All I could manage was to hold myself tightly and cry and cry until no more tears would come.

Chapter 35

I had to do something about these horrible feelings. I didn't feel like talking to anyone. I finally got out my journal and wrote.

September 23

I feel completely hysterical. He doesn't want to see me anymore. One minute he was saying I was his girlfriend, the next minute he's breaking up with me and blaming me for it. I'm so upset I don't know what to do. Am I such a bad person? Am I really all of those things that he said? Do I really expect too much of him?

Or is he running away from his own feelings? Does any criticism at all trigger some terrible feeling of inadequacy on his part, so that he has to attack and blame me instead of facing himself? He just can't seem to sustain the relationship. He withdraws for any little thing. He says that I expect him to be perfect, but it's he who runs away when I'm not perfect, when I don't support him the way he wants, or I criticize something he does. He just can't handle closeness. And I have been close to him. Closer than he ever got to anyone perhaps. He wants closeness, craves it, but then he can't handle it.

Maybe the intensity with which he pushes me away is concurrent with the depth of his need for me. He pulls me in then I get too close, or I ask for something, he feels uncomfortable, and he has to create a nightmare out of it and blame me so he can pull away and get back to his comfort zone again. But his comfort zone is so narrow, it never stays consistent. It shifts with his shifting emotions.

As I wrote I started to feel calmer. I realized that it wasn't some blazing fault of mine that made Ian do this. What I had written about Ian was the truth. He had to find a reason to pull away. I didn't expect perfection from him at all, far from it. I expected him to behave kindly and responsibly, but he couldn't do that in a consistent way. I didn't like what he had done with Nan, how could I? Who in the world would think it was ok to have sex with your best friend's wife behind his back? But I wasn't rejecting Ian. In fact, I stuck by him no matter what he did or how he behaved towards me. He was using the primitive defense mechanism of projection.

I put away my journal, feeling slightly better. Another thought occurred to me too. Ian would be back. This was just another episode in the game. He pushed me away because my reaction to what he had told me about Nan made him feel bad and inadequate. When that feeling passed, as feelings do, he would probably come back.

I knew intellectually that I should not be with him. I should move on, as he had said. I should find someone else. Not someone perfect, as he had told me sarcastically, but a mature man who didn't feel inadequate and who wasn't afraid of his own feelings. But I didn't think I could really let go. I thought it was just too late. Ian and I were intertwined.

Whether he would admit it or not.

Chapter 36

So, I waited. I was still very upset, but I wasn't going to do anything about it yet. I would wait. I would wait a week or maybe two, then if Ian hadn't called me or texted I would call him.

In the meantime, I was going to rekindle the friendship with Jerry. Just as Jerry had said, I would spend time with him while Ian had blown me off.

That didn't make me feel like a very good friend, but it was true enough, so I might as well be up front about it with Jerry, make a joke of it. I called him after work the next day.

"Jerry," I said when he answered, "Ian blew me off so I'm calling you."

I meant it to be a joke, but at first he didn't answer. "Jerry?" I said, getting worried.

"Well, I was wondering how long that would take," he said.

"I hope you realize I was kidding," I said, worried that his feelings would be hurt, then I qualified, "I mean, he did blow me off, but that's typical. But I wanted to see you anyway."

"Ok, when?"

So, this wasn't going to be difficult. Of course not. That's not who Jerry was.

"Do you want to meet for pizza tomorrow for dinner? My treat?"

"Sure, you owe me anyway." His voice was teasing. "The usual place and time?"

"Yes, 6:00 at the usual pizza place."

"I'll see you," he said then added, "Dana, are you doing ok?"

Jerry was so sweet. Why couldn't I be in love with someone like him? "I guess so, I mean, I'm upset but it's just the way he is, Jerry," I said. "I'm getting used to it."

"You shouldn't have to get used to something like that."

"Oh well, what am I going to do about it?"

I was afraid he would say leave the jerk, but Jerry didn't say that.

"See you tomorrow, Dana." We hung up.

Jerry was so supportive. Whoever dated him was a lucky woman. I could have been that woman but... you love who you love, as Bonnie had said that day.

I did meet Jerry the next evening and it seemed as though no time and hurt had ever occurred. We bantered and laughed. He told me more about Marcy and said that he couldn't see himself with her long term but wasn't quite sure how to tell her that.

"She really likes me," he said, a bit ruefully. "So now I'm in that same position as you were with me."

I protested, "But Jerry, I really like you too. I just was still hung up on Ian."

"I know," he said. It did occur to me to wonder whether he was still attracted to me, but if he was, he was certainly handling it well.

"So let me pick your brain a bit, Dana," he went on. "How do I break it off with Marcy without hurting her any more than I have to?"

It struck me suddenly like a blow to the stomach. Here was Jerry, all concerned that he might hurt someone that he didn't even love because he wanted to break it off with her, while Ian said he loved me then blasted me, insulted me, and broke things off with me in a harsh and hurtful way over and over again. Who was the better man?

I was such a fool.

Jerry was looking at me oddly. "Dana? What are you thinking?"

So, I told him. He was my friend, after all, why not?

"You are such a good person to even be worrying about her feelings, Jerry. Ian doesn't really give a crap about mine. He's harsh and mean and he just doesn't care how I feel in that moment, he just wants to blast me, so he doesn't have to face himself."

Jerry didn't speak for a moment then said, "That's the person you chose, Dana."

"I didn't really choose him, it's more like the whole thing chose me. I can't help who I love," I argued.

"No, but you choose whether to participate or not," Jerry told me. I was getting impatient. How did this conversation turn into a therapy session for me?

"Back to your problem with Marcy," I said. "Wouldn't it be better to be honest? I mean, you can be nice about it, but why let her hang on maybe thinking something more will happen between you? At least if you let her down gently she has the freedom to move on and hopefully meet someone who wants to be with her."

"I guess that makes sense," Jerry said, "But what do I say to her?"

We talked about specific things he could say to Marcy that hopefully would let her down as gently as possible. I found myself admiring Jerry all over again. I was lucky he had agreed to be my friend.

Yes, I had good friends. But I didn't seem to be able to have a good, solid, lasting relationship with a man who could be my partner in life.

Because I was drawn to men who were quite different, men who couldn't be stable partners, immature self-centered men. Was that something I could ever change? Or was I doomed to be with a man like Ian forever?

Chapter 37

Ian called.

He called on Tuesday night, after I had dinner and was trying to read a book. I was anxious of course. I had an underlying low-level anxiety all of the time now. I was lying on my couch thinking about Ian when my cell phone rang. I saw his name come up and thought about not answering, but then I picked up the phone and said hello.

"Dana, I need some help," he said. "I've got a problem."

I almost didn't want to hear it. "I thought you broke up with me." I said. I didn't want to let him off the hook quite so easily.

"Yeah, yeah," his voice was impatient. "I was just angry, ok?"

That was how he was going to characterize it? He criticized me, told me he was going to find someone else, broke my heart, just because he was angry? And why was he angry? Because I hadn't thought it was ok that he had sex with his best friend's wife??

But he was still talking. "I need your help."

"What, Ian?" I felt exasperated.

"Listen, if you don't help me I could go to jail."

Now he really had my attention. "What the hell are you talking about?"

"I got way behind on my child support when I wasn't working over the summer and it's caught up to me. They're asking for the back support and I don't have it."

"That's why you're calling me?"

"Who else am I going to call?"

That wasn't exactly the answer I wanted to hear.

"Listen, Dana, I know I handled it badly the other day. I was upset. I told you something about myself and you put me down. That hurt."

So now he was turning it around and telling me I'd hurt him? I felt a bit incredulous. But wasn't this how Ian operated, blaming others when it was his behavior that was questionable?

"I'm really behind and Julie is pushing the matter. So now the child support office is after me. You know that men can be put in jail for not paying, right? I mean, it's so stupid, how can they pay support if they're in jail and they lose their jobs? The system is really fucked up."

I almost said you're the one who's fucked up but didn't. "So, what are you asking me for, Ian?"

"I need at least $2000."

What? Now I was supposed to just hand him money?

"Dana, please. You know I'm working now; I can pay you back."

"That's a lot, Ian."

"But you love me. I know you'll help me. Do you want to see me go to jail?"

I wasn't sure if he was exaggerating, but if he wasn't, he was right. I didn't want to see him go to jail. The social worker part of me that liked to solve problems was kicking in.

Also, he was right about something else. No matter what, I did love him.

"I have to see if I have that much," I lied. I knew that I had enough to cover that amount and more.

"Please, Dana. I'm sorry," he now said, rather belatedly.

"When do you need it?"

"Right away. Look, I can come over tomorrow night, is that ok? Can you get it by then?"

I couldn't help myself. "You're coming just for the money?"

He hesitated then said, "Of course not, Dana, you know I want to see you."

I really didn't know that at all. But a small thrill went through me. Why did I have to respond to Ian this way? No matter what he'd done I wanted to see him. I felt lost without him. I had been so hurt by his words on Sunday, even though I thought I had coped well.

"Ian, I have to look at my bank account."

"Well, can you check?"

I sighed. "Just a minute."

I went to get my laptop and opened up my bank accounts. I wasn't sure exactly how much I had, though I knew I had more than enough to cover that amount. But I had told him I wasn't sure, so I would look at it anyway. Let him wait.

Giving him that much would make a dent in my savings, but I would still have plenty. I didn't make a huge salary, but I was pretty frugal, and made sure to put away some money every two weeks when I got paid.

"I guess I can do it, but we would need to set up a plan for you to pay me back." I was moving some cash from my savings account into my checking account as we were speaking. "I can write you a check tomorrow, I guess."

"Thanks, Dana, you're saving my life. I'll see you tomorrow. Around 7:00?"

"Fine." We hung up and I sat for a moment staring at my phone. What the hell? I didn't even realize he had to pay child support, but of course, that made sense, he did have a daughter and why shouldn't he help support her? I was sure that her mother wouldn't have let him off the hook for that even if he couldn't see the child. It just hadn't crossed my mind before.

But I wasn't all that happy with myself that I had given in so easily. Why had I?

The answer to that was obvious. I wanted to see him. I wanted him to love me. I knew what would have happened if I'd said no. He would have gotten angry, probably cursed at me, hung up, rejected me again. And maybe he would have gone to jail and what good would that have done for him, for the child, for me? I had to help him. I did love him. I wanted his love too.

More than anything I wanted Ian to love me.

Chapter 38

Ian came at the specified time the next night. He wasn't even late. His car pulled into the lot of my building right at 7:00. I had been watching for him, I couldn't help it. I wanted to see him so badly but felt stupid at the same time. Why was I so eager to be with someone who hurt me so badly, who rejected me on a regular basis?

I would take it up with my therapist. Right now, there was nothing but Ian.

He came to the door, walked in, and gave me a big hug. "Thanks for doing this, Dana," he said. "I really appreciate it."

Wow it felt so good to feel appreciated by Ian. If only it was this way all of the time!

Then Ian started nuzzling my neck. "You smell so good," he murmured. He moved to my mouth, nibbling at my lips, kissing me. "You taste so good," he said softly. I could feel his breathing getting heavier. He slid his hands under my t-shirt and over my breasts, making my nipples harden. "You feel so good," he whispered. He slipped his hands around to my back and pulled me into him, then kissed me harder, probing with his tongue. I responded, opening my mouth to his. We moved to the couch, pulling clothes off as we went. I was raging with desire, my heart pounding, my need for him intense. Ian always had this effect on me.

Later we sat at my table and had some wine and crackers. I asked Ian about the child support. He said,

"Julie took me to court after Emily was born. I was just a kid, remember, I didn't have much money. They ordered me to pay, but the payments weren't too bad back then. I was so pissed off that I had to pay but I couldn't even see her. It didn't seem fair. But I had to go along with it. I tried to pay, most of the time. I got behind before, but she didn't always push it. But this time she's being a bitch about it. I got a letter from the child support office threatening me."

I wanted to ask how he had managed to let it get that far. I remembered giving Ian money when he had lost his job the previous summer. What had he done with that money? He certainly must not have paid his support. He likely bought weed with it. But I bit my tongue. After that wonderful binding sex, I didn't want to start an argument.

"It means a lot that you're helping me, Dana," Ian was saying. He leaned forward to kiss me lightly. "I can stay tonight if you like."

If I liked? Didn't he know that he was food and drink to me, that he was the sun and the moon? It was like heaven to snuggle up with him all night long.

"Of course, I want you to stay. But you know I have to work tomorrow.""

"I know, so do I. I'll leave early."

Once in bed he turned to me again, kissing me softly, then more insistently. I had worn a light nightgown to bed, but he liked to sleep naked. I could feel his hardness against my leg. He pulled the nightgown up and I sat up so he could pull it over my head. We made love again, slowly, with less urgency than before. When it was over, I laid my head on his shoulder. He held my head and kissed my forehead gently. "Love you," he said. I felt tears come into my eyes. How I longed for these words, this gentleness, from Ian.

"I love you too," I said and curling myself into him, I fell asleep.

The next morning, we arose early. I gave Ian the

check I had written for him, and he thanked me again, hugging me tightly when he left. I got ready for work in a glow, feeling loved and satiated.

When I got to work, though, things changed. That was the nature of my work. Things could be going along fine for a while, but these kids were volatile, and their lives were often in turmoil. There was a new crisis that awaited me.

I saw another caseworker, Terry, on the way to my office. "Dana," she said when she saw me. "We have a problem. We're going to meet about it now." She gestured to the director's office. "Can you come in?"

"Sure," I said, feeling alarmed, fearing that something had happened to one of the kids. I walked into the director's office. She was there, along with the assistant director. Ginny was also there.

"Sophie is pregnant," the director, Ava DeSoto, said bluntly when we all sat down. "She doesn't know what she wants to do. As you know, Terry is her caseworker, but she's relatively new, so I'd like you both, Dana, and Ginny, to give her some assistance."

"That's fine," Ginny said, and I nodded agreement.

"You will need to meet with Sophie today, at least two of you, so she doesn't feel overwhelmed. When she decides whether to abort the pregnancy or keep the child, one of you can assist Terry in making arrangements." She looked at Terry, who appeared a bit flustered. "This will be a good learning experience for you, Terry, though I realize it's troubling. It isn't the first time we've been through this type of event."

She was right. I recalled about two years ago, one of the girls in our program had gotten pregnant. She had been only 16. She had chosen to have the baby and was now living with her grandmother and the child. She had dropped out of school at the time, but we had helped her sign up for her GED and she was now working on obtaining it. She no longer came to our program, but she had visited with the child, an adorable little boy.

Ginny spoke up. "Do we know who the father is?" Ms. DeSoto looked at her assistant, Carl Boyd. He nodded and said, "We think it's Brad."

Brad was trouble. Most of us had known it from the moment he had started our program over the summer. He had been mandated by the court to join after he'd been arrested for theft the previous June. He was a tall boy with longish blonde hair and rough manners, but he was cute and liked to flirt with the girls. A number of them had been attracted to him. Sophie was flirtatious and pretty, with short dark curls and an infectious laugh. I could see how the two of them had gotten together.

Ginny and I met with Terry to discuss how to proceed. It was decided that Terry and I would meet with Sophie when she came in and Ginny would work on helping Sophie to make arrangements when she decided what she wanted to do. When the kids started coming in after school Terry watched for Sophie and brought her to my office when she arrived.

Her usual brightness was gone when Sophie came in. She looked subdued and frightened. "Hi Ms. Taggert," she muttered, standing in the doorway.

"Please sit, Sophie," I said. Terry shut the door and took a seat too. "We heard the news," I began.

Sophie burst into tears.   "I was so stupid!" she cried. "I liked him so much, I wanted to hang with him but he…well, he pressured me, said I was a woman and why didn't I act like one…"

"Did he pressure you to have sex?" Terry asked.

"Well, I wanted to, you know, I liked him so much, but I was kind of scared, I didn't want to get pregnant. But he said I wouldn't, he knew how to stop it. I told him to use a condom, but he didn't have one."

Great, another irresponsible male, I was thinking.

Just like Ian at that age.

"How far along are you, Sophie?" I asked gently.

"About six weeks. My mom made me go to the doctor's." She
started crying again.

"Do you know what you would like to do?" Terry asked.

"Have you talked to your mom about it?"

"She's so mad at me! She's very Catholic, you know. To her I
committed a very bad sin."

"What does she say?"

"She says I have to have the baby. I did this and now I have to take responsibility. But I don't know!" she wailed and started to sob in earnest.

Terry spoke gently, offering Sophie a tissue. "I think it
would make sense to bring your mom in and we can talk to her with you," she said. "Would that be ok with you?"

Sophie sniffled and nodded. "Ok." Terry and I looked at each other and I left to call Sophie's mom. We knew we would have to speak to her because of Sophie's age but we hadn't wanted to push the issue until Sophie was on board with it.

Sophie's mother answered on the second ring. "I was waiting for you guys to call," she said. "I am so disgusted with my daughter. This is not how I brought her up."

"I know, Mrs. Rivera. I think she knows she made a mistake. But now we have to work out how to best help her."

I could hear the woman sigh. "Si, I know, but I am very upset."

"That's natural but we're here to help. Can you come in and talk with us and Sophie?"

"Sure, I guess so, I don't have to work until later. I've been
working the night shift lately, so she's been alone sometimes. That's why this happened!" she burst out. "I have to work, I have to support us, but then she must have started seeing this boy behind my back!"

I knew that Sophie's mom was divorced from her dad. She worked as nurse at the local hospital.

"It's very difficult when you're a single parent," I said soothingly. "What time can you come in?"

We settled on a time and I hung up, feeling a bit drained. There were so many problems in the world and in the lives of these kids and families that I worked with every day. I wished I could solve their problems, but I could only offer my meager assistance. I went to Terry's office to let her and Sophie know that her mom would be coming in soon.

When she arrived, it was an emotional and difficult meeting. Sophie's mom was angry at her daughter and showed it. She yelled at her and asked how she could have done such a thing, but then she started to cry. This seemed to impact Sophie as the yelling had not. She got up and hugged her mother and suddenly her mother was hugging her back. "I will help you; you know I will, mi hija," she said to Sophie.

After much discussion Sophie said that she did not want to
have a child now and that she wanted to go ahead with an abortion. She was teary but seemed resolute. Despite being a Catholic, her mother had come around to the idea of abortion.
She really did not want her daughter to become a

mother at this young age. I went to find Ginny, who was to assist in following up with the plan.

It had been a long and exhausting day. I was not happy about the idea of abortion, but I also realized that for a 16-year-old with her whole life ahead of her it did make sense. Her mother was upset but sympathetic and I felt sure they would get through this trying time together.

As I left work I wanted to call Ian, but I wasn't sure how he would react. This may cut too close to his own past for him to be comfortable with it. I decided not to talk to him. As I drove home I called Jerry instead and poured out the emotions of the day. I knew Jerry would listen and be supportive and he did not disappoint me.

As Ian so often did. No matter how much I loved him, I could not ignore that fact.

Chapter 39

I had an appointment with my therapist the next day after work. I had already had a number of insights with her help, but I resolved to delve more deeply into my attraction to Ian, to really try and understand myself better in relation to him. I not only kept running back whenever he called, even after a harsh rejection, but now I was giving him money again. And no matter how cruel he had been it still felt like coming home to be with him, to be close, to have sex with him, to sleep with him.

When I settled into my usual seat in Dr. Clarkson's office, I told her the latest. I did not leave anything out, including the fact that I had loaned Ian all that money for child support even though he had been irresponsible about money the previous summer and had gotten behind. She raised her eyebrows at me, one of her typical looks.

"Why do you think you do this, Dana?" she asked.

"I don't know!" I burst out, frustrated. "I just feel like he is... I don't know, he's like home to me. I really love him. And he tells me he loves me."

She looked at me for a moment then said, "I believe he feels something for you, Dana, I won't say that he doesn't. But his feelings seem to ebb and flow, they don't seem to stay the same." I started to protest, but she held up her hand and continued, "He is attached to you and you to him. But I believe you both have disturbed attachment. When this occurs, you may be drawn to someone who has similar issues. You may need to get something from a person who has trouble giving, recreating perhaps, something you did not receive during your childhood. But you may develop different strategies of coping. You tend to cling; Ian tends to run away. And when he runs, you panic, and you feel like the only thing that will save you from destruction is Ian himself, even though he is the one who is hurting you."

That was a long speech for Dr. Clarkson but what she said made sense. My childhood had been marred by a father whose behavior was erratic and who had broken my trust in a profound way. My mother had been distant when my sister and I were young as she attempted to deal with bringing up two girls whose father did not pull his weight. She was not like that now, but damage had been done. And Ian had a mother who had been abusive toward him and a father who abandoned him.

"It makes sense," I said, "but I don't know how to change it."

"It's very hard," she agreed. "The first step is understanding it, but it will not be easy to change. If you are with a partner who is also willing to do the work it would take, that helps." She stopped and looked at me, waiting for me to speak.

"No, I don't think so," I said slowly, "I can't see Ian being that willing to work on himself."

"From what you have told me so far that's probably true. But what do you want to do, Dana?"

"I want to try," I said. "I want to be better. But I don't know how to stop seeing Ian." I was a bit afraid she would tell me I had to do that, but I should have known better. She wasn't here to tell me what to do.

"You don't have to, that's up to you, Dana. But be more aware now. Be more aware of the choices you're making and the possible reasons behind those choices."

I nodded. That I could do.

The session ended and I drove home, thinking

intensely about what Dr. Clarkson had said. I thought that perhaps I had gotten closer than most people did to Ian and because of his feelings for me, I triggered his core issues more than his other girlfriends may have. And he got close to my core issues. We triggered each other. Could that be overcome? Perhaps not, but I would do as the therapist suggested and try to be more aware of my choices regarding Ian even if I continued to make the choices that brought me into his orbit. When he allowed me to be, that is.

I didn't hear from Ian that evening. I had not spoken to him since the previous morning, and I was starting to be a bit irritated. He could have at least called after the amazing sex and after I had given him all that money to help him out. I finally sent a text at about 10:00 at night as I lay in bed feeling anxious.

"Hi, what are you doing?"

No response for about five minutes, during which time my heart started pounding and my anxiety started climbing. I told myself to be aware, just observe what was happening. I went to grab my journal, thinking I would write about it. Then my phone pinged.

"Thinking of you," Ian wrote. Really? Then why the hell hadn't he called? I rang his phone.

"Really?" I asked.

"I think about you a lot, Dana," he said, which mollified me a bit.

"I think of you too."

"Thanks for the check. I sent off the money yesterday, that should keep the wolves from my door."

"Glad it helped."

"Do you want to come over tomorrow?"

I could feel my anxiety going down. He did want to see me!

We made plans and I hung up feeling better. I hadn't been abandoned again. Yet with Ian that fear hung in the air like a miasma because despite my happiness and excitement to be with him, I never knew when the abandonment might happen again.

I wrote about it in my journal:

September 28
I am starting to understand better what happens when Ian gets scared. I get to him, to his core issues and he both craves and fears that type of intimate contact. But when any little thing goes wrong he is afraid again, perhaps of being abandoned as his mother emotionally abandoned him, and he bolts. He can't handle those emotions, that fear. He doesn't ever work it through, so it happens again and again.

And me? Maybe I am trying to get the love that I didn't get properly from my father. So, I chase after a man like Ian who is fundamentally unavailable. There is something beautiful inside him, but then the walls go up and I am left pounding on those walls trying desperately to get back in.

Chapter 40

I went to Ian's on Saturday after running some weekend errands. It was a beautiful fall day, warm enough to sit outside eating sandwiches that he had made and drinking lemonade. He was smoking weed, as usual, but seemed relaxed and laid back. It was nice when he was this way, when the tension that was so often inside him was mellowed. He was joking with me and we were laughing, enjoying the day and each other. He asked if I wanted to go out for dinner that evening, and I was glad to say yes. "My treat," he said. "You deserve to be treated well, Dana."

Did that mean he would be treating me well from now on? I knew how quickly his mood could change, but I basked in the moment.

We went that evening to a casual restaurant on the other side of the lake. As the sun set, we feasted on pasta and clams and split a chocolate cake for dessert. Ian amused me by making up stories about the other patrons, telling me that that man over there was a spy and this woman was really a movie star, but she had disguised herself to go out without her fans bothering her. He had me in stitches. This was Ian at his best.

But his real best was yet to come when we got back to his cabin. He turned to me and took my hand, walking me into the bedroom. He undressed me slowly and lay on top of me, gazing into my eyes. He touched me everywhere, with his hands, with his mouth, the god worshipping the goddess. It was transporting, transcending. I saw the sun and the moon in his eyes.

The next day he made breakfast and we sat and talked and joked. I finally asked him if he would meet my friend Ginny. He said, "Sure, ok. I want to meet your friends, your family too, Dana." The weekend could not have been better.

I drove home on Sunday night feeling relaxed about Ian for the first time in a long time. Had we turned a corner? I had thought that before, true. But things had been so wonderful between us. Was he starting to trust me, finally? There was such a strong bond between us when it was good it was amazingly good. I wanted to trust that bond.

On Monday I saw Ginny and told her what Ian had said. She didn't look thrilled, but said, "Ok, I know it's important to you, Dana." We talked about getting together the next Friday night with her and Derek. She said she would check with him and I would check with Ian. I texted him to let him know. I knew he was working, and I didn't expect to hear back from him immediately, but he texted back quickly, "That works for me." I felt gratified.

Sophie's abortion was scheduled for the next day and Terry was going with her. Her mom, while she was on board with the plan, had opted out, feeling that she just couldn't be there while it happened. Terry came to speak to me that afternoon. "I'm really nervous, Dana, I've never done this before."

"Just be a support to her, Terry. It's too bad her mom won't go, but at least you can be there for her. You don't really have to do much, just reassure her and let her know she's doing the right thing for her."

Terry nodded, looking worried. "Sometimes I'm not sure I'm cut out for this job," she confided.

"I felt that way too sometimes, in the beginning," I told her, recalling my younger self. "When I first graduated and started working here I was so nervous, I didn't know if I could handle these kids or do what the job required. But it grows on you. The kids are so great, they really do appreciate what we do. At least most of them," I added, thinking of Brad, who had gotten Sophie pregnant.

Brad had been told of her pregnancy, as had his father. He lived with his father, his mother being out of the picture somehow, no one was sure why. Brad had reacted almost with pride, apparently feeling he was quite a stud to have gotten a girl pregnant. His father had not agreed. When Ginny and I had met with him and he was told what had happened, he smacked his son on the side of the head, albeit lightly. "What the hell did I tell you?" he had yelled. Brad seemed defiant. They did agree in the end to help pay for the abortion.

The week went on. Terry came back from accompanying Sophie for the abortion, and she seemed wiped out. She had brought Sophie home to her mother afterward. She said that Sophie's mom was solicitous, and she was sure that Sophie would be ok. She had cried and asked if she was doing the right thing, but in the end she had told Terry she was relieved. She didn't want to be a teenage mother and said that she was not going to have sex again until she was older and really ready. As for Brad she said she never wanted to speak to him again. We were planning to refer Brad to another program since it would not be a good idea for them to be there together.

Sometimes I could see Ian in Brad's defiance and anger. It wasn't a pretty picture. But I tried to shift my thoughts to the past weekend and how wonderful it had been. And he had agreed to meet my best friend!

I talked to Ian on and off all week. I didn't tell him about what had happened at work though, fearing it would trigger him. We made plans for Friday.

After work that day I rushed home to change. Ian was coming to my place and we were going to meet Ginny and Derek at a restaurant nearby. I got dressed, nervously waiting for Ian to arrive. He did, a few minutes late as usual. He was dressed in khaki pants and a button-down shirt. He looked so sexy I wanted to jump him right there but knew I had to wait.

Ian was nervous, I could tell. He didn't say much as I drove to the restaurant. Just before we arrived he said, "What did you tell her about me?"

"What do you mean?"

"She's your best friend. You must tell her about what happens sometimes, how I pull away. I'm sure you've cried on her shoulder."

"Ian. Sometimes I do talk to her, but I told her how crazy I am about you." I was trying to reassure him. Would he ruin this?

"Ok, ok," he said.

"They're really nice, don't worry."

"I'm not!" he said in a snappy voice.

"Ok." I didn't want him to get all upset now. We were just pulling into the restaurant parking lot.

But the evening went fine. Ian was polite and Ginny and Derek were too. It was a bit awkward at first, but we drank some wine and things warmed up. A while later Ginny and I both went to the lady's room and she said to me, "Ok, I get it, Dana, he's really hot," and we both started laughing.

"Told you," I said to her.

We went back to my apartment when the evening was over. It had gone well. Derek had paid the bill for us, amidst protests, but he was magnanimous that way. Ginny was lucky.

"It was great," I told Ian. "Did you like them?"

"Yeah, they were nice."

"Ginny thinks you're hot."

"Oh really? Do you think I'm hot?" he said teasingly?

"I do," I told him. I went up to him and put my arms around his neck. "I think you're super-hot."

"So are you," he murmured. He pulled me into him and started kissing me and we talked no more that night..

Chapter 41

Ian spent time at my apartment that weekend and things went well. This was the second weekend in a row! I felt heartened by the way we were getting along. I felt so close to him, it felt so good, so natural. He left on Sunday morning, kissing, and hugging me at the door. It felt wonderful.

I was going over to see my mother that afternoon. She had returned from her cruise and said she had so much to tell me. I had asked Ian if he wanted to come, but he said he had things to do at home and I hadn't pushed. Meeting my family could come later.

I drove over to my mom's place feeling so happy. If things could just stay this way with Ian my life would be perfect. I loved him so much. There was a niggling worry that things could not stay this way, but I pushed it aside, preferring to bask in the warmth of these present feelings.

My mother hugged and kissed me when I got there. She had fixed some snacks and we sat down. She was sparkling. "What's going on?" I asked her. "Your trip must have been great."

"It was, Dana," she said. "We went to so many Caribbean Islands, they were so beautiful. The weather was gorgeous, and the ship was amazing. I ate and ate, they had so much wonderful food. They held dances too, it was so much fun." Then she leaned in closer to me and said, "I met someone too."

"What?" I felt shocked. My mother was in her sixties, she wasn't supposed to be meeting anyone, though I knew she occasionally dated. But then I kicked myself mentally, thinking that after my father, she deserved to find some happiness.

"Who is it?"

"His name is Tom. He's a retired schoolteacher, he used to teach history. He knows so much about everything! We met at one of the dances. He asked me to dance, and we hit it off! We just talked and talked. You know I like reading about history, so we bonded over that. Then the next day when we went ashore in Jamaica, he asked me to come with him, so I did. We had so much fun! I don't remember ever having so much fun."

I felt a bit hurt, wondering whether she had fun with my sister and me when we were young, but didn't protest. She was so happy.

"Where does this Tom live?"

"That's the great part. He lives only about an hour from here! So, we're seeing each other. In fact, he's coming over later." She blushed. Oh my God. My mom had a lover. Unbelievable.

"Did you tell Tina?"

"I called her last night. I knew you were coming over, so I waited to tell you. Do you want to stay and meet him?"

"I guess so, what time is he coming?"

"He should be here around 5:00."

So, I stayed, and she told me more about the cruise and the places she'd gone. She said that the friends she went with were a bit jealous that she'd met someone, but happy for her. They were both widows too.

At exactly 5:00 the doorbell rang. My mother jumped up to open the door. "Tom!" she exclaimed. "They're beautiful!" She came back into the kitchen with a big bunch of pink roses. She got a vase out and filled it with water while saying, "This is my younger daughter, Dana. Dana, this is Tom." She turned and put the flowers on the table.

I held out my hand to Tom. He was a pleasant looking man, not very tall, slender, with grey hair and a short greying beard. He smiled at me and shook my hand. "It's wonderful to meet you, Dana."

He had a nice voice. "I've heard so much about you, your sister and your nephew. Your mom speaks of you often."

I felt warmth just radiating from him. This man was lovely! This was such a good thing for my mother, she had been alone for such a long time.

"Sit, Tom, I'll fix dinner."

"Can I help, Emma?"

"Oh no, no, you sit and relax, I'll do it. You can help me clean up afterward." She smiled.

"That's a deal." He smiled too. They were so relaxed with each other! And they had known each other for such a short time.

The dinner went beautifully. Tom was a wonderful guest. He was full of stories. He had taught high school, so he too had worked with teenagers and he had me telling stories of my own job, one of my favorite topics to talk about. After some time, I realized it was getting late and said goodbye to my mother and Tom. I whispered to her as I kissed her goodbye, "I approve!" She blushed again.

I drove home thinking about how wonderful it was that she had finally met someone so kind. But I couldn't help thinking that after all this time Ian still had not met my family and he had just recently met my best friend. And here was Tom who had just met my mother and already he had met me. They were driving up the next weekend to see my sister and her family. It bothered me, but I remembered that Ian had said he wanted to meet my family. I would ask him to make a visit with me to meet my mother the next time I saw him, and my sister sometime soon too. There was no reason why he shouldn't. After all, we had gotten over the hump. We were together now.

Chapter 42

I hadn't made any specific plans with Ian, but we talked during the week. I was hoping to see him soon, but he did not make that suggestion and I said nothing. I was assuming I would see him on the weekend. On Thursday night I finally asked about making plans. I really wanted to ask him if he was willing to come and meet my mother, but for some reason the idea of asking made me feel anxious. I figured it would be best to ask him in person.

So, when we talked that night I said, "I miss you, Ian. Do you want to get together this weekend?"

"Yeah, ok," he said. He didn't say he'd missed me, but I let that go.

"Well, do you want to come here?"

"Why don't you just come over here, Dana?"

"Ok, when?"

"Come on Saturday."

Tomorrow was Friday. Why wasn't he telling me to come then?

I hesitated, but then asked, "Why not tomorrow, are you busy?"

Now he was the one to hesitate. "No, not really, but I'm bushed, it was a busy week. I just wanted a night to myself. Is that ok?" His voice had that tone of annoyance in it. I didn't want to pressure him.

"Sure, we all need that once in a while, Ian, that's ok."

He sounded mollified. "Oh, then, come over on Saturday. I have some errands to run in the morning, but any time after that."

"See you then." I hung up, feeling a bit upset as only Ian could make me feel. He wanted a night to himself, after the past few weekends that had been so amazing? But wasn't that par for the course with him? He always started pulling back when we got close. I had hoped that it wouldn't happen, but wasn't this progress? That he was actually telling me that he needed a bit of space? And he wasn't rejecting me, he was still telling me to come on Saturday. I tried to relax about it.

But despite trying to talk myself out of it I was so antsy the next day I was afraid I wouldn't be able to sit alone that night. I called Jerry that afternoon on a break at work, but he said he was busy. He had made a date with a woman he had met online but not yet in person. He had broken up with Marcy and said she had not taken it well. I asked him what had happened.

"I told her in person, I felt like I owed her that," Jerry told me. "We'd gone out for coffee after work. I said I wasn't really ready to get into something exclusive and that things were getting too heavy between us. I told her I thought I was ready, but I realized I wasn't. It's not really true but I was hoping to let her down gently. She isn't that experienced with men, she's shy. I said that I hoped she would understand. She started crying, though, really loudly. People were looking at us. We ended up leaving the coffee shop and sitting in my car. It was pretty awful."

"Oh my God, that sounds terrible. Then what happened?"

"Well, I finally drove her home. I asked if she would be ok. She said she had feelings for me and now she was never going to meet anyone else. I felt sorry for her but what could I do? I don't want to get trapped in a relationship with someone I don't really care for. I just told her she would find someone someday. "

"There is no good way to break up with someone," I said, having been on both ends of the stick.

"I feel really badly, but I don't know what else I could have done."

"Sounds like nothing else, Jerry, you handled it well. You can't control how she handled it."

"No, that's true."

I asked him about the woman he was meeting tonight, and he told me a bit about her, then he said, "What's going on with you and Ian?"

"Nothing," I said. "He just wants a night alone. I'm going there tomorrow. Why?"

"A lot of times you call me when he's blown you off."

"No, he isn't blowing me off. I mean, he wants to see me, just not tonight. I mean, that's normal isn't it? We've been seeing each other, he even met Ginny and her fiancé last week."

"Oh really? Well, that's good, I guess."

"It is good. It went well," I said, feeling a bit defensive. "Anyway, have a good time on your date."

"Thanks. I'll let you know how it goes."

I agreed and we hung up. I still felt like loose ends. I thought of going out. Should I do that? It didn't seem right, yet it seemed better than sitting alone. I went back and forth. Why was I so antsy? Was it that bad that Ian was asking for a night by himself?

Was he by himself?

I didn't want to think along those lines, but it was hard not to. A few weeks of getting along didn't add up to a secure trusting relationship.

In the end I just went home and tried to keep myself busy. I cooked a rather complicated dinner for myself and after I had eaten, I put on a movie I'd wanted to watch. I tried to ignore my urges to call Ian. After all, I would see him tomorrow.

I hated that I had this response to Ian. I operated on nervous energy almost all of the time. The only time I could relax was when I was with him and things were good. I felt a loss when I wasn't with him, a discomfort. It was as though when that bond between us got stretched thin it was like a physical wound, deep in my gut. I had to be with him, in his presence. It was a need almost primal in its strength, like an infant needing her mother to survive.

The next day finally came. I hadn't slept well, I tossed and turned and dreamed of storms, dark clouds that hovered over me, threatening thunder and rain. I awoke feeling troubled and waited with trepidation for the time I could leave for Ian's. He had said he would be running errands in the morning, so I was planning to go in the early afternoon. I could hardly wait.

I tried to eat lunch but had little appetite. Why was I so nervous? I tried to reassure myself that nothing was wrong. Finally, I got in my car and drove to Ian's.

When I got there his car was gone. My heart stuck in my throat. He'd said he would be back late morning and it was going on 1:00. Where was he?

I called his cell, and it went to voicemail. Now I was sure something was wrong. I sat in my car for a few minutes waiting then I got out and went up to the cabin.

And I saw something on his door. A note. "Dana, be right back, door's open."

I let out a sigh of relief. What was wrong with me? He'd left me a note; he'd left the door open. I went back to the car, got my overnight bag, and went in. My heart started to slow its pounding. I sat on the couch and waited.

About half an hour later Ian drove up. I heard his car and jumped up to run outside. He got out and I covered his face with kisses.

"What the hell?" he said, laughing. "Dana!"

"I just missed you," I said, laughing too.

"Let me get my bags out of the trunk, will you?"

I helped him unload, seeing that he had purchased some tools and paint, and we went into the house. "I'm going to fix up a few things around here," he told me.

"That's nice." I was so happy and relieved that nothing was wrong I was almost giddy.

We walked around and he showed me the things he planned to work on to improve the rather shabby cabin's appearance. Then we sat on the couch ostensibly to watch a movie, but Ian's hand started slipping inside my shirt, then down past my stomach and into the top of my jeans.

"Thought you wanted to watch this movie," I muttered, just as his mouth closed on mine.

"Oh, I do," he said, as he slipped my shirt off over my head.

"It's a good movie," I said, my breath coming harder now.

"Yes, I'm really enjoying it," he said, his voice gruff as he unzipped my jeans, then his own. He touched my breasts, then put his mouth where he'd put his hands. His mouth slid slowly downward.

We lay on the floor in front of the TV and made love to the noise of the movie playing in the background, our sighs and moans drowning out the soundtrack. When it was over, Ian looked down at me. "I think that was the best movie I've ever seen!"

I laughed. He laughed too and pulled me up off the floor. I was feeling so wonderful, things were so good between us now. Why had I been worried?

But I would soon find out.

Chapter 43

We had been sitting at the table having some wine when my phone rang. It was in front of me, and I had been laughing at something Ian was saying. I looked down and froze. I saw Miguel's name come up on my caller ID.

Ian was also looking down at my phone. Oh my God.

I grabbed the phone and pressed the button to refuse the call. I looked up at Ian.

He had seen the name.

"Who was that Dana?" he said, his voice strained.

I tried to think, but my brain was a scramble. I heard my phone ping, which meant that Miguel had left a message. I couldn't think of anything to say, so I answered truthfully.

"An old boyfriend," I said. After all, he'd had an old girlfriend living with him. Why shouldn't an ex call me?

But when I looked at his face I felt afraid. His face was a mask of rage.

"Really," he said, his voice deceptively quiet. "An old boyfriend is calling you? His number is in your phone still? Why, Dana? What's going on?"

"Nothing," I said, but my voice was small and even I could hear fear in it. "He's called a couple of times to say hello." Then I felt a bit stronger, thinking of Patty. "It's nothing important, Ian. After all, you had your ex living here for a while. It doesn't mean anything."

He got up and towered over me suddenly.

"Really?" he was screaming now. "It doesn't mean anything? Are you cheating on me, you bitch?"

I got up and moved away from him, but he came after me. I was really frightened now.

"Stop, Ian, what are you doing?" I tried to shield myself, but he came up and raised his hand to me. I cringed, but the blow didn't come. Instead, he pushed me, hard, and I fell against a coffee table, slipping to the floor.

"You're cheating on me, you bitch!" he yelled again.

"No, no I'm not!" I thought of the time I had been with Miguel, but I had not been seeing Ian then. I started to cry.

"Get out of here! I knew I couldn't trust you! You're just like all women; you say one thing and then go behind my back! Get out of here! Go be with your ex!"

I scrambled to my feet, feeling pain in my back from falling against the table, but I ignored it. I grabbed my bag and phone and ran out the door. He was coming after me, yelling, "Get out! You bitch, get out!"

I was crying so hard I could hardly start my car. I finally managed and pulled out into the road. A car had been coming and I heard the horn blast, but it blessedly missed hitting me. I drove to the corner and pulled into the parking lot of a little store. I was crying so hard I couldn't see.

Finally, I got hold of myself and was able to pull out and start driving home. I couldn't believe what had happened. It had gone from hot sex to joking around to violence. He had actually been physically violent with me. How was I going to get my mind around that?

My heart was pounding, and my back was throbbing by the time I got home. I went to get a pain pill, looking into the bathroom mirror as I did so. I was a mess. My face was tear streaked, my mascara was running, and my hair looked wild. What the hell was I doing with a man who would physically harm me?

I didn't want to call anyone; I didn't want to listen to Miguel's message. I just wanted to sleep. I took a Benadryl tablet. I had some left over from an allergic reaction I'd had a few months ago to something I'd eaten. I normally didn't take anything to help me sleep but I remembered that the Benadryl had knocked me out. I needed something. I was so distraught. I didn't want to be conscious, didn't want to be inside my own skin.

I didn't know how I was going to bear this. Ian was harsh, he was cruel, he had physically abused me. But he was also the soother of my tension, the one who made me feel perversely safe. He was my passion and my bane, my salvation, and my destruction. No matter what, I still longed for Ian.

Chapter 44

I finally listened to the message from Miguel the next day. He was inviting me to visit him in New York City. I listened to his kind voice and felt tears well up. Even Miguel, who had hurt me so badly by leaving the relationship, was nicer and warmer to me than Ian. Maybe I should go and visit him.

I called him back. "Dana," he said, the pleasure in his voice apparent. "So, you got my message. Are you able to come?"

I wasn't going to tell him what havoc that simple phone call had caused in my life.

"I'm not sure, Miguel." I took a deep breath and decided to be honest. "I'm kind of upset right now."

"Que pasó, mi amor?" he reverted to Spanish. Between my relationship with him and hearing some of the kids at my job speak Spanish I understood what he was saying.

"Things with my...my boyfriend are pretty shaky," I started. "I'm feeling a bit fragile emotionally, you know?"

"Oh, querida," Miguel said. "Then come here and I will help you to feel better."

"I don't know if I can sleep with you," I said bluntly. I might as well lay it all on the table. "I just don't think I can right now." That might stop him from wanting me to come, but I didn't want to take a trip down there and feel like I had to have sex with him. I just felt too raw right now.

But Miguel said, "Dana, that's up to you, I would never pressure you. Come anyway. We will go out on the town, I will treat you to a nice dinner, I will pamper you for a weekend. Just come."

That sounded wonderful actually. To be taken care of for just a little while by a warm and good-looking man, with no expectations. It sounded lovely.

"Ok, maybe I will. When?"

"As soon as you can. I thought you could come down on a Friday afternoon on the train unless you want to drive. The train is easier. I will meet you. You can head back on Sunday."

I decided. "Ok, I will. Next weekend? I can get off work a bit early on Friday. I'll take the train; I don't like driving in the city and parking is so difficult."

"Bueno, I will meet you. Let me know what time your train will arrive."

"I will, Miguel. Thank you. Thank you," I was tearing up again. He could sense it.

"No tears, mi amor. We will have fun."

We hung up and I wiped my eyes. It would be a distraction. And I needed one badly. I was so distraught over Ian I could barely think.

I got through work that week, I wasn't sure how. I saw Ginny at lunchtime on Monday and she immediately knew something was wrong. I didn't want to tell her the details, it was too embarrassing, but just said, "Ian's done it again." She just looked at me with a pained expression. I knew she felt badly that I was hurting, but I also knew that she thought I was bringing it on myself because I stayed with him despite his mistreatment of me.

"Let me know if you want to talk about it," she said quietly so our co-workers wouldn't hear. I nodded.

I threw myself into work as best I could. I knew I was more subdued than usual. When Pedro remarked on how quiet I was that afternoon when the kids came in, I just said, "I'm not feeling that great, Pedro, just a little cold." I was troubled a bit by his perception because he looked at me oddly but said no more. I thought that he may well realize that it wasn't a cold that was bothering me. This kid had intelligence, awareness, and skill. He would go far in life. I couldn't help but feel a frisson of pride that I had played a part in that for him.

The week went on. I had an appointment with Dr. Clarkson on Thursday after work. I dreaded it, not sure what to tell her. I was so embarrassed to say that Ian had actually pushed me down, that he had gotten physical. After all, I was a strong and independent woman, a professional. My co-workers and the kids I worked with looked up to me. What was wrong with me that I was with a man who would do that to me? I was punishing myself for being so stupid.

But when I got to her office, I told her the truth. "We got into an argument," I said. I didn't even have to explain who I was talking about. By now she knew.

"And?" she inquired when I said no more.

"And he pushed me. I fell."

I waited, half expecting her to say something against Ian, but that was not her style.

"How are you feeling about that?" she asked.

"Stupid! I feel stupid, like, why am I with a man like that?"

"Are you blaming yourself?"

I had to think about that for a moment. I had been kicking myself all week. I answered, "Kind of."

"Who is responsible for Ian's behavior?" she asked.

"He is."

"Right. It was not your fault that he chose to do that to you."

"But why am I with him? Why? He never did that before!"

"No, but he has hurt you often in other ways."

"Exactly, so why am I with him? What is wrong with me?" I was becoming agitated; my voice was rising. "What is wrong with me?" I asked again.

"Dana, we've talked about this. You know that your upbringing and your dad's behavior contributed to the fact that you're drawn to unstable men like Ian. It isn't something that goes away in a flash just because you understand more about it."

Her calm voice was having an effect on me. She wasn't blaming me for Ian's behavior. She didn't think I was stupid.

"Dana, do you think it would benefit you to talk to some other women who have been through this type of thing? To attend a group perhaps?"

"Oh, I don't know, I would hate to…." I started. The idea scared me.
"I mean, I'm a professional in this town, I know a lot of people, parents of the kids I work with. Some of them have been through domestic abuse. What if one of them was in the group? I wouldn't feel right…." I trailed off.

"It was just an idea. Think about it. There are groups in other nearby towns if you wouldn't feel comfortable locally."

"I'll think about it."

"So, what are you going to do now, Dana?"

"I don't know. I know I shouldn't see him. Well, he was so angry that he probably wouldn't want to see me anyway," I said, realizing again that I shouldn't even want to be with Ian after what he had done.

But I did. I wanted him. I craved his touch. I yearned for him. I needed him.

I didn't say all of that to Dr. Clarkson.

We talked for a while longer and I told her I was going to visit my ex-boyfriend in New York. "Just as a friend," I told her, wondering if she would approve. Of course, she turned its back on me.

"Are you glad about that?" she asked.

"I guess so, I mean, he really wants to see me and that feels good. I told him I wouldn't sleep with him and he was ok with that."

"So, it might be good for you to get away," she said.

The session ended soon after and I left feeling a bit better. Ginny had been right; it was helpful to me to have someone to talk to who was a professional and not a friend. It helped me to take a more balanced view of what was happening.

And what exactly was happening? Were Ian and I done forever?

Should we be?

I was afraid I knew the answer to that.

Chapter 45

The next day I left work early. I had packed my bag and put it in my car that morning, so I drove directly to the train station and parked. I got on the train at the appointed hour and headed to New York City to visit Miguel.

I tried to read an e-book I had downloaded but I couldn't really concentrate, so I gazed out the window at the Hudson River. It was a beautiful sunny day and the river sparkled. It was mesmerizing, and I just stared for a long time as the train sped along. I tried not to think. I dozed a little.

At Penn Station I went to the lobby, texting Miguel that I was there. He texted back immediately, telling me where he was waiting. I went to the spot and saw him standing there, a big smile on his face. He embraced me, kissing my cheek, then reached down to take my bag.

"Dana, I'm so happy to see you!" he exclaimed. "We are going to have a wonderful time."

"Thanks for inviting me, Miguel." My voice sounded a bit shaky to my own ears. "I have to tell you the truth," I went on, "I'm not in good shape right now."

"Mi amor, it's ok, I understand. Don't worry about it. I am glad to have you here. I hope I can help you feel a little better." He took my arm, and we went outside to catch an Uber to his apartment.

We got out of the car at a pleasant looking brownstone in Brooklyn. "I live here on the second floor," Miguel said. "My brother lives just around the corner, a few blocks away. I really like it here, it's nicer than Manhattan. Quiet and a nice neighborhood."

"It's a beautiful building," I said. He unlocked the door and we walked up the stairs to his apartment.

"Here we are," Miguel said, opening the door. "I have a small study. I've made it into a bedroom for you if you like, Dana. As I told you on the phone, no pressure. I want you to be comfortable."

I felt reassured, but almost guilty. Why was Miguel being so kind to me? But then the thought came: did I feel I didn't deserve that? Was I so used to Ian's erratic behavior and cruelty to me that I now felt that it was normal?

"Thank you, Miguel," I said, putting my hand on his arm. "I want you to know I really appreciate this."

He smiled at me. "I want you to have a good time here with me, Dana. I care about you; don't you know that?"

"But you left me!" I burst out, then bit my lip. I hadn't meant to get into that now. What was wrong with me?

But Miguel did not get upset. "Yes, I did, and I have regretted my actions, Dana. I got scared, as I told you when I visited you. I have often felt I made a mistake. But" he went on, "let's not dwell on that now. I am sorry for hurting you, deeply sorry. I want us to have a good time now, let's not dwell on the past. Is that ok, Dana?"

I looked up into his dark eyes, so sincere and caring. "Yes, Miguel, you're right. I'm just a bit distraught over... over my boyfriend. Well, I guess I should say ex-boyfriend. Oh, I don't even know!"

"Do you want to talk about it?"

"No, not really. I want to focus on being here and having a good time with you. As much as possible, anyway." I gave a laugh, but it came out sounding bitter. "I want to try, Miguel, I don't want to spoil the visit by being upset and angry. And I'm not angry at you, not anymore. I understand what happened. I didn't mean to bring it up. Sorry."

"No, no, you don't have to apologize, Dana. Let me show you your room and put your things away, then let's go out to dinner. I want to take you to this wonderful little Brazilian restaurant nearby."

"Ok, I'll go and change," I said. He showed me the room where he had made up a twin bed for me if I wanted to sleep alone. I felt that he was really respecting my boundaries, while Ian trampled all over me. No. Stop! I wasn't going to think about Ian here.

I changed into a dress and jacket and went back to the living room. "Ready," I said.

Miguel looked me up and down appreciatively. "You look lovely, Dana." He held out his arm and I took it.

We walked a few blocks to a small but elegant restaurant. We had a delicious dinner of something called pato no tucupi, an amazing traditional duck dish. We were drinking wine, and I was loosening up and feeling better.

"Do you want dessert?" Miguel asked, as he sipped the last of his wine.

"Sure, let's be adventurous!"

I ordered Brazilian truffles and he ordered the coconut flan, and we fed each other pieces of our desserts, laughing. They were delicious.

I was actually having fun. Of course, Miguel picked up the bill. We left the restaurant laughing and I was in a much better mood. We held hands walking back to his apartment.

I started feeling a bit awkward once we were there. It was getting late, and I wasn't sure what to do. I didn't feel that I was able to have sex with Miguel, my feelings about Ian were still just too raw, but I didn't really want to sleep alone. I decided to be up front with him.

"I'm not sure what to do now, Miguel," I started. "I had such a wonderful time, I am feeling better than before, but... I just don't know if I can have sex with you right now. But..." I added, as he started saying something, "do you mind if I sleep with you rather than alone? Just to sleep?"

"No, Dana, that would be wonderful," he said. "We don't have to have sex. I would never pressure you. But to cuddle up with you all night, sure, that's great. I love cuddling with you."

I felt so reassured. He was so different from Ian. I wondered again about how this relationship had ended. I knew what he had told me, but while we were together, most of the time it had been so comfortable. He had a moody side, but it had come out rarely.

So, we did sleep together that night and it felt pleasant if a bit strange. I was used to Ian now. But my body seemed to remember Miguel, his large form wrapped around me in sleep. I felt safe. I slept well that night.

The next morning, we got up and Miguel made breakfast. He told me he had the whole day planned but wanted to make sure I was ok with it. He said that we were to go to his brothers for lunch, then into Manhattan to go to one of the museums. He suggested either the Metropolitan Museum of Art or the Guggenheim. I picked the first one. I loved the gorgeous paintings, the elegant rooms of historical furniture, and especially the hall of armor. For some reason I found it fascinating that people had actually worn that into battle a long time ago. I especially liked the armored horses.

I was a bit leery of seeing Miguel's brother. I had met him when we had been dating, but only once, when he had come to visit Miguel. He was a pleasant person, but I wasn't sure I was up to seeing anyone. On the other hand, I didn't want to be so rude as to refuse. Miguel was being so good to me and he was close to his brother.

So, we walked over to Diego's apartment later that morning. As Miguel said, it wasn't far. There was a chill in the air, but luckily it was another beautiful day. Diego lived in a building similar to Miguel's. He opened the door as we approached his apartment, with a big smile on his face. He resembled Miguel but was a bit shorter and stockier. "Hello, hello," he said to me, shaking my hand. "It's so good to see you again, Dana. I hope you like tacos. They're my specialty."

He was so warm and welcoming that I relaxed. We ate tacos and talked, and when Diego asked me about my work, I was happy as always, to talk about "my" kids and their problems and joys. In fact, I was going on and on, and Miguel finally said, "She really loves her job. She loves those kids." I blushed a bit.

"I know, I go on and on about them," I said. I do really love my job, though it's not easy at times."

Both men smiled at me. "It's good to hear that someone loves her work. So many people are unhappy with their jobs," Diego said.

"So, what about your love life, man?" Miguel asked Diego.

"Not so hot," Diego answered. "I met this girl, Milly, but I think she's got problems. She started calling me up all the time, asking me what I was doing, who I was with. And this was after only two dates! Too much." He shook his head.

"I did see the kids last weekend though, that was good," he went on. I knew of his problems with his ex-wife, as Miguel had explained that to me. "They're great but I wish I could see them more often."

"Yes, I miss seeing them," Miguel said. "Maybe next time you have them you can stop over."

Diego agreed. "I don't always know when I'm getting them, you know how that goes," he said ruefully. "But I'll let you know." He turned to me. "Let me show you some pictures." He pulled out his cell and showed me photos of two dark-haired young boys in baseball suits.

"That's Jeremy and that's Benny."

"They're so cute," I said.

"The divorce was hard on them," he said, and his voice was sad for a moment. But then he said, "You like kids?"

"I love kids," I said, and felt a pang. Would I ever have my own children?

The conversation moved on to other things, then Miguel told Diego we were going to the museum.

"Have fun," Diego told us. "Good to see you again, Dana." He gave me a hug as we left and clapped his brother on the back.

We left and took the subway into Manhattan. The museum was wonderful, as always, and being with Miguel was fun and easy. We held hands as we walked through, sometimes separating to look at different things, but staying close to each other. It felt good to be with him. I felt close to him.

That night we had sandwiches at his place. I knew that night I would sleep with him again.

And this time we would not be celibate.

Chapter 46

Sex with Miguel was gentle, comfortable. I didn't feel the feelings I had with Ian, but I was glad I had been with Miguel. I thought about this as I got ready to leave the next day. I packed up my clothes and Miguel came with me to Penn Station, calling an Uber for us. He kissed me goodbye softly and said, "Come anytime, Dana. It was wonderful to see you."

I thanked him and told him I'd had a wonderful time as well. I saw him watching me as I walked away to get on the train.

I watched the river and dozed as the train sped north. I was awakened by a ping on my cell phone. I fumbled in my purse and pulled it out, thinking it was probably Miguel texting me to say how nice it had been to see me.

It was Ian.

I felt a shock as I saw his name. My heart started pounding as I opened the text.

"Where were you last night?"

What?

Why the hell was he texting me? Why would he think I was anywhere but at home? How did he know I hadn't been?

My mind was racing. Should I even answer him?

How could I not? I was as hooked on him as ever despite his behavior toward me.

My fingers were shaking as I texted back.

"What do you care?"

I waited. Now I had probably pissed him off.

So what? I asked myself. Look what he had done to me!

The phone pinged again a moment later. Again, it said, "Where were you last night?"

I wanted to tell him to go fuck himself, but I didn't. I wasn't sure what to say. I was not going to tell him the truth. In fact, I deeply regretted telling him the truth the day I had been over there. When Miguel had called me, I should have told him it was someone from work. Why the hell had I told him it was my ex-boyfriend? Yes, sure, he had his ex actually living with him for a few weeks, but apparently the rules were different for me than they were for him. He was such a hypocrite!

I felt a wrench of pain suddenly remembering how pleasant the day had been before Miguel's call, how Ian and I had been sitting together and laughing. It hurt so badly. How had things turned so wrong?

I still hadn't answered his text, and the phone pinged again with the same question.

I texted, "At my sister's." I would just lie, who cared? He didn't deserve the truth from me.

Nothing happened for a moment then came, "I suppose u told her what a monster I am."

What to say to that? I had told my therapist something about what had happened, but Ian didn't even know I was seeing a therapist. I certainly hadn't told my sister or mother. Or Ginny for that matter. I was embarrassed to say anything to them. I could imagine what they would say to me if they knew how Ian had treated me.

"No, I didn't," I texted back.

I hadn't told Miguel either. I would never say anything to Ian about Miguel again.

Then I realized what I was thinking. I was thinking

that I would be back with Ian. It wasn't over. It wasn't over at all.

"Where are you now?"

I couldn't say I was on the train because there was no train to my sister's town.

"Coming back," I texted. My car was parked at the train station so he wouldn't know the difference. But where was he? At my apartment building? How had he known I wasn't home?

I waited, but there was nothing else. I was so agitated at this point that I couldn't relax. I wasn't sure what I would find when I got home. I wasn't even sure I wanted to see Ian. I was so sick of his erratic behavior, his cruelty to me, his moods. It was such a contrast to be with Miguel, who was kind to me, who treated me respectfully. But I was in love with Ian.

There was no denying it. I was in love, wildly, deeply, insanely in love with Ian.

To my own detriment.

When the train reached its destination, I went to my car and just sat for a moment. I was afraid of what I would find when I got home. I wanted to see Ian, but at the same time didn't want to see him. What the hell would I say? He had pushed me; he had physically hurt me. He had chased me away- again. I was so sick of it. I wanted to see him. I didn't want to see him. My emotions were in turmoil.

I started the car and drove toward home. Where else would I go?

But when I got there I didn't see his car. I wasn't sure if I was disappointed or glad. I went inside and unpacked, throwing things in the washer and taking a bath to try to relax. Then I heard a knock on my door.

I was still in the tub. I got out and hastily dried off, pulling on my robe. I peeked out the window and saw Ian's car in the lot.

Oh my God.

Did I even want to answer?

How could I not?

I went to the door and opened it.

He was standing there looking so abashed I caught my breath. His hair was rumpled, he had a couple of day's growth of beard on his face. He looked like a lost boy.

He looked sexy as hell.

What was wrong with me?

I opened the door, and he came in. I said nothing.

"Dana," he said. It came out almost like a moan. "You drive me crazy. What are you doing to me?"

That got me angry. "What am I doing to you? Seriously? You chased me away, you hurt me!" Suddenly it all started pouring out. My hurt over all of the things he had done for all of the time I had been in and out of this ridiculous travesty of a relationship.

"You get crazy when I tell you an ex-boyfriend called when you had your scummy ex-girlfriend living with you. Living with you!" I turned on him, furious. "You chased me away that time I came to go out on the boat with you for NO REASON!" I was really yelling now. "You hang up on me when you don't want to bother with what I want to talk about, even when I really need you. You haven't met my family yet after all this time. You bring me to your friend's house and don't even tell me that the slut of a wife had a fling with you, that's she's still hot for you, then she acts all weird with me and I didn't even know why! Then when I didn't think it was ok to fuck your best friend's wife YOU GOT MAD AND BROKE UP WITH ME! You suck! I hate you!" Now I was crying. I sat down on the sofa, worn out by my tirade.

Ian just stood there, his shoulders slumping.

"Well?" I asked, "What are you even doing here? You're constantly leaving me. How did you even know I wasn't home?" I was getting wound up again. "You pushed me, you jerk, you hurt me!"

He finally answered. "I know."

"That's it! What is going on with you?"

"Can I sit down, Dana?"

I gestured toward a chair. "Go sit there then."

He sat and said, "I came here late last night. I was upset, I knew I had lost my temper with you and I felt bad. But you weren't here. It made me sick. You weren't here and I didn't know where you were, I thought…"

He stopped. I knew what he thought. That I had been with someone else.

Which of course, I had. But I was never going to tell him that. I said nothing.

"You went to your sister's?" he asked. "Why?"

"Do you have any idea how much you hurt me?" I deflected the question.

"Yes. I do. I don't know what comes over me. I never reacted so strongly to anyone before. You make me crazy."

You are crazy, I thought, but didn't say it.

"I don't know what to do with you. I think I should get out; I get so upset with you that all I want is to get away, then I miss you and I wonder what you're doing, and I can't focus on anything and I… I came over last night and you weren't here, and I went nuts. I didn't even go home. I went to a coffee shop and then sat in my car the rest of the night. I tried to sleep but couldn't sleep much. I didn't know what to do."

"Why the hell don't you try behaving like a normal boyfriend? So, my ex called? So what? I didn't call him. I didn't do anything. I could have just called him back to say hello and that would have been the end of it. I would have told him I was with you. That's it. What is so terrible? You were with your best friend's wife, for God's sake, and you thought that was ok, but I can't have an ex call me? I didn't change my phone number, so he still had it. So what?"

"Why did you still have his number then?" Ian

sounded accusatory but I wasn't having it.

"Because I never deleted it. So what?" I said again. "Patty obviously still had your number! What did you do when she was living there? Did you fuck her?"

"No, I told you I didn't!"

"Sure, but the rules are different for you than for me, right?"

"Maybe they are." He sounded angry now.

We were at a standoff. If he believed that the rules were different how the hell was I supposed to live with that?

I was still angry, but I was also feeling sad, terribly sad. I almost wanted to fling my arms around him, drag him to my bedroom, forget all the pain and just lose myself in him again.

As I always lost myself.

"Ian," I said, and my voice sounded desperate.

He just looked at me. "It's not going to work, is it?" I felt something pierce my heart.

"Why are you so jealous?" I asked him. Why do you always push me away, then you come back, I don't know what is going on with us at any given moment, you're in, you're out. It's insane."

"I realize that. I can't change the way I am."

"Are you sure? Do you want to change it? We were getting along so well for a while." My voice caught in my throat, I felt tears welling up. "I still love you," I said, my voice softer.

"What do you want to do?" he asked.

"I don't know what to do."

He got up. He came to me. He just stood for a moment then he reached down and drew me to my feet. He slid his hands beneath my robe. I started to melt against him then pulled away. "Ian, this is what always happens. We have this horrible scene then we have sex. I don't know…."

But then he stopped me with his fervent kisses, sliding off my robe, pulling my body against his, and I stopped protesting.

Chapter 47

Ian stayed the night. I wasn't even sure I wanted him to, I was so filled with conflicting emotions. Yet it felt so good to feel him clinging to me in the dark. I finally slept, fitfully.

In the morning I woke up to get ready for work. Ian was still asleep, and I nudged him softly, knowing that he didn't like to be awakened out of a sound sleep.

"Ian," I said, then, "Ian."

He stirred, opened his eyes, and looked up at me. "What?"

"I have to go to work. And don't you have to get up too?"

He sat up slowly. "Not really."

"What do you mean?"

"Listen, Dana, why don't you call in today?"

"Why?"

"I want to talk to you."

"Didn't we talk yesterday? I have to go to work!"

"Can you call in? I want to talk to you," he repeated.

For some reason I felt a quiver of fear.

"About what?"

He was getting irritated. "Can you just do that for me?"

"I guess so." I wasn't happy about it. I had already taken a half-day off the previous Friday and I never felt ok about blowing off the kids who depended on me.

"Just tell them you're not feeling well."

Not exactly a lie. It was just that my upset was emotional, not physical.

So, I called in a little later when I knew someone would be in the office. I reached the assistant director, Carl, who was my supervisor.

"Hi Carl, I'm sorry, I'm not feeling well this morning," I said to him, feeling guilty.

"Sorry to hear that, Dana," he answered.

"If I feel better I'll try to come in later."

"Don't worry about it, stay home if you need to. Do you have any appointments today?"

"Nothing special, just the usual this afternoon when the kids come in."

"I can get someone else to cover. Just feel better." Carl was a nice man and a good supervisor.

"Ok, thanks, I will. I'm sure I'll be better by tomorrow."

Ian was looking at me when I hung up. "Who was that?"

"My boss." I looked up at him. What was he getting at?

"A man."

"Yes, a man. Carl."

"And how do you and Carl get along?" His voice was full of innuendo.

"Very well. And I don't know what you're trying to imply. He's a very nice man. Happily married with three children. His wife is nice too, I've met her a number of times."

Ian looked at me and shook his head. "Nothing. Nothing."

"What do you want to talk about?"

We were in the kitchen and I was fixing some toast. I didn't feel like doing up a big breakfast for him. I was still upset, despite the sex having been as wonderful as always. Sometimes I wished it wasn't.

"I want to try and see Emily."

It took me a moment to recall who Emily was, then with a slight shock I realized he was talking about his daughter.

"Ok," I said slowly. "But I thought her mother doesn't want you to see her."

"She doesn't. But I'm tired of it. I always tried before to talk her into it, and she always said no. I pay her all that money and that bitch won't let me see my own child!"

His voice sounded angry and harsh. I didn't think calling the mother names would be conducive to his case.

"What do you want to do then?"

"I was thinking…" he looked at me intently, "I was thinking that we should get engaged."

What?

I said it out loud: "What?" Then, "What does that have to do with seeing your daughter?"

"I thought maybe I should try to go to court and ask for visitation. I was talking to some guy I know about it. His ex-wife was giving him a hard time and he went to court and he got to see his kids. I thought if I was engaged to somebody like you I'd have a better chance. You're smart, you're educated, you work with kids. I'm just a poor slob who works in construction. I've been late with support payments sometimes. I'd have a better chance with you."

I didn't know what to think or say. My heart was pounding. Was Ian asking me to marry him? Or would this just be a sham?

I finally said, "So we get engaged, you go to court. Then what? We get married? Or we're done? You just said last night you didn't think this relationship was even going to work."

"I said that because I was upset. We could get

engaged and take it from there." He must have seen the look on my face. He added, "Look, Dana, I told you I love you. I was upset when I tried to reach you and you weren't home. I want to be with you, you know that it's just.... just so hard sometimes. I explained it all to you, my background. But I do love you. Don't you want to get engaged to me? I thought you wanted to be with me."

He was somehow turning this around. "I wanted to be with you from the beginning of this, Ian. But you keep pushing me away. I would like to be engaged to you. But only if it's real."

"It would be real," he said softly, and reached out to touch my face. "I mean it."

"But only so you can get to see Emily!"

"No, no... not just because of that. Maybe if I know there's a commitment...maybe that will make a difference."

I got up from the table, turned my back. I wasn't sure what to do. My emotions were churning, as they always did with Ian. Did I want to get engaged; did I want to marry Ian? I loved him so much, so passionately! But I was also afraid.

I changed the subject. "Don't you have to go to work today?"

Silence. I turned from what I was doing and looked at him. "Ian?"

"Uh, not really."

I didn't like the sound of that. He had said it earlier too.

"What happened?"

"The job wound up and...well, there's no work right now."

"They don't have anything else?" I felt a bit incredulous. He had told me that he was working for a busy company.

"Maybe soon...look, I had words with the boss.

They were screwing up something and I tried to tell him, but he didn't like it. He thinks he knows it all," he said, in a sneering tone.

"So now you have no work?"

"What are you harping about? I'll get something."

"So, you ask me to get engaged so you can get your daughter, but you have no job? How do you think that will go over with a judge?"

"Well, it would give me time to spend with her."

"I think they like to see stability." I knew something about judges after all. I worked with disadvantaged teens and had been to both criminal and family court with various cases many times over the course of my job.

"I fucking know that ok? That's my point too."

So now he was getting angry. Always getting angry. That was his modus operandi.

I said nothing. I sat back down.

Ian was silent for a moment, then said, "Look, I realize that I have to get a job. I will. I didn't say this was happening right now. I would have to apply to the court in the county where she lives and wait for a court date. I want you to come with me. As my fiancé. Will you?"

I felt my heart soften a little. After all, he was doing something noble. He was trying to see his own daughter. And he was asking me to be part of it. How could I refuse to help him?

The answer was I couldn't. I could not refuse Ian anything.

"Ok," I said. It was almost a whisper.

He leaned forward. He took my hand, kissed me gently. "So, we're engaged."

"Shouldn't I have a ring?"

He put his hand in his pocket and brought something out. A box.

He opened it and took out a tiny ring, a diamond. He held it out to me.

"Oh my God!" I couldn't help but feel thrilled. This was real!

I held out my finger and he slipped on the ring. It was a bit tight, but fit.

"Oh my God!" I said again. I got up and almost leaped into his lap, kissing him wildly. He started laughing.

"Ok, Dana, ok," he said. "I told you, I love you. You know I love you."

We just held each other for a moment. "I love you too, Ian, I love you so much." I buried my face in his chest, listening to his heartbeat. "This is all I want."

Ian said he could spend the day. I asked him if we could visit my mother. He had still never met her.

"We don't have to tell her about this yet," I said. For some reason I felt hesitant to tell anyone. "But she hasn't ever met you and I think it's time. I can take the ring off when we go. It's too much just yet."

Ian agreed, quite readily. I was actually surprised.

I called my mother and told her, and she asked us to come for lunch. I turned to Ian when I got off the phone. "She's making lunch for us," I said. "She loves to cook for people. We can go around noon."

That morning we ended up back in bed. "Let's celebrate," Ian had murmured, nuzzling my ear, slipping his hand into my bathrobe. We did. Then we showered together, laughing as we soaped each other up. I still could hardly believe what was happening.

Just before noon we drove over to my mother's apartment in my car. "We won't tell her," I told Ian again. "I just want to introduce you." I had taken the ring off and left it on my dresser.

"Fine," he said.

My mother was standing there as we walked up to the apartment door. "Hi darling," she said brightly to me and looked at Ian. "Ian, it is so nice to meet you. Come in," she said. She was good with people; she knew how to make them feel welcome. I knew Ian was nervous and she was setting him at ease.

We sat in the kitchen and my mother served lunch. She told Ian about her recent cruise and how she had met Tom. He told her he loved English history and would like to go to England someday. She knew something about the topic because of her extensive reading, and they got talking about some episodes in English history that I had never heard of. The lunch was an unmitigated success.

When we left I was excited. "She liked you!" I told Ian.

"Well, why wouldn't she?"

"I didn't mean that. I mean, you had such a good talk with her, talking about King John and the Magna Carta and Agincourt and…well, I don't know much about English history, but my mother loves to read about it. It made me happy, that's all."

"I liked her too. It was an interesting conversation. There aren't a lot of people who know about those things."

When we got back to my place, Ian said, "Look, I'm going to send in that application for visitation. Then we'll have to wait and see." I nodded. I was feeling so happy. Ian had met my mother, they had hit it off, and I had a ring. I had a ring! I went to get to my bedroom to get it and put it back on my finger.

Ian said he was leaving, and I reached up to kiss him goodbye. "I love you," I told him.

"Love you too," he said.

Chapter 48

For some reason after Ian left, though, I didn't feel elated. I felt afraid. Ian was so unstable. Was this even real? Suddenly he decided to go to court for visitation when he had never done so before? And suddenly he thinks being engaged to me is the answer? Had he even asked me to marry him? No. He asked me to get engaged to him and come to court with him. Not exactly romantic.

I looked down at the ring. I knew Ian did not have much money, but this ring looked real. It was a diamond, albeit quite small. It had a silver setting and it sparkled on my hand. When the hell had he bought it? And with what? I thought cynically that he had probably used some of the money I'd lent him.

Did this ring symbolize a moving forward with Ian? Or was it just a sham?

I thought about him getting angry and pushing me. That was what had precipitated my trip to New York to see Miguel. I hadn't expected Ian to seek me out after that. I had thought it was over.

But it never seemed to be over no matter what happened. Ian came back, then pushed me away again.

Would that happen if we were engaged? Would we really get married? Dared I hope?

For some reason I decided not to wear the ring to work. I didn't want Ginny or the kids to see it. Then I would have to explain. And what if something went wrong?

Did I really want to marry someone who had treated me the way Ian did?

I was a social worker, I had studied psychology, I worked with troubled kids. I knew human nature. I'd had a troubled childhood myself. I was aware that Ian hadn't changed. He had gotten irritable only this morning when I questioned him. Was getting engaged or married going to change that?

Of course not.

On the other hand, I loved Ian. I wanted to see him be able to have a relationship with his daughter. The fact that he did not want to abandon her, that he did not want to give up on her spoke well about his character. And I was flattered that he wanted my help. I could not deny him.

He had said he loved me. He had said it over and over.

Ginny had told me love was action, not just words. But these were actions. Ian had looked for me, after he knew he had hurt me. He had bought me a ring. He had asked for my help. He wanted to get engaged. I loved him so much. I would have to believe it would work out for us.

Chapter 49

All that week at work I said nothing. I saw Ginny at lunchtime, and we talked but I did not report what had happened between Ian and me. I did tell her about my weekend with Miguel though, because the first thing she asked me at lunch on Monday was "How did it go?"

"Very well," I told her. "He was such a gentleman, so kind to me. I was upset when I went and I wasn't sure how I would feel being with Miguel, but it was very easy, actually."

Ginny looked around the small room to make sure no one was listening, then whispered, "So? Did you have sex with him?"

I was a bit embarrassed. "Yes," I whispered back. She pumped her fist in the air and the other caseworkers in the lunchroom looked over at her, startled.

"Nothing," she mumbled, smiling broadly.

"Why are you so happy about that?" I asked her, trying to speak quietly.

"You know why. You need someone who treats you better."

I knew what she meant. But I said, "Miguel left me, remember?"

"Yes, I'm not saying I want you to get back with him permanently, unless that's what's happening between the two of you. I'm just glad you had fun and got away from…" Her voice trailed off, but I could certainly fill in the blank.

But I did not tell her what had happened with Ian. I did not tell anyone, not my mother, not my sister, not Jerry when I spoke to him that week.

Jerry was now dating the woman he had met after he broke up with Marcy, so he was not as available as before. But we still talked on the phone and once in a while got together for coffee. He asked how things were going after he had called me on Tuesday night. I told him I had gone to New York City to visit my ex-boyfriend.

"Oh really," he said slowly, "and how was that?"

"Very nice," I answered, laughing. "Get the leer out of your voice, Jerry."

"I just want you to be happy, Dana," he said.

"I know. I'm not getting back with Miguel, but it was a great visit, and I was glad to see him."

Jerry was not as crude as Ginny, he would not come out and ask if I had sex with Miguel. He started telling me about his new girlfriend.

"I really like her, Dana," he said. "Gloria is smart and funny. We're getting along and we like a lot of the same things."

I was happy for Jerry. He was such a good man, he deserved someone who loved him and treated him well.

I spoke to my mother later that same evening. She mentioned the visit with Ian, and I asked how she had liked him, my heart in my throat. I heard her hesitate a moment, then she said, "Well, I liked him well enough, Dana, but I know you haven't always been very happy with him."

"I know, Mom." I thought momentarily about telling her we were engaged, but something stopped me.

She said, "I am a little worried, I can't deny it."

"Ok." I wasn't sure what else to say.

"You love him, don't you?" she asked.

"Yes, I really do." I felt a sob trying to rise out of my throat and I pushed it back. I loved him so much.

"I hope it works out for you, Dana," she told me.

We chatted for a few more minutes. She told me that she was going away with Tom for the weekend. Things between them were going strong. I was glad for her but when we hung up I felt a sadness sitting on my chest. Was I happy with Ian? I was happy when things were good between us but there was always a dark cloud hanging over my head, waiting to burst.

Because Ian was unstable. Ian kept leaving me. Ian kept hurting me. What would stop him this time, engaged or not?

Nothing.

Chapter 50

I spoke to Ian the next evening and he told me he had filed the paperwork with the court.

"I sent it off yesterday," he told me. "I should hear back soon."

"That's good," I said. "So, what's next?"

"They should be giving me a court date."

"Don't you need a lawyer?" I asked him. I knew he had little money and it had occurred to me that he might end up asking me to pay for a lawyer. But he didn't.

"They should be able to appoint me one because my finances are short right now."

"Good." I felt a modicum of relief that he wasn't going to ask me. Lawyers were expensive and he might have quite a battle on his hands.

Ian said nothing about getting together as we spoke, so I finally asked him. "Do you want to get together on Friday?"

"Sure," he said, which put my mind at ease. I never knew quite how he would react. "Come over here."

"I'll come after work," I said.

On Friday I raced home from work to change and drive to Ian's. I made sure to put the ring back on. I had left it at home when I worked all that week.

But when I got to his cabin on Friday evening I saw another car in the driveway behind Ian's. It looked like the same car that had been there before. Doug's car.

Oh no, I thought. Why the hell was Doug's car in

the driveway? Was Nan there too? I did not want to see her again.

I went to the door and knocked. Ian opened it with a big grin. I could smell liquor on his breath. He said, "Look who's here, Dana."

Doug was sitting on the couch. I did not see Nan.

"Hi Doug," I said tentatively. I wasn't sure what was going on, but Ian appeared somewhat drunk.

"Hello, Dana," Doug said. "We've been having a little party, join us." He pointed to the table, where I now saw bottles of vodka and empty glasses.

"Have a drink, my darling," Ian said, swaying a bit as he walked toward the table to pour me one.

I wasn't sure I liked this at all. I had seen Ian high but not drunk. I felt uncomfortable.

But I wasn't going to make a fuss, not now.

I took the drink and asked for juice as well. I wasn't going to drink straight vodka. Ian scoffed a bit but got some juice out of the fridge and I poured some into my drink. I sipped slowly, determined not to have too much. Someone needed to stay sober here. I wondered when Doug was leaving. But should he even be driving?

Ian sat on the couch next to Doug and patted the seat. "Come here, Dana, sit with us."

I sat and put my glass on the table next to the couch. Ian pulled a joint out of his pocket and lit it. He took a hit, then put it in front of me. I shook my head and he handed it to Doug, who took a long hit.

"What's going on?" I said. I could hear the irritation in my own voice.

"We're having a party," Doug repeated.

"Where's your wife?"

"Oh, she's home with the kids. She lets me out now and then," Doug said, and laughed. He took another hit on the joint, then a long drink of the vodka.

"How are you going to be able to drive home,

Doug?" I said. I must have sounded like a killjoy, but I wasn't going to let him do that if he was drunk. On the other hand, I certainly didn't want him to stay over. I wanted private time with Ian. And yet, I didn't like being around Ian when he was like this either.

Ian said, "We're celebrating my pending visitation with my daughter. Don't be a party pooper. Drink up," and he indicated my glass on the table.

I picked it up and took another sip, but the liquor burned my throat and seemed to curdle in my stomach. I hadn't eaten, since I had expected to have dinner with Ian. I put the drink down again and said,
"Ian, I got home from work and didn't eat, do you have anything?"

He waved a hand loosely at the fridge. I went and looked inside and found a packet of cold meat. "Do either of you want a sandwich?" I asked, getting out the bread and mayo.

They both snickered. They were acting like the kids I worked with.

"We want something else," Ian said. I thought he meant drugs and booze and didn't say anything.

I sat and ate my sandwich, feeling increasingly upset. I hadn't seen Ian since he left my apartment the previous weekend. I had expected to have a nice evening with him, and certainly expected to stay over. I didn't think I would be sitting with two grown men who were acting like 15-year-old boys who had raided their parent's liquor cabinet.

But I didn't want trouble with Ian, especially now. I twisted the ring on my finger.

"Doug," Ian was saying, "Did you hear the news about us?" he indicated himself, then me.

"What?" Doug asked, looking at me.

"Dana, come over here."

I got up slowly and walked over. Ian grabbed my

hand so Doug would be able to see the ring.

"Wow," he said, looking at Ian then at me. "You getting married? Are you kidding? Ian I never thought I would see the day!" He was shaking his head in wonderment.

Nice response. I was getting upset and disgusted.

"Come on, Doug. I just hadn't found the right woman before."

At least Ian was sticking up for me. I went back to the table and finished my food.

After cleaning up, I went back and sat next to Ian. He and Doug continued drinking and smoking weed. As the night wore on I wondered if it would ever end. They started talking about women in a crude fashion and laughing uproariously. I was tuning out, scrolling on my phone, trying to ignore them.

Ian put his arm around me, and we sat this way for a while. Then he began fondling my breast.

"Ian!" I protested, pulling away. But he pulled me roughly back.

"What?" he said, "We're engaged, Dana. I can touch your tits if I want to." He pushed his hand inside my shirt and roughly grabbed my breast.

"I can touch anything I want," he boasted, and slid his hand down to my crotch. I tried to jump up, but he held me down.

"Ian, Doug's right here!" I protested. "Stop!"

"Doug?" Ian said drunkenly. "Oh sorry, Doug, I didn't mean to ignore you. Why don't you join in?" he said and started pulling off my shirt, holding me down as I struggled. "Come on, Doug!"

Ian managed to pull my breast free. "Here, Doug, touch her, go ahead. I give you permission."

"Stop!" I screamed. "Stop!" I was really struggling now. I saw Doug's hand reach out to touch my breast and without thinking I bent my head to try and bite him. But he pulled away as he saw the move. Ian only laughed.

"She's a spitfire, isn't she, Doug?" he asked. "She wants it, but she doesn't want to admit it. Too righteous. Dana, the big savior of everyone." But he let go of me and I jumped up off the couch.

"You assholes!" I screamed. I pulled my shirt together and ran into the bathroom. I could hear both of them laughing.

I was a mess. My hair was sticking up all over, my face was red with anger, my makeup was smeared. I urinated and washed my hands and face, then went out of the bathroom, grabbed my purse, and rushed out of the door.

"Dana, what the fuck, where are you going?" I heard Ian say. But I ran to my car. I sat there for a moment, breathing hard, not knowing what to do or think. I even waited a moment, wondering if I was doing the right thing. Would Ian try to come after me? Would he apologize, tell me he was wrong, beg me to stay?

But no one came out the door and I started the car and left to go home. My heart was pounding so hard I thought it would burst out of my chest.

What the hell had just happened?

Even as I drove home I found myself making excuses. He was drunk and high; he didn't realize what he was doing. His boundaries were thin, maybe non-existent because of his abusive background. He'd had sex with this man's wife, after all, maybe in his world sharing a woman was just fine.

But I knew in my heart what had just happened wasn't ok, not at all. Not at all.

Chapter 51

I took a Benadryl when I got home and went right to bed. I didn't want to think about anything, and I knew I wouldn't sleep at all without help. I was able to fall into a drugged sleep. I awoke with a start in the morning just as it was getting light. My heart started pounding as I recalled what had happened the night before.

I twisted the ring, which was still on my finger, my mind racing. Ian was drunk. That's why that had happened. We were engaged! Why would he disrespect me so badly? What an asshole! And Doug was a husband and father of two gorgeous children, what kind of a way was that for him to behave? Idiot! Of course, he didn't know that Ian had ever had sex with his wife. What was wrong with both of them? Jerks. But Ian and I were engaged. How could I marry someone like that? But I loved him so much. But he had so disrespected me. Yes, but he was so drunk, maybe when he sobered up he would feel terrible.

My mind spun around and around and around until I felt dizzy. Would I really make excuses for Ian's horrific behavior last night?

I feared the answer was yes. Even though I was very angry and upset- the answer was yes.

Because I loved him so much, I was so hooked on him, it was as though a spell had been cast on me. I didn't want to let go of him. Even now.

I dragged myself out of bed, took a shower, tried to

eat breakfast. During every moment of each task, I remembered that I was supposed to be with Ian last night. I had anticipated staying over, I had anticipated that wonderful earth-shaking sex, I had anticipated waking up with him, having breakfast with him, spending the day with him.

And here I was alone. Alone. I could hardly stand it.

I was going over there.

When the thought popped into my head I pushed it away, thinking no, that was ridiculous, why would I go back after what he had done?

Then I thought of him trying to go to court to get visitation with his daughter, how noble that was. I looked down at the small diamond on my finger. He had given me this. He wanted my help. He wanted me.

How could I not follow through with that?

I was going over to see him, confront him.

I moved with more purpose now, managing to eat a bit, drink some coffee, get dressed. It was too early to go now, so I tried to do some chores, tried to settle my mind. But it kept racing around and around, so I just let go and let it race. I wondered if Doug had stayed the night. He'd been so drunk I imagined that he might have. I really did not want to see him again. I would have to wait. I thought he would likely leave that morning after he had sobered up.

The minutes dragged like hours. Finally, later that morning I got in my car and drove to Ian's.

My heart was pounding so hard I could hear the whoosh in my ears. My mouth was dry. I didn't know what I would say but I knew I had to do this. Somehow I had to make this right.

Because I just could not let go of Ian.

When I pulled up to his cabin I saw only one car, his. Good. Doug was gone.

I parked and went up to the door and knocked.

Nothing happened for a moment and I knocked again. Was he asleep? He was like a bear if he got woken up.

So, what, I thought. Too bad. And I knocked again.

Finally, I heard noises and Ian opened the door. He was a mess. His hair was rumpled, and he still reeked of booze. He just looked at me and I thought for a minute that he would shut the door in my face. But then he opened it wider, and I went inside.

I said nothing for a moment and neither did he. Then it all came pouring out.

"What the fuck was that Ian?" I blasted him. "What the fuck did you think you were doing?"

"I was drunk," he said, sounding sullen. "I suppose the holy Dana never got drunk."

"Don't turn this on me," I said furiously. "You and Doug were complete and utter assholes last night! Drunk and high and stupid! Did you never learn that no means no? That was disgusting!" I spat out. Worn out by my own tirade I abruptly sat down at the table. I felt hot tears burning my eyes.

"Ok, ok, I know I was wrong. I was drunk," Ian repeated. "And if I'm such an asshole, what are you doing here?"

I looked up at him. He was standing over me. What was I doing there? I felt a bit stupid too. Most women would have kicked him to the curb long before this.

"You know why I'm here," I said. The fury had gone out of my voice. "We're engaged, you're trying to see your daughter. I love you; you jerk. To my own detriment."

I felt defeated. He was just going to make excuses for his behavior last night. But I was going to accept those excuses. I could do nothing else.

Ian sat down too. Neither of us spoke for a time. Then he said, "You want some coffee? Or tea?"

I accepted tea and he got up to make it. He poured

coffee for himself and we sat drinking in silence. Then he said, "Look, I know I was wrong. I knew Doug when we were teenagers and sometimes when we get together we still act that way, ok? Stupid, I know. Nan is going to be furious with him too. He didn't even go home until this morning."

"I figured that," I said.

We were silent again, sipping our drinks.

Ian said, "Stay, Dana. Stay with me today."

I could not resist him. I knew I should not be with this man. But I could not resist him.

Chapter 52

I stayed and things were subdued. I was still upset and angry, but I pushed those feelings down for the sake of peace. Ian was hungover and didn't feel well but said little. It was uncomfortable but better, I told myself, than being home alone with my fears and my anger.

I stayed the night too. We had sex but it was perfunctory. I couldn't help but remember the previous night and I felt myself hold back. Ian didn't seem to notice. He finished, rolled over, gave me a quick kiss, and turned away from me. Soon he was snoring lightly.

I lay awake, looking up into the dark, eyes wide open. I was not happy with this man. I was angry, upset, disturbed, thrilled, excited, sad; but not happy. He was too erratic, and his behavior was too disturbing. Was I really going to marry him? Did he really want to marry me? What kind of man would do what he had done to his fiancé? Did he only want to marry me to help him to see his child? If we did marry, where would we live? Here? He lived an hour away from where I worked when my apartment was only fifteen minutes away. Did I really want to commute? What kind of a husband would he be? Well, what kind of a boyfriend was he? Half the time I didn't know if I even had a boyfriend when he rejected me. Would that happen if we were married?

My thoughts went around and around, like a cat chasing its tail, until finally I dozed off. I slept fitfully the rest of the night. I dreamed of a dark shadow that was chasing me, something fearsome, but I could not see its face. I awoke, startled, when dawn was just breaking, my heart pounding, Ian still sleeping next to me. I lay until my heartbeat slowed, then lay awake until full light.

Things still felt tense between us when we got up the next morning. We spoke little. Ian made some breakfast, just toast and coffee. I told him I had to leave early. He did not protest.

But when I was getting ready to leave, I could not help myself. "What happens now, Ian?" I asked him.

"What do you mean?"

"What are we doing? I don't know what to think!"

"Don't start, Dana," he said, but his voice sounded tired, not angry.
"Nothing's changed. Not unless you want it to. We're engaged. I'm going to court for my daughter. Nothing's changed," he repeated. Then he looked sharply at me. "Unless you've changed your mind," he said, a question in his voice.

I sighed. "No, Ian, I haven't. But I don't ever want a repeat of the scene from the other night."

"Fine, ok, fine, I said I was wrong. I was drunk," he said. Now he was sounding irritated. In Ian's mind, apologizing once was enough. I was supposed to erase the whole event from my memory now.

I didn't want to make him angry. "Fine," I said. "I have to leave, talk to you later."

He didn't protest. He gave me a quick peck on the cheek, and we said our goodbyes.

When I got home I collapsed on my couch, my mind spinning. My anxiety had gone down, but I couldn't help arguing with myself. Was anything really going to change with Ian? Was he ever going to behave differently? What was I getting myself into?

Yet I knew deep in my heart that I was not going to let go. Any sane woman would have. But I was not sane when it came to Ian. This would have to play itself out. I would go ahead with the plan. I would follow his lead and see what happened next.

Chapter 53

Ian called later that week in the morning to tell me that he had a court date in two weeks. He had been assigned an attorney and would be meeting with her just prior to the hearing.

"I want you there, Dana," he said. "As my fiancé."

"I will be," I told him.

"And wear your ring," he said. He knew I hadn't always been wearing it.

"Yes, I know." I hesitated, then asked, "What about a job, Ian?" I didn't want to anger him, he angered so easily, but I had to know.

"I have a lead," he said. "I'll follow up later today."

"Ok, that's good."

"Well, are you coming over?"

I felt a thrill go through me. I still reacted like a kid with a new puppy when Ian wanted my company.

"When?" I asked.

"How about tonight?"

I had to work the next day and going to his house meant a much longer drive to work, but I didn't want to spoil things by asking him to come to my place. He might say no.

"Ok, I can come after work."

"I'll make something for dinner."

"See you later."

We hung up and I got ready for work, feeling glad that I was going to see him. I had to let go of his behavior the other night. He'd been drunk and I had to forgive him. After all, now we were engaged, I was going to try and help him to see his daughter. We were moving forward.

Together.

That night when I arrived at Ian's he had made sandwiches for dinner. Nothing fancy, but he had a bottle of my favorite wine. When I finished my sandwich, he said, "I have dessert for you. Chocolate mousse." He got it out of the fridge and put the dish in front of me.

"My favorite!" I said, taking a spoonful of its sweetness.

"I know," he said, and he sounded serious. "I know you, Dana." I looked up into his blue eyes. "I know what you like, I know what kind of person you are. That's why I love you."

Ian loved me! My eyes began to tear up with emotion and I looked back down at my dessert. "I love you too, Ian," I said and starting wolfing down spoonfuls of mousse.

"What about you, don't you want dessert?" I asked, my mouth full.

"You're like a little kid with that stuff," he said, and laughed.
Then in a more serious voice, "Yes, I want dessert." I looked up at him again. "I want dessert, Dana," he said, his voice low and sultry. I felt a sexual frisson down my whole body. I finished the rest of the mousse quickly and got up.

Ian came to me and swept me up in his arms, kissing me deeply, with hot promise. He carried me into the bedroom and started undressing me slowly, his lips moving down my body. He stopped to pull off his shirt and slide down his pants, then lay naked on top of me, kissing and caressing. I responded with intensity, thinking, this is it, this is why I'm with this man. This is my reason for being, my reason for living, this closeness, this passion, this intimacy. This is why. We are meant to be together.

Chapter 54

The next morning, I had to get up early to go to work. Ian handed me coffee and asked if I wanted breakfast, but I didn't have time. I hadn't wanted to leave the warmth of his bed, his body next to mine. As I was rushing out the door, he called, "Dana?" I turned and he grabbed me, hugging me tightly and kissing me with a butterfly kiss, nipping lightly at my lower lip.

"You're going to make me late!" I said to him, laughing. He just grinned, a sexy sweet grin, and I went out to my car.

I felt a glow all day long, the glow that always surrounded me when I had a good time with Ian. He meant so much to me. It was because I was in love. I was so in love with him, a love like I had never felt before. When things were good I was in heaven. When things turned sour I was in hell. There was no stopping it. It was a force with its own power, its own will. I could not stop it. And right now, I didn't want to.

I still had not told Ginny about the engagement, but I was in such an afterglow that I had forgotten to take off the ring. No one else seemed to notice but when I saw Ginny walking toward the lunchroom and fell into step with her, she suddenly stopped.

"What?" I asked. Then I realized she was staring down at my left hand.

"Oh," I said, flustered.

"Oh? That's all you can say, oh? What the hell, Dana? Were you even going to tell me?"

Her voice was too loud, and I said, "Hush, the whole office will hear you. We were keeping it a secret. But I was going to tell you." As I spoke, I was pulling the ring off my hand. I slipped it into my purse.

"Let's go eat in my office, then we can talk," I told her. We got our lunches out of the fridge and went back to my office.

"Ok, what's the deal?" Ginny said as I shut the door.

"We got engaged, ok? It just happened." I stretched the truth a bit, not wanting her to feel too left out.

"With Ian?"

"Of course, Ian," I said. "Who else would I be engaged to?"

"Somehow I didn't think he was the marrying kind," she said, with a bit of scorn in her voice.

"Ginny!" I admonished her. "I told you, he said he loves me. Why shouldn't we get married?"

She gazed at me for a moment, not speaking. I thought I saw the answer to my question in her eyes. I looked down, away from her gaze. When she spoke, her voice was softer.

"Dana," she said, "I worry about you. I know you love Ian; I really understand that but… well, he doesn't always treat you right, he keeps breaking up with you. Do you think…I mean, why aren't you telling people? Do you think…?" She broke off the question.

But I knew exactly what she meant. Did I think Ian would actually follow through?

I wanted to say yes, I wanted to say I was sure, but I couldn't. I couldn't lie.

"I don't know, Ginny." I sat down heavily in my chair. I picked up my sandwich and took a bite. Then I went on.

"I'm not sure. I want to be, but I'm not. I won't lie to you. That is why I haven't told anyone yet. And he's going after visitation for his daughter too. I'm going to be helping him with that."

Ginny sipped her drink, then said, "Well, you are a stabilizing influence on him, Dana. I mean, I'm not saying I didn't like the guy when we met him, but I just don't like how he treats you sometimes. I hate to say it, but marriage doesn't mean that will change."

I sighed. "I know, I'm not an idiot, Ginny. I love him so much, but I realize he has issues." I stopped for a moment, then added, "Please don't tell anyone, ok? I just forgot to take the ring off this morning." I couldn't help adding, "We had a pretty awesome night last night. Pretty amazing." I felt my cheeks flush with remembering.

"Nice," she said slowly. She didn't say anything else. We finished our lunch and went back to work. I felt a bit relieved that Ginny knew.

But I wasn't going to tell anyone else, yet not even my mother or sister. I wanted to wait.

I wanted to wait to see if the marriage really did happen.

Chapter 55

Ian and I were spending quite a bit of time together. I went to his place at least once during the week and on weekends. He was spending less time coming to my place and although it would have been much easier for me, especially during the week when I had to work, I didn't push. I knew he got upset when I pushed, and things were fairly peaceful between us now. I didn't want to upset that. Ian was also getting more and more nervous about the upcoming court date and I didn't want to add to the pressure. He had even found work, although it was a temporary job working on a construction crew that was building a barn near where he lived.

I was nervous too. I was nervous about how court would go, about Ian's job, hoping he wouldn't blow it, and most of all, about whether or not we would actually get married. I just didn't trust it.

I didn't trust Ian.

I didn't want to feel that way, but it was hard not to. He had stopped talking about us getting married and was focused more and more on what might happen in court.

"The judge could be biased, Dana," he told me one night as we ate dinner in his cabin. "The judge probably thinks I'm just a deadbeat dad who never bothered to see his kid. I tried but of course, I never went to court before. I'm screwed."

I tried to reassure him. "Ian, you did try to see her, you just didn't try through the courts." Privately I was wondering why he hadn't done so before this, but I certainly wasn't going to say that to him.

"You have a lawyer; the lawyer will take your side. You have a right to see your child."

"Yes but she barely knows me. What if they decide it's better if she doesn't see me?"

"I think the courts would prefer that a child have access to both parents," I told him. "Even though she doesn't know you well, hopefully the judge will give you a chance to get to know her and for her to know you."

He just looked at me for a moment, then said, "I hope you're right."
But he was in a low mood and quiet as the day drew near.

The night before I had stayed over at Ian's since I had taken the day off from work to go with him. We were mostly silent on the drive over, just paying attention to the GPS as it gave directions to the courthouse. We had left early to ensure that we got there on time. Ian was to meet with his lawyer prior to the hearing. He had wanted me there and introduced me to the lawyer as his fiancé.

"This is just an initial hearing," the lawyer told us. "The judge will hear both sides. Probably not much will be decided today. The law guardian will also have a say. He will have met with your daughter by now and will report to the judge. Since the child is older, she will have a say in what she wants to do."

After the meeting with the lawyer, we sat in the waiting room. Ian was clearly nervous and so was I. His ex, Julie, the child's mother, would be there and I was not looking forward to that. I felt insecure and wondered if my presence was really going to matter one way or the other. But I wanted to support Ian.

We sat in nervous silence until he whispered to me, "I just saw her."

"Who?" I whispered back.

"Julie. She just walked by."

"Oh." I hadn't seen her. I wondered what she looked like, whether she was attractive. Then I wondered why I was even thinking about that. But I felt a visceral jealousy of anyone that Ian had been with in the past.

Our hearing was called, and Ian and I went in. I sat in the rows of seats while Ian sat up front with his lawyer. I now could see Julie clearly. She was attractive, a pretty woman with short blonde hair and a trim figure. She was younger than me, having been quite young when she gave birth. She was sitting with an older woman who must have been her lawyer.

The hearing proceeded, with both sides presenting their cases. I thought Ian's lawyer did a decent job. I heard Julie's lawyer stating that the child Emily barely knew her father and thought to myself, isn't that why we're here? Ian's voice was a bit shaky when he was asked questions, but he answered well, telling the judge why he had applied to have visitation and explaining that he was engaged and that he had a regular job. I saw the judge, an older man, glance over at me. The law guardian, a young man, also presented information about his meeting with Emily. It seemed that it wasn't clear yet how she felt.

All in all, I thought it had gone rather well. Nothing was yet resolved, but we had known going in that it would take more than one hearing.

I hadn't counted on Ian's response. When we got to the car, we had barely shut the doors when he exploded.

"That bitch!" he yelled. I told him to keep it down, since we were still in the court parking lot. He continued, "She's a lousy bitch and always has been. She just doesn't want me to see Emily." He started the car and backed up abruptly. I heard a nearby car sound its horn.

"Ian, be careful!" I exclaimed, seeing a car coming up behind us as he had been backing out.

"Fuck!" Ian said. He didn't seem to have heard either me or the horn of the other car. "Fuck!" He pulled out onto the road and gunned the car.

"Ian!" I yelled again. "We're in a city, slow down!"

"Fuck off, I'm pissed." He kept going faster than the speed limit.

"What are you so mad about?" I asked, clutching at the door as though this would slow the car down.

"She said she didn't think Emily was ready to visit. She said she doesn't even know her own father!"

I thought, well, she doesn't. I tentatively said, "Ian, I really don't think it went that badly. It's going to take time, like your lawyer said."

He seemed to be calming down a bit now, was driving more carefully.

"Yeah but...I don't know what I expected," he finally said.

"Keep the faith, they have to be careful when it comes to a child's welfare, you know," I told him.

"Ok, ok, but..." his voice trailed off, then he said, "When the hell am I going to get to see her? She should know she has a dad."

"She does. The law guardian spoke to her, she knows what's happening. She's not sure yet, she's only a kid. Give her time."

He said nothing for a moment, then said, "What if Emily decides that she doesn't want to see me?"

I thought that might actually be a possibility but hesitated to say so. "It's going to be up to the judge. They might have to go slowly, but hopefully she will want to get to know her dad."

"You are so naïve, Dana," Ian said scornfully, "Don't you think her bitch of a mother and grandmother have poisoned her against me?"

"I really don't know." I felt stung that after I had taken the day off to come and support him, he was insulting me. I had just been trying to calm him down and be positive.

We drove in silence after that. Ian got on the highway and I noticed again that he was speeding, but I was afraid to say anything. The tension was too thick. When we got to his cabin I started to go in, but Ian said, "Maybe you should just go home, Dana. I want to think."

Again, I felt stung, but said nothing. I thought this did not bode well for our getting married. He wasn't going to be able to chase me away if we were living together. What then? I said, "I have to get my things inside." I went in, used the bathroom, then picked up my overnight bag. I gave him a quick kiss on the cheek and left, mumbling, "Talk to you later." He was preoccupied and just nodded.

I drove home feeling letdown. Somehow I had thought this whole thing would bring us together. Instead, Ian had shut me out again.

Chapter 56

When I got home I wasn't sure what to do with myself. I felt edgy, as though every nerve in my body was tingling. I tried to eat something for dinner, but the food caught in my throat. All I could do was to eat a bit of soup. I tried to read, but the words just blurred in front of my eyes. I turned on the TV to watch a sitcom, but I couldn't concentrate. I just wanted to run away from my life.

Run away. To where?

For a moment I thought of Miguel. The time with him had been so wonderful, so peaceful, even healing. But I couldn't run to him now. I was engaged to Ian. Wasn't I?

I tried to reassure myself that even if Ian had asked me to leave, it didn't mean anything. He just needed to process what had happened. But the fear coiled in my stomach, that particular anxiety that Ian brought on in me. Only Ian. He evoked so many emotions, many of them not good.

Run away. The thought kept churning in my brain. I needed a break from everything, from my life.

Maybe I should run away. Maybe I should just leave, just get in the car and drive.

But I had to work tomorrow. What about work?

I didn't even want to do that. I just wanted to get away.

I went into my bedroom, pulled out an overnight bag, and started packing. I could always call in sick. Why not? I had sick time coming. I almost never took any of it.

Why the hell not?

I put jeans and tops, sweat pants, socks and underwear in my bag. I threw in my cosmetics bag and zipped it closed. I grabbed my jacket and my cell phone and charger and walked out the door.

It was evening by now and getting dark. I didn't even know where I was going, but I got in the car and headed for the thruway. I turned south, just driving. Then I knew where I wanted to go.

The ocean. I wanted to see the waves striking the shore. I wanted to hear the seabirds. I wanted the ocean, grey in the autumn light. When the turnoff came, I headed east.

The night was dark by now and there were few cars on the road. I drove in silence, not wanting music. I felt more peaceful, the motion of the car soothing the rattling of my nerves. I drove and drove.

The trip took hours. I had decided to head toward Cape Cod. I had been there before when I was younger with some friends and had loved it. I would be able to find a place to stay.

Eventually I crossed the bridge that led to the cape. I found a place to pull over and checked my phone for local motels. Finding a likely one nearby, I set my GPS and drove there.

After checking in, I took a long hot bath and put on t-shirt and sweatpants. I lay on the bed and just looked around. The room had a nautical look, typical of places on Cape Cod. It was very near the ocean. I could hear the lapping of the waves and it was very soothing. I fell asleep.

The next morning, I awoke with a bit of a shock, surprised that I had slept so well. I listened and heard the sound of the waves again. I pulled myself out of bed, got dressed, and went to the lobby for the free breakfast that the motel offered. It was very early, and I would have to call in to work a little later. Then I had the whole day to do whatever I wanted. I was going to put my anxieties and worries, and fears away and just enjoy the day.

It was cloudy and grey, the sky matching the ocean. I walked on the beach before returning to my room. The slap of the waves, the seagull's calls, soothed my mind, blanked out my thoughts. I stood on the beach for a time, letting the sounds and the salt breeze wash me clean. Then I went back to my room.

Almost inadvertently I checked my phone, which I had left in the room. There were no calls, no texts. Well, I wasn't going to worry about it.

I took a shower, turned on the TV and lay on the bed, waiting until it was late enough to call in to work. I felt a bit of trepidation. I wasn't sick, but I was going to lie about it. I remembered when Ian had urged me to call in sick that day and I had. But I pushed the thought away. I had a right to take a day to myself. It was Friday, so I would only be taking this day off. I would be back by Monday.

When 9:00 came, I called. Carl wasn't in yet, but I got the office manager. I told her that I wasn't feeling well and was taking a sick day. She said she would give the message to Carl. It was easy.

I wondered if I should call Ginny, but I didn't really want to have to tell her anything. I didn't want to talk about the court experience the previous day, and I was afraid she would ask. She knew that I had gone with Ian to court. I didn't want to tell her where I was. I didn't want to hear her ask what was wrong, since I had called in sick, and she would be concerned about me. I didn't want to talk to anyone, so I didn't call her. She might call me later, I realized, but I would wait and see.

I didn't even want to talk to Ian. Not right now.

I got my phone and checked out places that were nearby. I decided to go to the glass museum in Sandwich. It was only a few miles from the motel. I would go to lunch afterward, then take a long walk on the beach.

That was what I did. It was thoroughly enjoyable. The museum was unusual and interesting. I stayed for a couple of hours, then left and went to lunch at a restaurant nearby. It was a relaxing and enjoyable meal of local seafood. Then I drove back to my motel and went out to the beach.

The waves were coming in more strongly now and the wind had picked up. I just sat in the sand, my eyes closed, immersing myself in the chill wind and the salty smell of the ocean. Again, I felt washed clean. When I opened my eyes, a seagull was nearby, just standing there, majestic, and unafraid. I watched it for a time, then with a squawk, it flew off, hovering over the waves. I got up, brushed the sand off my clothes, and walked down the beach for as far as I could go. I walked slowly, my feet making prints in the sand. There were only a few people out, some with their dogs. I was mostly alone with the ocean and the sky and the wind and the gulls.

I finally got back to my room. I had left my cell there while I walked on the beach and now I checked it. Ian had not called or texted.

That bothered me. But Ginny had texted. "How are you feeling?" the text read. She had been worried; she knew I rarely called in sick. I texted back, "Better." I didn't want to tell her where I was. I would tell her the whole story next week.

It was close to dinnertime by now and I was hungry. I walked over to a nearby restaurant and got a meal. I was beginning to feel lonely. The peace of the ocean was fading. It bothered me that Ian hadn't bothered to contact me, not even with a short text. But I didn't want to contact him. Not yet.

I ate my food quickly and went back to my room. I was feeling antsy now. I got out my notebook, which I had brought, and sat down to write.

I wrote about Ian. The words flowed out of me, without conscious thought.

I sit by the ocean
And you are with me
I hear your voice in the waves
I see your footprints in the sand
I feel you beside me.
I want to walk with you
Along the shore
To make love with you
Where the rocks would hide us
From stranger's eyes
To sleep with you
Under the stars
Of tomorrow
And Always.

I could not banish Ian. Not from my mind, not from my heart. Ever

Chapter 57

That night my sleep was troubled. I tossed and turned for a time, then finally fell asleep. I dreamed of Ian.

The dream was murky, blurred. He was there in the dream with me, but I wasn't sure where we were. We were making love and I could feel him around me. But it was not peaceful. It was wild, it was stormy, like the sea when it rages in a strong wind. When I awoke I could hear the sea in my ears. My heart was pounding. Ian was in my brain, Ian, with his strong body, his flat abs, his wide chest, his shaggy hair, his craggy face. Ian. I wanted him so strongly I almost felt faint. I had to get back to him. I had to see him.

I got up and packed. I took a quick shower and blow dried my hair in haste. I stopped at the motel breakfast to grab a few things to eat on the way and checked out. I was in a rush. I had to see Ian. Not only to see him, but to touch him, to feel him inside me, to find that profound connection that flowed between us.

I had not been feeling it lately. Sex had been more perfunctory. He had been so preoccupied with the court hearing that he was not all there. But I needed that connection, I craved it as I craved air. I needed Ian. I was not myself without him. I could not breathe freely without him. I needed him. More than I needed myself.

I drove. I drove faster than usual, though not so fast I would get stopped by the troopers. I drove, one thought in my brain. Ian. Ian. Ian.

It took a few hours to reach his cabin. His car was there. He was home. I got out of my car and ran to the door, knocking loudly. I was sick with anxiety. I felt almost panicky, needing to see him so badly.

There was no answer for a moment, and I started looking around wildly, wondering how to get in. I tried the door, but it was locked. I was not leaving without seeing him. I was not.

He opened the door.

I lunged for him, throwing my arms around him, kissing him hungrily. He stepped back for a moment, startled, then grabbed me and kissed me back. We staggered to the couch and fell upon it, pulling off clothing as we went. We came together like an explosion. My need felt so great I could hardly breathe.

When it was over, we lay panting, him on top of me. Then he looked down and said, "Dana. What's going on?"

"I just missed you," I said, and the tears started. I could feel them sliding down my face. "I just missed you," I repeated.

Ian just looked at me, then got up slowly. He sat on the edge of the couch, his hand on my leg. Then he said, "I'm here. I was just thinking about everything. You could have called or texted. I just had to think."

I felt relief flood me. When I didn't hear from him I always thought he had gone from me. But he had not.

"I know, but I just wanted to see you, to do…well, to do this."

Then Ian looked at me and we both started laughing. "Yeah, that was pretty great," he said.

I sat up too and snuggled into him. We just sat for a while, then Ian said, "Want something to eat?"

I was very hungry for food, I realized now that my other appetite had been satisfied for the moment. "Sure."

Ian fixed some sandwiches and we sat and ate. I wondered whether I should even tell him of my trip. I never knew how he would react to anything. I decided not to say anything. I wanted peace between us and right now

I felt very close to him.

I stayed for the rest of the day and Ian asked me to stay the night too. I felt content. I felt happy. I felt fulfilled with him beside me. This was all I wanted out of life. Him and me. Together.

The next day after breakfast Ian said he had some errands to run. "Do you want to come?" he asked. I was happy that he had asked, he normally didn't want company when he puttered around at the store. But I hadn't been home for a few days, so I said no.

"Thanks for asking," I added. "I love spending time with you."

Ian smiled, though he did not say the same. But he kissed me deeply and gave me a huge hug to say goodbye. I drove home content.

After unpacking and throwing clothes in the wash, I called Ginny.
She answered, asking immediately, "How are you feeling?"

"I wasn't really sick, Ginny," I told her.
What?" I could hear the surprise in her voice.
"I had to take a day to myself."
"Did court go badly?" Ginny knew me so well.
"Not the way Ian wanted it to. He was upset."
"So, you stayed to comfort him."
"No, actually, he didn't want me there. I went to Cape Cod."
"What do you mean?"
"I mean I got in my car and drove to Cape Cod. I needed a break. I was antsy, Ian wanted to be alone, and I just couldn't stay home by myself. So, I got in my car and drove, and I ended up there. I've always liked it there and I just needed a break."

"Wow. I was surprised, you hardly ever call in sick. But I guess it's ok, you have time coming."
"Right."

"So, what's going on that Ian wasn't happy with court?"

"Nothing happens fast in court, you know that. It was just preliminary. He doesn't have a lot of patience. They must be wondering why it took him so long to file too. I mean, the little girl is nine."

"I can see that."

"And Ian tends to shut down, so he didn't want me there when he was upset."

Ginny said, "He wasn't.... did he...I mean, was he really nasty, like he can be sometimes?"

I knew what she was asking. Had Ian been abusive? "No, he just said he wanted time to himself. I guess he has a right to that."

"I guess," she said. Then, "Well, I'm glad you're not sick. How was Cape Cod? Did you just get back?"

"It was nice, beautiful but lonely. I missed Ian. I drove back yesterday and went over there. And it was fine," I added before she could ask. "I stayed over, I just got home."

"Well, that's good."

For a moment there was a pause. Then Ginny said, "I'll see you tomorrow then, right?"

"I'll be in, see you."

We hung up. I held my cell for a moment, wondering what the slight awkwardness had been. I didn't like it. I had always been so close to Ginny. But I realized that she was trying to accept my relationship with Ian without saying how she really felt about it. She didn't like it, and with good reason. But she was not telling me so right now and I did appreciate that. Nothing she said could change my mind about Ian anyway.

It was far too late for that and it had been for a long, long time.

Chapter 58

The time for the second court date was coming up. Ian had been working a lot of hours, trying to keep busy and to save up some money. Feeling a bit guilty for taking time off to go to Cape Cod, I had come in early the Monday after my trip and caught up my paperwork before the kids came in after school. Right now, things at work were going smoothly and none of the kids were in crisis. It was just the usual teenage angst and issues. I was grateful for that since I didn't want any additional stress.

I had seen Ian a few times a week for the past couple of weeks. I was still going to his place. I had asked him once to come over to my apartment during the week, but he had told me he had to get up for work early. Of course, when I stayed at his place, I had to get up early for work too, but I had said nothing and had driven over there without protest. That was just how it was between us. I gave, he took. I felt it was worth it to keep the peace. And things had been more peaceful between us.

I had requested a personal day on the date that the court hearing would take place so I could attend with Ian as before. Again, he was very nervous, hoping things would go in his favor. I was anxious too, knowing how badly he reacted when things did not go his way.

The hearing was stressful, as before, but the judge seemed willing to hear Ian's side. After hearing both sides, with testimony similar to the last time, the judge said, "Well, I have also taken into consideration the feelings of the child involved. It appears that she would like to see her father." I was watching Ian and saw the tension in his face relax. The judge went on, "I am ordering that the child be allowed to visit with her father and his fiancé this afternoon for three hours. You may pick her up and take her someplace that is local, then return her home after the visit. I would like to see how this visit goes, then I will consider having her come to your home for an overnight visit the next time if all goes well."

I heard Ian say, "Thank you, Your Honor," in a soft voice. I glanced over at Julie. She appeared to be angry and opened her mouth as though to speak. I saw her lawyer lean over and whisper something and she sat back. Her lawyer then asked to speak, and the judge agreed. The lawyer rose.

"Your Honor, the child has not seen her father for many years, and she is rather shy. It may not be in her best interests to go on a visit alone with two people who are virtual strangers to her."

The judge responded. "I have spoken to the law guardian, Mr. Peterson, and at the last meeting with the child she expressed an interest in getting to know her father, as I said. I will allow it and review the case again after the visit today."

It appeared that the hearing was over. I saw Ian and his lawyer rise and the lawyer had a smile on his face. Apparently this was a victory for our side. We went into a nearby conference room.

"This is a good sign," the lawyer told us. "The judge is granting you a visit alone with Emily."

"But I don't want to take her out and bring her back to her mother's, I want to bring her to my home!" Ian burst out.

"I realize that," the lawyer replied, "But this is a first step and a good one. Just pick her up, as the judge said, at the stated time and go and do something with her.

Make it low key. Maybe bring her to get something to eat, ice cream, something quiet but fun. Don't grill her, just tell her that you really wanted to get to know her, keep it light." I thought that was good advice.

Ian was quiet for a moment, then said, "Fine, ok." He thanked his lawyer, as did I, and we left. We had to go pick up Emily in about a half hour and she lived close by, so we sat for a few minutes in the car. Then Ian said, "This isn't what I wanted but..." He didn't say anything else. I tried to reassure him.

"This is a good thing," I told him. "The judge is trying to allow you to establish a connection with Emily. That can only lead to eventual visitation."

"It's so fucked up that they have to make me jump through these hoops."

I wasn't sure what to say. I didn't think the hoops, as he called them, were unreasonable for a man who had rarely seen his child, but I didn't want to get Ian upset. "Maybe we should go," I said instead. "Do you know how to get there?"

"Yeah, she still lives in the same place," he said, and started the car. We drove in silence. A few minutes later he pulled up to a pleasant house in a residential neighborhood. "She still lives with her parents," he said scornfully, and I realized he was talking about Julie. "What a loser."

"Ian, be careful," I admonished him. He glanced at me.

"Don't worry, Dana, I'm not stupid for Christ's sake. I won't say anything in front of Emily."

"Ok, ok," I said, trying to appease him.

At that moment the door opened, and the little girl came out, along with her mother. She was a slight little thing, with shoulder length blonde hair. She was wearing pink skirt and tights and a warm jacket and was carrying a small backpack. She looked up at her mother questioningly, then they came up to the car. Ian got out.

"Emily," I heard Julie say, and her voice sounded strained, "this is your father."

"Hi," the child's light voice said.

"Be careful, Ian." The mother's voice was hard.

"Yes, I will. Hi, Emily, I'm so glad to see you." Ian answered, looking down at his daughter. "Are you ready?"

"Where are we going?" Emily asked, but her mother said, "Make sure you bring her back on time."

"I will," Ian said, and opened the back door for Emily to get in the car. "This is Dana," he said to her, motioning to me. I turned.

"Emily, it's great to meet you," I said.

"Hi," she answered quietly. I thought that this must be hard for her, but she was doing well.

"Would you like to go and get ice cream, Emily?" Ian asked.

"Sure," she said. He backed slowly out of the driveway and headed toward the center of town. He knew the area. I noticed he was driving more slowly and carefully than usual, and I was glad to see that.

I turned to talk to Emily while Ian was driving.

"What's in your backpack?"

"Oh, I brought my iPad. I wasn't sure what we were going to do," she said, looking up at me. She had big blue eyes. She was quite a pretty little girl. My heart warmed to her.

"Well, we're getting ice cream first. Then is there anything else you'd like to do?"

"Maybe go to the park?"

I looked at Ian, and he nodded. "Sure."

We pulled into the ice cream shop and we all went inside. It felt a bit awkward, but it also felt good. It felt like a family. Ian asked Emily what she wanted, and she said without hesitation, "A chocolate mint cone." He ordered, then ordered a hot fudge sundae for himself and looked at me. "Hot fudge sundae too," I said.

We took our ice cream and sat at a table. Emily was licking her cone, when she suddenly looked at Ian and said, "How come you never came to see me before?"

Ian looked a bit shocked for a moment, then said, "I did, Emily. I did come to see you. The last time I saw you was when you were only six years old. But well...." He hesitated and I realized he wasn't sure what to tell her. He knew that he couldn't put down her mother.

"Things weren't so great between me and your mom. So, I decided to go to court to try and work something out. I really wanted to see you and get to know you." He added. I thought he had done well, and my heart swelled with love for him.

"I wanted to have a dad," Emily said. "All my friends have dads, even though some of their moms and dads are divorced. Did you ever marry my mom?"

"No," Ian answered, "We were pretty young."

Emily seemed ok with that answer. She licked her cone then said, "Yeah, that's what my mom told me. She had me really young."

Ian went on eating his sundae, his head down. He seemed a bit overwhelmed. I said, "Emily, it's so good to be here with you now."

"Yeah," she said and kept eating her ice cream. She seemed surprisingly relaxed, more so than Ian, who was clearly tense at being questioned. I wasn't sure what he had expected. This child was nine, not a baby. She wanted some answers. But she seemed to be fine with the answers he had given.

After we finished, we got back in the car and drove to the local park, which had a playground. Even though it was November, it was a fairly mild day and there were quite a few other families there. Emily went on the swings and I went with her. We were laughing by the time we were done. Ian wasn't saying much. We took a walk around a little pond, watching the ducks, then it was time to bring Emily home.

When we pulled into her driveway, Ian got out and opened the door. I turned and said, "Emily, I hope we see you again very soon." She nodded and smiled. I heard Ian tell her the same as he walked her to the door. It opened before they got there, and Julie came out. She took her child's hand and went inside. I heard Emily call out, "Bye, Daddy."

Ian's eyes were full of tears as he got back in the car. "She called me Daddy. Did you hear that? Did you hear, Dana?"

"Yes," I told him, and my eyes were tearing up too. "That's wonderful. You've made a good start with her, Ian."

Ian was much happier as we drove home, and I was happy for him. And for Emily. Maybe having a relationship with his daughter would make Ian a softer, kinder man.

Chapter 59

Ian was quiet on the way home, but it was not a tense quiet. He seemed to be thinking, and he seemed satisfied with the way the visit had gone. When we got back to his place, I went inside with him and he didn't tell me to leave. He sat and smoked a joint while I perused my phone checking my emails. I didn't say much, not wanting to interrupt his mood. Later, he cooked some pasta, and we ate. He finally started talking.

"It went well, didn't it, Dana?" he said.

"Yes, it really did."

"Maybe I'll get to bring Emily home next time."

"I hope so. She seemed to enjoy the visit," I told him.

Not much else was said, but again, Ian seemed content. We watched a movie and went to bed. I was waiting for him to make a move toward me, but he gave me a quick kiss and turned over. I felt a bit rejected but told myself he had a long and intense day, and I didn't want to make a fuss. I turned over too and went to sleep.

The next day I had to work so I left early. Ian kissed me goodbye and said, "Thanks for coming, Dana. It was good to have you there." I felt warm inside and again thought that perhaps having a daughter would mellow Ian. I could only hope.

The next couple of weeks went by with little drama. Thanksgiving came and went, and I spent it with my mother and Tom at Tina's home. I had asked Ian to come, but he said that he was going to Doug's and I didn't push the matter. I certainly didn't want to go with him and run into Nan again.

Ginny's wedding was coming up in early December and I was supposed to be the maid of honor. It was to be a small wedding with just family and a few friends. I had asked whether Ian could come. Ginny looked at me for a long moment and said, "Of course you can invite him." I realized that she thought he might not come. I was irritated, but I knew she was right. Whether he came or not would depend on his mood at the time. She agreed to send him an invitation and I gave her his address.

I approached asking him when I went over to his place that Friday. The wedding was next weekend, on Saturday afternoon. I asked with trepidation, since I never knew how Ian would react.

After dinner I said, "Ian, you know that Ginny is getting married next Saturday."

He looked at me. "That's nice."

"Well, you're invited to come with me."

"I didn't get an invitation."

"She's going to send you one, but I wanted to ask. I wasn't sure…"
I hesitated. I didn't want to imply that I wasn't sure he would want to come. I didn't want to offend him. Even though things had been stable between us lately, I was usually walking on eggshells with him, never knowing when one of his bad moods would flair up.

"I guess I could go. Maybe."

"I have to tell her one way or the other, Ian."

"Look, Dana, I'm not sure what's going to happen by next Saturday."

What the hell did that mean? Why couldn't he plan for a week ahead with me? But I didn't want to argue and ruin the night.

"Fine, but can you let me know in a couple of

days?"

"Yeah, I guess so."

Things were a bit tense after that. Ian got up and went to his cupboard, pulling out his weed. Every time things got tense he had to smoke. Without thinking I blurted out, "You know, you can't smoke if Emily comes here."

He looked at me with derision. "You think?" he said sarcastically.
"You don't give me any credit, Dana. You think I'm an idiot."

"No, I don't."

"Whatever. I'm not going to be smoking weed in front of my nine-year-old daughter. What the hell. If you think I'm such an idiot what are you doing here with me?"

"Forget it. Sorry I said anything." I was afraid he would blow up, but he let it go. He sat and smoked, and I finally grabbed the remote and turned on the TV just to have some noise. The tension floated in the air between us.

We spoke little until he said awhile later, "I'm going to bed. I turned off the TV and got up too. We lay down, but again, he made no move to touch me. I felt on the verge of tears. I wanted to be close to him, but any little thing made him pull away. I told myself that at least I was here next to him, he hadn't completely rejected me, as he used to. I tentatively reached out and touched his abdomen, rubbing a bit, then sliding my hand down. He didn't stop me. I pushed my body against his, and I could feel him getting hard, hear his breathing getting heavier. It was clear that he wasn't going to reject my advances tonight.

The next day, Saturday, things were still tense. Ian was quiet and I was not sure how to approach him or what to say. We ate breakfast together with him scrolling on his phone. Afterward he said that he had errands to run that day. He didn't invite me along. "I guess I'll just go home then," I told him. He did not protest.

I drove home feeling upset and hurt. We were supposed to be engaged, but Ian was not being loving. The sex had been perfunctory. What was going wrong? I felt tears burn my eyes, but I didn't want to overdramatize this. I would just hang out by myself for the rest of the weekend and wait. The tension would blow over, it always did. Maybe it was best that we weren't together when things were so tense. But what would happen if we were married and living together? I pushed that thought away. Right now, marriage to Ian seemed to be a distant dream, hardly a reality at all.

Chapter 60

Ian did not call or text for the rest of the weekend. I went to see my mother on Sunday morning, and she fixed breakfast. She was going out with her boyfriend later that day to a local music festival. She never used to do things like that, but Tom had opened up her horizons and she was having fun. I was glad for her, but I couldn't help but be a bit jealous too. Why couldn't Ian and I do things like that together?

Tom arrived at my mother's just as I was getting ready to leave. She and I had discussed Ginny's wedding and other topics, but I had not told her about Ian's court battle to see his daughter, nor had I mentioned that we were engaged. I tried keeping it light. When Tom arrived, he gave me a hug and said, "Why don't you come along, Dana?"

I turned him down, laughing.

"No, no, you two go ahead. I have things to do." I was thinking about what a kind man he was. Things were easy between him and my mother. They laughed together, they talked, there was no tension between them. Tom was kind, he was giving. She was lucky.

I wanted to call Ian as I drove home. I missed him and was feeling resentful that I was spending this beautiful sunny weekend alone. But I didn't give in to the impulse to call or text and tried to busy myself with other things.

When I went to work the next day, Ginny came to my office all aflutter. "Oh my God, Dana, do you believe it's this week?" she said. "I can't believe it!"

"I know," I told her, "I don't even know why you're here this week."

"I don't need to take the whole week, I'm taking the last few days off, then next week of course, for the honeymoon." They were going to Bermuda; a place Ginny had always wanted to visit.

"I don't think I'll get much done this week!" she said.

"Neither will I if we keep talking," I said jokingly. She laughed and left my office and I tried to do some of my paperwork, but I felt distracted. Not only by Ginny's excitement, but about my own anxiety over Ian. There had been no contact since Saturday morning, and I had no idea what was going on. Shouldn't a fiancé be more attentive? My cynical persona kicked in and a voice in my head asked me who I was kidding. If we really were engaged wouldn't he want to tell the whole world about it? Not just the courts as a means to an end.

Wouldn't I want to tell the whole world too? But no one in my life knew except Ginny, and that was only because I had mistakenly had the ring on, and she had seen it. Shouldn't an engagement be more like hers? Out in the open, shared by others?

I tried to focus on my paperwork and put aside these troubling thoughts. But they kept niggling at my mind like little flies, buzzing in my head.

Chapter 61

Ian came over on Tuesday.

There had been no contact from him at all on Monday. I wanted desperately to call or at least text, but somehow I managed to hold off. I had called Jerry on Monday night and told him some of what was happening, but not about the so-called engagement. He was supportive, as always. His new relationship was going well, and I was happy for him.

After work on Tuesday, it was snowing lightly. I drove home slowly and made a quick dinner of pasta. I was eating when I heard the doorbell. Surprised, I got up and peeked through the peephole. Ian!

I opened the door and he grabbed me, kissing me hungrily. Saying not a word, he shut the door behind him, took me by the hand, and pulled me to the bedroom. He yanked my t-shirt over my head and pulled down my jeans, putting his lips where his hands had been. I was immediately lost in a sea of wanting, his urgency quickening my desire.

The pasta sat cold on the table as we made love.

Afterwards, Ian gathered me in his arms. "I missed you," he said, as though there had been something keeping us apart other than himself. When I said nothing, he looked down at me. "Dana?" he questioned.

"I was here," I told him.

"Yes, I know I haven't called or anything, you know what I'm going through, Dana." He kissed my head and said, "No fighting. I'm here now."

A bit later we made our way to the kitchen and I heated up the pasta, fixing a plate for him. I felt physically satiated and although I had been upset at the lack of contact, this was Ian's pattern and he had tried to make up for it by coming to my place. He hadn't been here in a long time.

We chatted about inconsequential things. I wanted to mention Ginny's wedding, but I didn't want to disturb the peace, as usual. Ian said he had to leave because he needed to get up early for work, and I didn't argue with that either. I let him go with a lingering kiss at the door.

I had to satisfy myself with that.

Chapter 62

The week passed and Ian made no mention of Ginny's upcoming wedding. I finally asked him on Thursday when we spoke on the phone. He hesitated, then said, "I don't think I can make it."

"But why, Ian?" I heard the sound of my own voice and didn't like the begging tone.

"I just can't. I'm too busy. It's nothing to do with Ginny, she's ok."

"What do you mean, too busy? Doing what?"

"Listen, Dana, I've got projects around the house and I'm working a lot trying to earn money, so the damn judge doesn't think I'm a deadbeat dad, ok?" He was getting aggravated by my questioning, as usual.

"But you're my fiancé! I don't want to go alone to a wedding!"

The words hung in the air for a moment, seeming to be out of a dream. He didn't feel like a fiancé. Not at all. And he did nothing to reassure me.

"Then don't go."

"I have to go, she's my best friend and I'm the maid of honor for God's sake, Ian." I was getting aggravated too.

"Then go, do what you want. I can't fucking go."

"Thanks a lot, Ian, really. What the hell."

He had hung up. I was so upset and angry, my heart was whamming in my chest. He was so fucked up, he was crazy, he was mean. He didn't care about me, just about himself. I threw the cell phone on the bed where it bounced and fell on the floor. I picked it up quickly to make sure it still worked. It was fine. But I was not fine. Ian was so damn hurtful. The anger was subsiding, and tears came to my eyes. Why had I even thought he might come with me to Ginny's wedding? It was pretty clear he hadn't wanted to from the time I brought it up.

It was also clear that I wasn't going to see Ian the next night, Friday. Just as well, it would give me time to calm down and get ready for the wedding on Saturday. But my heart kept pounding and my eyes kept tearing up. The rejection had made me want Ian more than ever, made me long for a more normal relationship where I could count on him to be by my side. But that is not what I had. Not at all.

The wedding was small but beautiful. Ginny looked ravishing in an off-white gown that was simply cut and stunning. My own gown was lavender, and the color looked well with my dark hair. Ginny's groom, Derek, looked so handsome in a white suit. What struck me the most as I stood by the couple while they said their vows, was how happy Derek looked, how in love with his bride.

During the reception I ended up being paired with the best man, Derek's brother, Brent. We sat with other members of the wedding party at a table near the bride and groom. Brent was quite good looking and unmarried. He had not brought a date to the wedding and was paying attention to me, asking me frequently to dance. I tried to put on a happy face for Ginny's sake, though my insides were doing a slow bleed for the fact that Ian was not there. I got through it. It was even fun at times, dancing with vigor to the band that was playing, reminding me of times before meeting Ian when I had gone dancing with friends, carefree and young. That seemed to be a long time ago.

When I got home late that night I vowed to think of anything but Ian and to focus on my friend's happiness. I even succeeded and was able to fall asleep. But waking up brought me back to reality.

I wasn't sure what to do. Should I call Ian and apologize? But for what? I had done nothing wrong. Yet the lack of contact and the knowledge of his anger weighed me down like a large rock in my gut. What should I do?

It was Sunday, so I spent the day alone. Ginny and Derek were off today for their honeymoon and my mother had gone away for the weekend with Tom. I thought of driving to my sister's, but it would have taken a few hours and she likely had plans. So, I did chores and felt the rock in my gut grow heavier. Should I go there? Should I just wait? I wasn't sure what to do.

I realized that I should not chase Ian down. When he was upset, he withdrew, but he came back. He always came back. Best not to push.

So, I sat alone while it seemed the rest of the world was made up of happy couples. I sat alone and pondered how I had come to this.

I had stopped seeing my therapist for a time. Part of the reason I had stopped was that it seemed unnecessary when Ian and I had been getting along better, especially when he had asked me to marry him.
But perhaps it was time to start up again. I would give Dr. Clarkson a call during the week.

That decision made, I felt slightly better. I could wait this out. Again.

Chapter 63

I went to work Monday and forced myself to get through my day by focusing on my job. The holidays were coming, and we normally put on a party for the kids, so I had to help plan for that. When I left and was driving home, I considered whether I should just keep going and drive to Ian's. I didn't, however. I drove home and made a rather complicated dinner for myself to keep my mind occupied, even though I'm not crazy about cooking. I realized that I could call, but I wasn't ready yet. I wanted to stick to my previous decision to try and wait it out.

After dinner I tried to read a book, but my mind kept jumping to Ian. I was thinking about what he had said about being broken, that we were broken people. I had been bothered by that characterization, but I had to admit there was a grain of truth in it. Ian had been damaged by his mother's treatment of him and I had been damaged by my father's abuse of me. Neither of us reacted in a normal way to the upsets of relating, we both overreacted.

But I loved Ian. How I loved him, in my flawed and damaged way. He was in my mind, my heart, my guts. I got out my notebook and wrote down a new poem.

Take this,
This imperfect love
Deep and lasting
But from a flawed being,
A wounded heart

A heart
That has ripped open, then repaired
Over and over again.
Take this love
Flawed and imperfect though it may be
Like a flower
With a brown and wrinkled petal
But the other petals
Are beautiful.
This love
From this flawed and imperfect being
Is yours
Is unconditional
Is forever.
Take this
This imperfect love
From this flawed and imperfect being
With this torn but mended heart
That is so full
Of love
For you.

I sat back, exhausted for some reason after writing, and put my pen down. I loved Ian, I loved him, I wanted to communicate that to him. I wanted to give him this poem. I wanted to get to his heart, that heart that he so often shut down when he shut me out as he was doing now.

But I would wait. I would wait. I shut my notebook and lay down to sleep.

I was awakened by the ringing of my phone. I sat up with a start, my heart pounding. Ian!

But I realized in another moment that it was not Ian's ringtone. I answered slowly, not sure whether it was the middle of the night or still evening.

"Hello?"

"Dana." I heard Miguel's familiar voice. I tried to shake away the sleepiness.

"Hi Miguel, sorry, I was sleeping."

"Oh no, I'm the one who is sorry, I didn't mean to wake you. But it's only 8:00."

I had been sleeping for the past hour. I shook my head again. "I was just really tired," I said.

"Well, I have some news," Miguel said. "I wanted to tell you."

I waited, wondering whether he would be coming up to this area again and perhaps wanted to see me. But the news that he told me surprised me completely.

"I am getting married," Miguel said.

I didn't answer. I wasn't sure what to say. On some level I had felt that Miguel was a sort of backup, someone I could run to if Ian hurt me or abandoned me. I was shocked by his news. After all, he hadn't been able to commit to me. And suddenly he was getting married?

"Dana?" Miguel questioned.

"I'm here, I'm… just really surprised."

"I know, I know, it was so unexpected, especially because, well, I know I've had issues with commitment but… I just know it's right this time."

Again, I felt hurt. Obviously with me it hadn't been right. What was wrong with me? But I pushed down the thought.

"Who is she?"

"Her name is Anita, I met her through work. She's also a buyer but for another company. We were at a convention and, I mean, we just looked at each other and we knew. There was this connection. It's hard to explain. She lives in New Jersey, so we started dating and we realized pretty quickly that we wanted to make it permanent."

"That's great, Miguel," I forced myself to say. He was quiet for a moment.

"Dana, is something wrong? I know I woke you up but… is something else wrong? You aren't upset at my news, are you?"

I was, a bit, but I didn't want to say that. It would have been too selfish of me. "No, but, well, it's Ian again." I was embarrassed to tell him, but what the hell. It was status quo.

"Again?" Miguel said. There was a bit of scorn in his voice. "Dana, really, this guy doesn't sound good for you."

"Yes, yes, I know." I was sick of hearing this. "But never mind about that. I guess I should say congratulations."

"Yes, thank you. We are getting married next month. Just a very small wedding, nothing fancy, just family." I realized he was telling me that I was not going to be invited. I didn't think I could handle another wedding soon anyway.

"That's wonderful, Miguel, I am happy for you, truly."

"Ok, well, goodbye Dana. Please take care of yourself. Ok?"

"I will, Miguel, thanks. Bye."

He hung up and I realized that he had also been telling me that he was not going to maintain contact any longer. I had been his ex-girlfriend and occasional lover. He did not want to maintain that type of relationship when he had found the love of his life.

I had also found the love of my life. But I sat here alone, again. Alone.

Chapter 64

I had cried myself to sleep after Miguel's call. I slept sporadically, restlessly, with vague disturbing dreams that went unremembered when I awakened. I went to work on Tuesday and again tried to immerse myself, focusing outward on what I needed to do, on the kids when they came in, on anything but Ian or even Miguel's surprising announcement.

At lunchtime I called Dr. Clarkson's office to make an appointment. Unfortunately, she was fully booked, but put my name on a waiting list.

I got through the day and drove home again that night feeling so empty. I could not face another night alone. I simply could not.

I would call Ian.

I realized, pulling into my parking lot, as I had realized before, that an intimate relationship should not be so painful. Calling your boyfriend, lover, fiancé, should be simple, always accessible, not an excruciating decision about proper timing, planned ahead like a major life event. But sometimes calling Ian felt so fraught with significance, that I had to get it right, that if I said the wrong thing or called at the wrong time, it could have a profound impact on my very existence.

I ate dinner first, trying to fortify myself and giving him time to get home from work and settle in. I cleaned up, went and sat on the couch. I resolutely picked up my phone and dialed his number. My heart was slamming my chest as I waited for him to answer.

No answer.

It was only about 7:00. I would wait. Maybe he was driving and didn't want to pick up.

At 7:30 I called again. No answer. I dialed again at about 8:00. No answer.

I was getting jumpy and distracted. Was he still out? Had he forgotten his cell? Was it out of a charge? Why did he not answer?

I kept calling until 11:00 that night. I thought of driving over but put that out of my head. I finally gave up and tried to sleep but could not. I lay there, thoughts spinning around and around. I dozed at times. I kept looking at the clock, just waiting until it was time to get up again and go to work.

I moved through my day, feeling like an automaton, just trying to focus on doing my job. I had a splitting headache and took some ibuprofen to try and stop the pounding in my head that came from my lack of sleep and lack of contact from Ian. I finally told Carl that I wasn't feeling too well and was going home an hour early.

I started calling when I got home. I heard the ringing in my ear again. No answer. Again.

The same routine as the night before. I didn't even try to eat or read or watch TV. I called over and over again, telling myself I was being obsessive, I was being crazy, what the hell was I doing? Then I would press redial again.

After trying to call on and off for four hours I was about to give up. I put the phone down and went to take a bath, hoping it would relax me. I vowed not to call again that night. After my bath, feeling a touch calmer, I went to my bedroom, deciding to lie down and rest, telling myself that Ian was just being Ian, he needed space for whatever reason. Five minutes later I picked up the phone and dialed again.

He answered. "Hello." His voice sounded so tired.

Now I didn't know what to say. I felt like a fool.

"Ian, I was trying to call…"

He cut me off. "I know. You've called about 50 times; I know you were trying to call. I was… look, I'm discouraged, they cancelled court again. I was going to tell you."

"What do you mean?"

"I mean they cancelled…well, I guess I should say postponed, but I'm getting pretty discouraged about this whole process, it's just not working. I didn't feel like talking about it, Dana, I still don't. But you have to push, you always push."

I was getting angry. "I didn't push, I just hadn't heard from you. I mean, haven't I been trying to help you with this whole thing?" I could hear my voice rise up.

"Oh, yeah, savior of the world, Dana, that's you," he said sarcastically. "Look, it's late, I'm going, talk another time." Ian hung up.

Even though Ian had been abrupt, and I was upset, I felt perversely relieved. I was used to this, to his moods. Nothing was really going on. He was upset and when he was upset, he withdrew. Normal behavior for him.

I lay back on the pillow and finally was able to go to sleep.

But I had no idea what was coming next.

Chapter 65

I decided I would give Ian time to get over his mood and let me know what was going on. Maybe we could get together this weekend and talk about it. I went to work with a lighter heart the next day.

The week proceeded and Ian did not call, but I thought to myself that at least now I knew what was happening. He was in his dark hole; he would call again when he pulled himself out. I wanted him to let me help him, but that was not how Ian operated.

When Friday came and I hadn't heard from him, I called him again. The pattern was the same as earlier in the week. No answer.

This was getting old. When the hell was he going to come out of this? I wanted to see him, I wanted to give him the poem I had written. I wanted to make love with him, to touch him, comfort him, tell him I was there for him, that eventually he would get to see Emily again, that we would fight this fight together. Also, the holidays were coming up and I was hoping to spend some time with him, maybe have him come with me to meet my sister.

But my calls still got no answer. The anxiety was rising again.

On Saturday morning I tried again.

On Saturday afternoon I was back to regular robotic dialing of Ian's phone. At one point, it didn't ring. He had shut it off, or maybe it had just run out of juice.

That evening I tried again. That time it rang. And he

answered.

"Look, Dana, I just need to be alone, let me be, will you? Stop calling constantly. Cut it out."

I was about to answer when I heard a sound. I stopped and listened. A child's voice. Probably the TV. Then I heard, clear as a bell, "Daddy?"

The line went dead.

I froze, the phone in my hand. That had not been the TV.

That had been Emily.

What?

How could Emily possibly be there at Ian's? He had not been granted visitation yet. Had he kidnapped her?

That horrific thought crossed my mind, then fled. Of course not. She hadn't sounded upset at all. And even Ian would not go that far. Then how...???

Another realization began to dawn. He had somehow worked something out with her mother. Outside of the court. But she hated him! How?

I couldn't figure that out and I didn't want to push, he said that I pushed too much. I would have to wait until he saw fit to tell me. I wasn't going to drive over there, not if Emily was there. I didn't want to pull the child into the middle of this.

But I couldn't wait. After a time, I called again, determined to get answers. Predictably, the phone was shut off. I had no choice. I would have to wait.

Ian called me on Sunday. I jumped to grab the phone when I heard his ringtone. I had barely slept again the night before, the questions going around so fast in my head I felt dizzy. Maybe now I would get an explanation.

"Dana, look, I don't know how to tell you this," he started. I waited, holding my breath.

"You did hear Emily. She's here with me. And her mother," he went on. "I... well, I don't want you to call me anymore. I'm going to try with Julie."

My ears were buzzing, I felt like I was in an alternate universe. What had he just said? Was I in a dream, a nightmare? Julie hated him! She was there?

In all of my meandering thoughts of the past few days, I had never dreamed of this.

"Ian…" I said, "Ian, we're engaged… I was helping you…" I could barely get the words out of my throat. I was in shock.

"Don't call me anymore, Dana," He said. "I'm with my daughter and her mother now."

I heard no more. There was silence on the line. He had gone. He hadn't just withdrawn this time. He had left me.

He was with someone else.

How? How had he gotten Julie, who had hated him, to come and bring her beautiful little girl? Were they living with him now? What about all the promises he had made to me?

Empty. Lies. Nothing.

There was nothing.

I couldn't breathe, couldn't think. I went to my medicine cabinet and grabbed a bottle. I had some Benadryl left. I shook the pills out. For a moment I thought of taking all of them. Then I grabbed two, washed them down with water, and lay down, waiting for oblivion to catch me.

Chapter 66

I woke up the next morning though, still feeling drugged. Oblivion faded and the horrible reality faced me.

It was Monday, I had to go to work. I dragged myself up, ate a piece of toast, put on makeup, got dressed. I looked terrible. I didn't know how I would get through the day.

I managed to get to work and tried to focus. Ginny was not back yet and I was glad. She would have known in an instant that something was very wrong.

But of course, Ginny was not the only one who noticed me. The kids could be very perceptive. Especially Pedro. He always noticed. That kid was so tuned in to other people, he had a remarkable instinct.

"What's up, Ms. Taggert?" he had asked. "You ok?"

I wasn't sure how to answer. I wasn't ok. But I couldn't share that with Pedro. He was my client, not my confidant.

"No, I'm fine, Pedro, just…tired," I told him, knowing it sounded lame. He looked at me oddly but didn't comment. I knew that he knew I was lying.

The week dragged on in a similar manner. I would do my work as best I could, knowing that I was falling short. I muddled through. I went home, tried to eat something like soup or a sandwich, and took a couple of sleeping pills. Then I would do it again the next day.

But the worse came that Friday when my supervisor, Carl, asked me to come to his office.

"Dana," he began when I sat down, "I'm not sure how to say this. You have always been an exemplary employee, but…" he paused. I was cringing inside. What the hell? Carl went on, "You've seemed a bit short lately, not yourself. Some of the kids have remarked on it."

"You mean they've complained?" I heard my voice rise and I hated how I sounded.

"Well, a couple of the girls felt that you answered them rather abruptly. And some of the other kids were asking if you were sick."

I was silent, my heart pounding, trying to figure out what could have happened. Two of the girls had come to me the other day to ask me for help with another girl they were having problems with. Had I been abrupt with them? I had been so upset, so distracted. I could barely remember what I had said. And Pedro had asked me what was wrong, though I hated to think that he had complained about me to someone else.

Carl was going on, "Dana, if something is wrong, if you need some time off…"

I interrupted. "No, no, I don't, but I have been really…tired lately," I went on, giving the same lame excuse I'd given Pedro. Carl looked at me sharply.

"Perhaps you should take off next week." Carl was in full boss mode. I was embarrassed beyond belief. This had never happened to me before.

"But the holiday party is next week!" I exclaimed. I had never missed that before.

"Dana," Carl's voice softened, "if something is wrong, then I understand. But it can't affect your work with the kids. They need us, they need us all. No one expects you to be perfect, but you have to set the example for them. You have to be there for them. I know it's not always easy, we all have our own lives."

"Carl, you know I love my job," I burst out, feeling humiliating tears burn my eyes.

"Yes, I know," he said. "We will manage the party. Take some time off, sort things out."

"I will," I said. What choice did I have?

"Take care, Dana." I was being dismissed. Again, I felt the tears burn my eyes. I turned to go, hoping that I didn't run into anyone in the hallway. I headed for the bathroom, where I sat on the toilet and put my head down in my hands. I couldn't believe it. Never had such a thing happened before. Now my pain at Ian's betrayal was affecting my job performance. I had been reprimanded by my boss when in the past I had been complimented and praised, I had been asked to train new caseworkers. What had I become?

When I had composed myself, I went to my office, gathered my things, and left for home, where I lay on the couch in a sort of stupor. My life was falling apart. I had done all that Ian had asked, but he had left me, he was with someone else, the mother of his child. It felt as though my life, my world, was falling apart.

Chapter 67

I took pills and tried to sleep away the weekend. The weekend bled into Monday, but I didn't have work to distract me, I had to take the days off that Carl had given me to sort things out. Sort things out. How was I to do that?

I felt numb. I had accomplished nothing that weekend, spoken to no one. Monday passed the same way. Numb. I was barely eating. Monday slipped into Tuesday. My mom called me that evening to find out how I was, since she hadn't heard from me. I couldn't even lie this time.

"What's wrong, Dana?" she asked, hearing it in my voice.

"I'm taking a few days off from work," I told her.

"Why, are you sick?"

"No, I'm…. I'm upset." I stopped, not wanting to tell her what had happened.

She was silent for a moment, then, "Dana, what is going on? You're so upset you had to take time from work? Do you want me to come over?"

"No, you don't…" then to my chagrin I burst into tears.

"I'll be right there," she said and hung up.

A little while later she rang my doorbell. I had dried my tears but knew I looked a mess. My mother walked in and said, "What the hell is going on?" She rarely swore and I was surprised. "Come sit down, Dana, and tell me.

Let's sit in the kitchen, I'll make some tea." She marched off and I followed her.

As she bustled about, I finally decided to tell her the whole thing. I couldn't hide any longer. When I told her the last part, I choked on my tears. She sat down beside me.

"I'm sorry, Dana, but he is not good for you, and what he has done is terrible. I tried not to say much before, and I know he's good looking and likeable, but for you to get upset like this, well, it reminds me…" she trailed off, then went on, "It reminds me of your father. He was not a good man."

That was the first time she had ever come out and said such a thing. She was not finished. "I never knew what a good man was until I met Tom. And now…well, I'm so sorry I didn't up and leave your father. I'm so sorry that I let something bad happen to you. And to myself and your sister."

I was surprised again. She had never referenced any of the terrible things that had happened, preferring, I supposed, to forget them and put them behind her.

"Maybe that's why you're drawn to men like Ian. Even your ex, Miguel, he was charming, but he wasn't going to commit to you, that was clear. Maybe it's my fault for not getting out of that terrible marriage. I'm sorry, dear."

She had gotten back up and had turned away from me as she spoke, making the tea. Now she turned to face me with two cups in her hands.

"I'm sorry, Dana," she said again. She brought the tea over and sat down. "But you have the chance, Dana. You don't have to put up with bad behavior from any man."

"I love him." I said. My voice sounded flat and weary.

"I know you do," she said gently. "I once loved

your father too. Very much. But having a man like Tom made me understand that no matter how much you love someone, you can't change them. You can't make them into what you want and need them to be."

I picked up my tea and sipped. I could hardly believe my mother was talking to me so openly about this when she never had before. I knew she was right. But I felt no more capable of giving up on Ian than I felt I could open my window and fly out. Even though he had given up on me.

"I don't think I can let go of him, even now," I mumbled, the teacup to my lips.

"I hate to see you doing this to yourself. I knew something wasn't right, Dana, but I didn't want to say anything."

"I'm not sure what to do." I put the teacup down.

"He is not good for you," she said, and I heard the echo of Ginny, who had told me the same thing.

I didn't respond and we sat in silence for a time, sipping our tea. I was grateful that she was there. After we finished, she said, "I can stay for the afternoon. Do you want to watch a movie?" I agreed, and we went into the living room and picked out a comedy to watch. It distracted me for a time, and I felt comforted with my mother sitting nearby.

When she left, she hugged me and said, "Call me if you need me, ok?" I said I would. I was still reeling from the fact that she had talked to me about my father. But even though I knew, and had known for some time, that I was attracted to Ian for some of the wrong reasons, I could not fight it. I felt bound to him by an unbreakable tie. I felt bound. And it was a bind I could not break. Even if he had broken his end of it.

Chapter 68

There was nothing I could do. Ian was with someone else. I had no part of Ian's life now. It seemed surreal, but he had made another choice. I had lost him, but I could not afford to lose the other parts of my life too, like my job, which I loved. I had to pull it together.

How? I cried. I moved through my apartment feeling like I was moving through sludge. Every step was painful. I had to return to work the next week and behave as though everything was ok, but how? How?

Christmas would be coming soon and then the new year. How would I cope? Everyone else close to me had someone, everyone was happy. Even Miguel was finally making the commitment and getting married. My mom had a lovely boyfriend. Jerry had a new girlfriend. Ginny was a newlywed. My sister had been happily married for many years. And Ian now had someone, he had a family, a girlfriend, and a daughter. I hurt so badly it was hard to stay awake, hard to fall asleep, hard to wake up. But I someone had to cope. I had no other choice.

I thought of harming myself but brushed that thought away. I couldn't think of that. Some of the kids I worked with had been suicidal and I had helped them. I thought of Jaime. She had tried to harm herself and had come through it and was thriving. I couldn't do that to them. The news would get out and then how would they feel? Betrayed by someone who had always been there to help. How would Pedro react? He trusted me.

Then I caught myself, realizing how low I had come to even be thinking along such lines. Had I no resourcefulness, no pride, no self-esteem? I could get through this.

But it felt as though every breath I took said, "Ian." Every beat of my heart said, "Ian." The blood that pulsed in my veins said, "Ian." And he was no longer mine.

I slept and dreamed. I dreamed that Ian was hovering above me. I could feel his breath on my face, feel his energy flow into me. In my dream he whispered, "Dana." His voice was soft, like a caress. I awoke with a start. It felt as though he was there, he was with me.

I awoke thinking, no, I have not lost him. I thought I had but I have not.

How could that be?

I knew I had to get through this time somehow, to get through the holidays, to not ruin them for my family. I would do that somehow. Somehow.

The week off went by with me continuing to feel like I was plodding through mud. My mother came over again on Wednesday, bringing a few holiday decorations. We put them up together, but I felt numb, looking at the bright glinting lights. Nothing could get through to me, my body felt robotic, my mind was numb, my feelings were frozen inside me, as cold as the frozen ground of December.

My mother told me that Tina and her family would be coming on Christmas. Tom was going to be with his own children but would be coming over that night. "You are coming, right, Dana?" she said, looking at me with a worried expression. "You know we all love you. You should be with your family."

I reassured her that I would be there. In body at least I would be there. I would get through the day, as I got through life now, with nothing inside to give.

Carl called the next morning to find out how I was doing. The party had gone off well the day before, he said, but many of the kids had been asking for me. Especially Pedro, who had seemed very concerned.

That sparked some interest in my numb brain. "What did you tell them?" I asked.

I told them you had some minor medical issues, that you are fine, but you needed to stay out of work for a time." He laughed lightly, clearly embarrassed. "I'm sorry, Dana, I should have known they would question your absence at the party. I didn't think it through very well. They really love you; you know. I hope what I said was ok. They put me on the spot."

I could feel a slight thaw in my frozen chest when Carl told me that the kids loved me. "That's ok, Carl, what could you say? I really love those kids too."

"When do you want to come back, Dana?"

"I thought you wanted me to stay out for the week."

"Well, if you need the time, but if you want to come in sooner…"

"I can be back tomorrow if that's ok. I miss the kids. I'll uphold your story; I can just tell them I felt better sooner than expected."

"It's fine." Carl hesitated then said, "Are you doing ok, Dana?"

I told him the truth. "Not really, but I can still do my job."

"Ok then, see you tomorrow."

I hung up, feeling a slight bit better. Ian had done a number on me, he had crushed my spirit, but I still had love in my life. My family loved me, the kids at work loved me. I still had something to give, at least to them. Ian had blocked me out, he had turned the sun off for me, but I still had the light of these others. I would have to cling to that for now.

Chapter 69

So, I went in to work the next day. I had lost weight, and my pants felt loose. My skin was pale, and my hair looked a bit lank. But I put on some make-up and brushed my hair and I drove to work feeling like I had been given a second chance. Carl's fiction actually gave me an excuse for looking less than my best.

The kids were off from school for Christmas vacation so a few of them were there early. Pedro and George were among them. When they saw that I was in my office, they rushed in. "Ms. Taggert! We missed you at the party! Where were you?" Pedro said.

"Didn't Mr. Boyd tell you?" I asked, pleased that they cared so much.

"He said you was sick," George said. They both looked at me, as though assessing whether I looked ill or not.

Pedro said, "Yeah, you look a little bit pale," he decided.

"I was sick, but I'm getting better, and I missed you guys," I told him, trying not to tear up in front of them. "I got better more quickly than I thought, so I came in today. How was the party?"

They interrupted each other, both trying to tell me about it, and I felt gratified. I even laughed a few times at their descriptions of one of the male caseworkers playing Santa Claus and the crazy things the kids had been asking him for as gifts for Christmas. When they left my office I felt momentarily cheered, like myself again for a moment, that caring, competent professional self. It was much better than the miserable, numb, rejected self that I had been since Ian threw me away.

But I knew that self would return.

Chapter 70

Christmas was the next Tuesday. I had to buy presents that weekend, since I had done nothing yet, so I busied myself with that on Saturday and Sunday. Jerry called me on Sunday night. I told him I wasn't seeing Ian anymore. He asked if I was ok and wished me happy holidays. He was going with his new girlfriend Gloria to meet her family, who lived in Ohio, and was excited. I wished him well.

On Tuesday I drove to my mother's apartment. Tina and her family were there already, having arrived the previous day. We exchanged gifts and had a lovely meal that my mom and Tina's husband Lenny had cooked. Collin talked about his new girlfriend nonstop, with good natured teasing from his dad.

After the meal I was headed to the bathroom when Tina pulled me aside into my mom's bedroom.

"Dana," she said, "You look kind of pale and you seem to have lost weight. Is everything ok?"

I wasn't sure what to tell her. "I'm...well, I had a..." I wasn't sure why I was stumbling. I should just say that I was ok. But when I tried to speak again I was dismayed to feel my eyes well up with tears.

"Dana!" she exclaimed. She shut the bedroom door, then turned back to me. "What is it? Are you sick?"

"No, I....my boyfriend and I broke up."

"Oh, Mom mentioned him," she said. "It sounds like he was pretty unstable."

I wasn't happy, realizing that they had talked about me and Ian.

"I'm really upset."

"I can see that" Tina told me, looking closely at me. "Well, we're all here for you, you know that, right?"

I looked at her. Suddenly I needed to ask her something, something I had never in all these years asked before.

"Tina, did you know what happened that night?"

She stared at me. She knew exactly what night I was referring to.

"Not at first," she answered slowly. "Not right away. But when I thought about it, I figured it out. I was so angry I didn't know what to do." She looked down at the floor, then back up at me. "I wanted to kill him. And I confronted Mom."

"What?" I had never known that.

"I asked her how the hell she had let him back in the house. That's how she knew that I knew. She said she had to; he was her husband. I was so angry at her then too, for a long time. And I watched to make sure nothing else ever happened."

"I never knew that" I said again.

"No, you didn't. You were so traumatized, I couldn't talk about it, but I did watch. I did care. And so did Mom. I was mad at her, but I saw her watching. We both made sure nothing ever happened again. Then he got really sick. I was glad."

I looked at her. She had a look on her face I had never seen before, my kind, loving sister.

"I was glad. I knew the watching was over. He couldn't do anything ever again."

"I'm sorry, Tina," I said.

"No, Dana, I'm sorry. I was sorry such a thing had happened, and all because I wanted my own room. But I was your big sister, I had to watch out for you."

"Thanks," I whispered, because I couldn't find my voice any longer.

She hugged me tight and left the room. I sat for a moment, wondering. She had protected me, and I had never known. So had my mother. I felt the hurt inside me, that very old hurt, shift and alter a little then.

When I went back out to the living room, I sat quietly with my family watching some Christmas movies on TV. Tom came later that night and we had leftovers for a light dinner. He was full of stories about his children and grandchildren. It was warm and pleasant and lulling. I drove home that night and fell into the least troubled sleep I'd had since Ian had left me.

Chapter 71

I was dreading New Year's Eve. That was the night when the world celebrated, when lovers should be together, kissing at midnight to see the old year out and the new one in. I wondered if Ian would be kissing Julie. I knew that my mother and Tom would be going out to dinner and spending the night together. Tina would be at home with Lenny and Collin's new girlfriend Briana was going to be there too.

Ginny and Derek had returned from their honeymoon and would be spending the evening with a few friends. Ginny had called me to let me know she was back and to tell me about how wonderful and romantic the honeymoon had been. She had asked me to come on New Year's Eve, but I told her I couldn't manage it.

"We broke up," I had told her.

"Dana," was all she said. She didn't ask what had happened. I knew she probably thought it was the same as all the other times. I couldn't talk about it, even to her.

"If you change your mind, just come over," she told me. I knew that I wouldn't. I just could not bear to see the happy couples together.

I planned to take some pills and sleep the night away. I had purchased more Benadryl. That was my plan. Pills would be my companions.

So, I slept as the old year bled into the new. I slept and I dreamed.

Again, I heard Ian's voice in my mind. I saw his

blue eyes staring into my eyes. I felt his body move against mine. In the dream he was saying, come to me, Dana, come to me. You are mine. You will always be mine. I am yours; I will always be yours. Come to me.

I awoke. The morning was dark still.

In a strange fog I arose. I got ready. I ate a piece of dry toast. I drank a sip of coffee. I brushed my teeth and showered. I dried my hair. I got dressed. The day was getting lighter as I got in my car and drove to Ian's house.

I didn't even think it through. I felt as though I was still dreaming, that he still hovered nearby. I would obey the dream. I would go to Ian. I drove.

I didn't think about the fact that she might be there, that he might be with her and her daughter. I thought of nothing. I just drove. I felt that he had been calling me. Calling me to come to him.

In less than an hour I pulled into his driveway. His car was there, but just his car. I got out and like a zombie, walked to his door. I knocked. Then I knocked again.

Ian came to the door and opened it. He looked rumpled, unwashed. I peered inside. I saw no one else. I walked through the door.

I turned to Ian and slapped him across the face.

I hadn't known I was going to do that. He looked stunned, then he grabbed my hands, pushing at me. We stumbled to the couch. He was holding me roughly, harshly, looking at me with hatred in his eyes, but something else too, something painful.

"Let go of me," I said, almost snarling at him. He let go and I slapped him again. He immediately grabbed my hands again, twisting my wrists around. I gasped in pain and kicked out at him. He pushed me and I fell against the couch. I kicked out again and he was upon me, grabbing my throat, tightening his grip. I tried to breathe and started seeing black, but he released me. He flung himself on top of me and kissed me, biting my lip so hard that I tasted blood. I struggled, but then was kissing him back. He grabbed my shirt and I felt it rip. He pulled at his jeans, dropping them to the ground. He yanked at my pants and I slid out of them. He thrust inside me with no foreplay, forcefully, violently. I grasped at his head, pulling his hair, pulling his head down to mine, moving along with his thrusts, screaming, screaming in rage and passion and pain.

Then it was over. He slumped against me, then lifted his head and looked at me.

"It's not over," I said, "You son of a bitch, you bastard, it's not over, how could you do that to me?"

He looked weary.

"I had to see my daughter," he said. "I didn't know how else to do it. I couldn't risk you coming here. I had to..." his voice trailed off.

I screamed at him, "How could you do that to me?"

"Stop, stop!" he got up off of me, pulling his jeans back on and sat down at the table. "I told you, I had to. I had to tell you not to call anymore, she was right there. I had to make her think... that I wanted her back. I had to make her think that so she would bring Emily."

"You bastard," I shrieked again, hardly recognizing my own voice. "You bastard, you lousy son of a bitch, how could you do that? How? I was helping you! I've been good to you! I hate you!"

"Calm down, calm down for Christ's sake," Ian said. "I told you, the courts postponed the hearing, it was the holidays, I wanted to see Emily. So, I told Julie that seeing her made me realize what a mistake I'd made and that I wanted to see if we could work it out for Emily's sake."

"Is she that gullible? Or are you lying, you bastard?"

"She always had a thing for me."

"What the fuck does that mean? All these years

later?"

"Look, she's a loser, she still lives with her parents, Dana. I guess she had a serious boyfriend for a long time, that's what she told me, and they were supposed to live together, but it didn't work out. So, when I told her that, she said she'd come up with Emily and we would see how things went."

"You bastard!" I yelled at him again, but I was losing steam.

"Yeah, you said that already," he replied wearily.

"But we were supposed to be engaged," I said, and now I could feel the tears starting.

"Oh, fuck, come on, Dana. What are you trying to do here?"

"What?" The rage was starting to rise again.

"Never mind. Look, they're gone, at least for now. But they're supposed to come back, Emily is on Christmas vacation until Thursday. What do you want me to do?" He asked, holding his hands out in a supplicating manner. "I need to see my daughter, and she is getting to know me."

"You were supposed to go through the courts," I said flatly.

"I tried; you saw that. But it was taking too long, and I thought this might work. And it did. I'm not going to fuck that up. Do you get that? Do you?" His voice was starting to rise.

"You are despicable. You don't give a shit what you're doing to me, to us!"

"It's nothing against you," he said. "I just wanted to see Emily. Her mother's not a bad person, she's ok. I had to make her believe that I was regretful, that I wanted her here too. She never would have let me see Emily otherwise."

"Is she stupid?" I asked scornfully.

"Maybe a little," Ian admitted. "She was never the brightest bulb in the box. She always had a thing for me," he repeated. "She was devastated when I left. She figures that now we're older, we're smarter, maybe things could work."

"Speaking of work, how is your job going?"

"It's fine."

"That's nice," I said sarcastically.

"What the hell are you doing here, Dana?" His eyes pierced mine. "I told you not to come, but you're here. And you're violent toward me? You come and start beating on me, what the hell?"

"Fuck you, Ian," I said, angry again, "I had to know what was going on. You're supposed to be my fiancé, you bastard. I had to know."

He was silent for a moment, then said, "Well, now you know. Yeah, it's screwed up, but it got me what I wanted. I spent time with Emily. She is a great kid, she really is." He looked at me again, "And it was nice to fuck you, Dana."

I flushed and fingered my lip, which was sore, but had stopped bleeding.

"It's always great to fuck you," he went on, "No matter what else is going on, we always have that."

"That's not why I came over," I snapped.

"Well, it's a benefit then."

"Right," I said, sarcastic again. Then we sat quiet for a moment, me still on the couch, him on the chair. I felt like I had come back to life. I was so angry I could barely sit still, but the very fact that I was sitting in his presence, in his house, and he hadn't kicked me out, was making me feel calmer. Even though I knew he had been with Julie, that he was still planning to be with them again. How was I going to live with that?

Chapter 72

I sat for a time and neither of us said anything. I sat, reluctant to leave, not finished with being in Ian's presence, yet feeling a rage and hurt that threatened to overwhelm me. Then I spoke. I hardly knew what words were going to come out of my mouth until I said them.

"My father molested me."

Ian, who had been sucking on a joint and staring out the window, looked up at me in shock.

"What the hell?"

"He molested me," I repeated. "That's why I'm 'broken,' as you tell me. That's why I'm fucked up. He was a drunk. He came into my room. I never got over it. I never got over it." My voice cracked on the last word. I buried my face in my hands.

"What the hell?" Ian said again. "You never told me this, Dana? You tell me now? When I told you all about my fucked-up childhood, my fucked-up mother, you never said anything, you just pretended you had this great life, this ideal family. You liar!" He looked really angry, his craggy face, that face I loved so dearly, twisted in rage.

"I didn't tell you, I couldn't. I don't know why. I feel…damaged by it. I feel like something was wrong with me."

"There is something wrong with you!" Ian cried out. "Oh, don't look like that, not because your drunk dad molested you, that's on him. But look what you've done. I tell you all about my past and you hide yours from me!

And you tell me now? Now? When I'm trying to make peace with my ex so I can see my daughter? Is that so wrong? You think I'm such a mess, don't you Dana, with your perfect life, your perfect job, those kids you work with. They're all screwed up and the wonderful Dana gets to help them. Well, you're just as fucked up as they are, more! Because you hide. You pretend. You just as broken as they are. And you aren't even willing to admit it."

He seemed to run out of steam then and took another hit on his joint. He turned away from me to look out the window again at the cold white day.

I felt that I couldn't breathe, my chest was so tight. I sat, as stiff as the cold ground outside, barely moving. Was he right? He had been harsh, but was he right? Was I a phony, had I been moving through my life pretending I had it all together when inside I was just a mess? Look at how I reacted to him? Were these the actions of a normal person, a person who had it all together?

I finally made myself move, made myself get up. I walked closer to Ian. He saw me and cringed, as though he expected to be slapped again. But I stopped before I reached him and said, "Is that why you don't love me, Ian?"

He looked at me and I thought I saw a fleeting look of something in his eyes, not anger, not scorn, but a sadness. He looked at me without speaking.

I asked again, "Is that why you don't love me?"

He looked away then. "I didn't say I don't love you."

"Oh, yes, great way to show it. Go back with your ex behind my back. Lead me on, tell me we're getting married, then back out. Great way to show it."

I felt so defeated then. There was no answer. There was no resolution. I didn't know why I had shared my deepest secret with Ian, only to be attacked. Attacked, but perhaps with a truth I had been denying. I was shattered. I was broken. There was nothing else to do right now.

But instead of leaving, I sat back down on the couch. He didn't say anything. He didn't ask me to leave. He said nothing. The time passed that way, both of us almost petrified. He finished his joint and still he sat. I sat, staring at nothing, feeling the brutal impact of his words, of the circumstances.

Finally, Ian said in a softer voice, "Look, they're supposed to be coming back later, you need to go home."

I got up and left without speaking another word.

Chapter 73

I managed to drive home. When I arrived, I got out my journal, which I had not written in for some time.

January 2
I know he said it's over. I know he's with her. But it isn't over. It isn't. It can't be. We're both in too deep. He is part of me and I am part of him. We are bonded together. We fit together, albeit with jagged razor edges. We fit at the broken places.

What else was there to say?

The next day I had to go to work, and I went through the motions like a zombie. I had to keep myself together for the kids and I would do that. I would pretend to be ok; I would pretend that my pretend medical condition was better, I would pretend I was normal. I would pretend. At least my care and concern for these kids was not pretend.

Ginny was back at work. When she saw me, she flung her arms around me and hugged me tightly. She then backed up and peered into my face, my eyes.

"Dana," she said. That was all. It was enough. I knew she knew what I was going through and I knew that she cared. She let me go and fumbled in her purse, bringing out a necklace made of beautiful tiny shells. "Just something for you," she said, dropping it into my hand. I felt tears burn my eyes. "Don't cry, Dana," she said, brushing her hand across her own eyes. "You'll make me cry too."

I turned and got a tissue off my desk, wiping my eyes. "This is beautiful, thanks," I told her.

"I'm here for you, Dana, you know that" Ginny said. Then she left to go to her own office. I sat at my desk, looking down at the paperwork I had to complete, thinking again that I was certainly blessed with my family and friends, if not with a life partner. With their help I would keep going.

Two weeks passed, then three. I did not hear from Ian. I felt as though I was living in some kind of suspended animation. No part of me felt that it was really over. I was just waiting for the next installment.

But there was a flame that burned me from the inside out, a hurt in my deepest core. It throbbed and ached, but I could do nothing. I did not feed it and I did not try to put it out. It lived inside me, it had become part of me, that agony of being without Ian. So, I waited.

Then Ian called me.

It was evening and I had just finished a light dinner. I wasn't eating well and had lost more weight, but I kept trying, not wanting to hear the alarm in my mother's voice or in Ginny's when they saw how thin I was becoming. I forced food down, barely tasting it. I had washed the dishes and was walking into my living room when my cell rang. I knew it was Ian by the ringtone. I picked up calmly but said nothing.

"Dana, are you there?" I heard his voice. Still, I did not answer.

"Dana? Dana?" There was an urgency in his voice. I finally said, "I'm here."

"Well, you didn't say anything. Anyway, I need your help. I need you."

I wasn't even surprised. Of course, he did. He could do anything to harm me, anything at all, but he still fully expected me to be there for him, no matter what.

The sick thing was that he was right.

"What, Ian?"

"Court was scheduled again."

That did confuse me. Wasn't he back with Julie? Court was irrelevant now, wasn't it?

"What do you mean?"

"Remember it was postponed? Well, they finally have a date."

"But why do you need to go to court? You see Emily now."

I felt him hesitate.

"Not really."

"What?" Now I was really confused. Wasn't that why he had blown me off, ripped my heart and soul into a thousand pieces?

"It didn't work out very well. Julie accused me of using her to see Emily. She's a bitch," he added. I thought, but isn't that what you were doing? I didn't say it.

He was still talking. "I need to get a court order. Then she can't fuck with me."

"What am I supposed to do? You blew me off, you said we weren't together anymore."

"Come on, Dana, I told you why I did that. It wasn't against you. I just wanted to see Emily."

"So, you scammed Julie and broke my heart?" my voice was louder now "You treated me like garbage? You lied to her?"

"What do you care if I lied to her?" he yelled, missing the point, probably deliberately.

"Why the hell should I help you, you son of a bitch?" I yelled. "Why?"

I heard nothing for a moment, then Ian answered in a soft, seductive voice. "Because you love me, Dana. You love me. And I need you," he said. "I need you."

I felt a burning inside my gut. He was right. I was a fool, a complete fool, but I did love him. I could not refuse to help him. Self-esteem and pride be damned. I was going to help him no matter what. No matter what he had done to me.

"When?" I asked.

"Next Wednesday."

"What time?" I asked.

"At 10:00. We should be there at least by 9:30. Will you do it? Will you come?"

"I'll be there," I said, and hung up.

I sat there, staring into space. I was being used; I knew that. And yet, there was a niggle of hope inside me. Maybe we would get back together now. Maybe this was the start, maybe he realized he had done the wrong thing. Maybe we were back on track.

Maybe he had been right. I had been hiding, hiding from myself, pretending to be all put together when I wasn't. Maybe I needed to be with him to help me face the truth about myself.

Maybe I deserved no better than this.

Maybe I shouldn't be helping someone who had harmed me the way Ian had.

But I would do it. I would help him.

Chapter 74

The day came.

I drove with trepidation to Ian's that morning. He had not asked me to come the night before, so I had to leave quite early, when it was still dark. But I did it. I had taken the day off work to do it. He had hurt me, shattered me, broken me, but I would go. I was compelled to go. I could not say no to him. I had to help him, to try to find the self I had lost by re-connecting to him in whatever way I could. I was no longer myself without Ian.

I arrived at his cabin and he was waiting for me. He looked at me as I walked in the door, just looked at me for a moment, as though he was re-memorizing my face, as though he had thought I was a dream he was having, as though I would not have come when he called.

But I was there.

Then Ian took my arm and said, "Let's go."

We walked to his car and got in. He drove in silence, heading toward the highway to take us south.

It was cold and the road was a bit wet from snow the previous evening. I was not sure what to say or whether I should say much of anything. There was a jagged place in my soul, a place that Ian had carved. I had already been wounded, but he had not put salve on my wounds; he had taken a knife and cut them deeper. They were not scarred over.

So, I remained silent.

The sky was lightening above as we drove along.

Finally, Ian said, "Did you eat? Are you hungry? We're early, we can stop."

"I just had coffee."

"So, you want something?"

"Sure."

We had almost arrived in the city where the courthouse was, but as Ian said, we were early, so he pulled into a little diner just outside the city.

We went in and sat down. I ordered a muffin and he got coffee. It felt stilted, neither of us speaking much, saying much. I ate as he drank his coffee, then he looked at me, staring into my eyes.

"Are you still my fiancé?" he asked.

"Do you want me to be?"

"Dana. When I was with Julie I thought of you. I couldn't even… I was thinking of you."

I felt my blood rise.

"And that makes it ok?"

"No, no, I didn't mean that I mean… I can't get you out of my head, Dana, you are in my head, like no other woman ever has been."

I wasn't sure what to say to that. I believed him. But it did not make him treat me like someone he loved. Not at all.

I finally said, "You treat me like shit, Ian, not like I'm important to you."

"But you are."

I suddenly felt very tired.

"Look, I'm here, I think you're doing the right thing by going to court to get visitation. I told you that from the beginning."

"Ok." He looked as though he wanted me to say more, but I had nothing more to say. I finished my muffin and said, "I'm done, are you ready?"

Ian paid the bill and we left.

I waited with him in court, as I had before. I had my

ring on, but it felt awkward, unreal. Since the last time we had been here, he had been with Julie, he had her and Emily staying there, he had slept with Julie, had sex with Julie. What in the world would she think if she saw us together now? She would think Ian was so erratic, so unstable.

But wasn't he? Wasn't that the truth?

And could that be used against him now? Would Julie be willing to show how she had been humiliated by Ian in order for things to go her way?

I was suddenly afraid that this would go badly. And how would Ian react to that?

We were called into the courtroom for our case. Ian's attorney looked hopeful, and I wondered if he had been told what had transpired over the Christmas holidays with Julie and Emily. I doubted that Ian had told him.

I was right.

Julie's attorney slammed Ian. She brought up the fact that Ian had contacted Julie, that one minute he was engaged and bringing me to court with him, the next he had contacted Julie and asked her to come visit with Emily, implying that he wanted a relationship with her.

And Julie had another weapon up her sleeve.

Her attorney was telling the court that Ian had used drugs while Julie was present. Emily had been asleep, but Ian had smoked weed while Julie was there with him. It was still illegal in this state.

I looked at Ian's attorney. He appeared flabbergasted. Ian had not bothered to tell him anything.

I was afraid to look at Ian.

When Julie's attorney was finished, and the judge was asking Ian's attorney to speak. He did not say anything for a moment, then asked for a quick recess to speak to his client.

The judge looked a bit surprised but granted it.

We left the courtroom. Ian's attorney blasted him

when we got to a private area.

"What the hell, Ian! You never told me any of this. Is it true?"

"Yeah, but..."

"This puts a whole different spin on things. What were you playing at? And smoking? Look, I know most people think weed isn't a big deal, but it is still illegal here and you're going for visitation, it does not look good!"

Ian looked sullen. "I'm still her father. We were getting to know each other."

The attorney just shook his head. "Listen, you screwed up, man. I'm not sure how to fix this." He then looked at me. "And Ms. Taggert, is it? Why are you here with him again?"

I felt foolish. Was I supposed to say we were engaged now? After that shit show in the courtroom. But I tried.

"We were engaged. And I know that Ian had Julie and Emily over but... well, he was just trying to get to know Emily. He didn't want to spend another Christmas without knowing his daughter."

"So, this was ok with you?"

"Well, I understood that he wanted to spend time with Emily."

The attorney looked at me, then shook his head again.

"Ok, but to smoke weed in front of the mother, well, not a good decision."

Ian's face was infused with red, but he asked, quietly enough, "What happens now?"

"I'm not sure," his attorney said, clearly disgusted with him. "But we have to go back. I can argue that you were trying to make amends with the mother and spend time with the child, but..." He trailed off.

We went back to court and the attorney spoke, but it came off as stilted. The judge appeared somewhat incredulous. When Ian's attorney was finished, the judge said, "I was going to allow visitation to begin, slowly at first, but I'm afraid I must reconsider. I realize that the child has been getting to know her father, and I am not saying that I don't think that should continue, but I feel that any visits must be supervised at first. And Mr. Bothwell," he said, addressing Ian directly, "You do realize that you cannot use any type of illegal drug while your child is in your care, do you not?"

Ian's voice was subdued, "Yes, Your Honor."

Finally, court was over. The judge was true to his word and had ordered that visits could occur, but that they would take place in this town and be supervised by the law guardian.

Ian and I walked back to the car in silence. My stomach was churning, waiting for him to blow up, as I knew he would. I wondered if I should drive, knowing how upset he was. Hesitantly I offered, but he snapped at me, "I'm fine. I'll drive."

It had been snowing lightly and there was a coating of snow on the car. Ian brushed it off with his gloves and got in. He started the car. Then he said, "Fuck! Fuck, fuck, fuck!"

"Ian..." I started, but he was yelling.

"That bitch! She turned on me! And I know why."

"What do you mean?"

He turned to look at me.

"She really wanted me back," he said.

"I thought you said she accused you of lying to her to see Emily!"

"Yeah, she did, but... she was happy, she really believed that we were getting back together. I led her to believe..."

"What?" I asked sharply.

"That we would get married."

I was shocked. I had no idea it had gone that

far. I felt sick.

"I'm not doing this, Dana," he was saying. He backed the car up and started to pull out. "I am not fucking doing this. I'm not doing supervised visitation as though I'm some kind of…pariah, some kind of bad influence on my own daughter."

Ian pulled out sharply onto the street. The road was a bit slick. "I'm not doing it," he said again. He steered toward the highway. He pounded on the steering wheel.

"Ian!" I was feeling fearful. He was too volatile to be driving right now.

"Don't preach to me, Dana, I'm fucking furious."

"Well, what can you do?" I needed to try and calm him down. "If the visits go well the judge will end up allowing unsupervised visits, just give it time."

Ian was pulling onto the highway now. He sped up the car.

"No, I have to do something else."

"What can you do?" I was getting frustrated. Did he think he could control the outcome of this after what he had done?

Ian didn't answer right away. He was driving, faster now. There was light snow on the road, and he was passing other cars.

"Slow down, Ian!"

He didn't. He didn't say anything for a time, and I clung to the purse on my lap, frightened, but not wanting to push him too hard and make things worse. As we drove north the snow had started up again, but Ian did not slow down.

Then Ian said, "I'm getting back with Julie. That's what I'll do. I can do it. She was really upset but she wants to get married. That's what I'll do. I'll offer to marry her. That's what she wants."

I felt something in my head explode. I was sitting here, as his fiancé, I had thought we were getting back together. And now this? He would blow me off, actually marry someone else, just to get what he wanted? It was beginning to seem that this wasn't just about seeing Emily. This was a power play. He was losing and he couldn't allow that. He couldn't allow someone else to have control over his life.

Suddenly I couldn't take anymore. I could not go through that pain again. I could no longer take the come close go away, the abuse, the constant rejection, the pain that Ian could inflict, pain that cut into my very soul. Never again. Never ever again.

"No, Ian." I said. "No. That is not what is going to happen."

And I leaned over and grabbed the wheel.

Epilogue

Ian was with me now.

I had moved into a larger apartment in my building to accommodate both of us. During the day, when I went to work, I had hired an aide to help care for him. When I arrived home from my new job as a social worker at the rehabilitation center where he had been a patient, he would smile vaguely up at me. The aide would go home then, and I would take over his care.

That day when I had grabbed the wheel, that, combined with the excessive speed, Ian had lost control of the car on the slippery road. It had veered off, went down an embankment and had struck a tree. No one knew what I had done. The accident report completed by the police had merely stated that the car had gone off the road and struck a tree due to the slippery road conditions. Ian's car had been totaled.

I had gotten off with some broken ribs and was otherwise just bruised. But Ian had been propelled sideways and then forward and had hit his head badly, causing a closed head injury. He had been in a coma for the better part of a month. Surgery had to be done to reduce the swelling on his brain, but he had frontal lobe damage and had lost the ability to speak intelligibly. He lived in a twilight world now, a world of images that he could not really connect together. He required assistance for the simplest of everyday tasks. He did not remember how to do them and had to be shown, over and over.

So, I would come home, and he would smile at me from the recliner I had bought for him and placed in the living room so he could watch TV. He did not know who I was or what I had been to him. He only knew I was a familiar face.

Emily had been visiting occasionally. Her mother would bring her. Julie had contacted me after she learned of the accident and I had realized that she was not a terrible person, nor as stupid or as vindictive as Ian had painted her. She wasn't sure if it was a good idea to bring Emily, but we discussed it and decided to try. So, she brought her, having explained to Emily what had happened to her dad. Emily was a great kid, and strong. She accepted Ian for what he was. She would sit with him, holding his hand and telling him about school and her friends. He would listen attentively, not really understanding, but happy to be with her, even though he did not know who she was.

I still saw some of the kids I had previously worked with around the town. Pedro and George had graduated high school and were planning to start college and I was so proud of them. Ginny and Derek had a baby boy now. My mother had married Tom and moved into his house.

So, I had my life, my new job, my friends, and my family.

And I had Ian. He was with me. He lived with me now. I wore the ring that Ian had given me on my right hand now. I never took it off. There was no more back and forth, no more up and down. No more breaking my heart. No more rejection.

I would never marry. I would never have children. That was the penance for what I had done.

But Ian could never leave me now.

He would never be able to leave me again.

The End